ROSEMARY
for
REMEMBRANCE

a supernatural war torn love story

NIKKI BROADWELL

Airmid Pubishing
Tucson, Arizona

Formatting by Perry Elisabeth Design
Cover design by http://www.stunningbookcovers.com/

Library of Congress Control Number: 2017907036
Airmid Publishing, Tucson, AZ

ISBN: 978-0-9979941-6-2

FOREWORD

This book has been many years in the making. It was originally inspired by my father's POW journals that were found in a cardboard box after his death. He never spoke of them. In my first draft I depicted events as closely as I could, trying to stay true to my parents' relationship before and after the war. But it proved too emotionally draining. In the end I opted for two main characters who bear little resemblance to the real persons and whose story is very different from theirs. As soon as I made this decision the characters took hold and wrote it--that was when I knew I was on the right track.

The heavily redacted writings were kept during the three and a half years my father was held by the Japanese, and are not only a record of the situation, but also love letters to my mother. Major John Ramsay Pugh was aide-de-camp to General Jonathan Wainwright and took part in the surrender to the Japanese forces on May 6, 1942. For more on this please visit: http://www.historynet.com/a-dreadful-step-surrender-at-luzon.htm

Three and a half years later, then Colonel John Ramsay Pugh, made it home, lucky to be alive. Many of his journal entries are included within, and are in his own words.

ACKNOWLEDGEMENTS

To my father, who spent three and a half years as a POW held by the Japanese and lived to tell about it. Without his return I would not be here. I thank him for the use of his eloquent words to enrich this novel.

I hate war as only a soldier who has lived it can, only as one who has seen its brutality, its futility, its stupidity.
Dwight D. Eisenhower

CHAPTER ONE

Washington, D.C.
Late May 1957

The dream took her over…*soft caressing music, as though from ancient instruments, fading as she walked away from the house. Looking back she could see the gas lights flickering in the early evening dusk, a feeling of despair rising up as it always did, to consume her. The garden lay in shadow now, the beech trees and berry bushes softened around the edges. She took the trail that led through the woods, hoping to dispel the sadness. It was like a heavy weight around her neck. Would she ever be free of it? Her life was encircled within a claustrophobic world that pressed on her from all sides. Her father's house stood behind her like a prison, each brick a reminder. No longer beautiful to her, it was like a dark and malevolent creature that held her in its heavy talons.*

"Rebecca?"

The voice echoed out of the dark, propelling her forward, but her foot caught on the hem of her dress and she fell, landing in an untidy heap on the ground. Before she could rise, strong arms took hold of her.

"The carriage is here. It is time."

"Why, Papa?"

"Because my reputation is being ruined by your antics."

"If you mean my grief, I cannot help it."

"Public displays of that sort are simply not done in polite society."
"But I have suffered a terrible loss!"
"That loss rests squarely on your shoulders. It is your hysterics that caused it."

When Rosemary Hughes woke, her face was wet with tears. She wiped them away with her sleeve. A wave of ineffable sadness washed over her. The dreams were like waking memories, each one another slice of a life that had been lived years before—parts of a story she had read but couldn't recall.

She sighed and kicked off her shoes, folding her legs under her pleated summer skirt as she settled back against the wicker chaise. The glass of Pinot Grigio was where she'd placed it a half hour before, the pale liquid now warmed by the late afternoon humidity. She'd discovered the bottle in the pantry, but instead of drinking it when it was still crisp, she'd fallen asleep, only to be revisited with the same unrecognizable house, and the same feelings that had held her captive for a decade. She had yet to discover if the house was a real place, or even if the person she inhabited in the dream could be traced to anyone. The only link she had was the locket she wore around her neck, the necklace her husband Dylan discovered in an antique store years before and presented to her before the war—a gift given the day he proposed. "It had your initials," he'd told her. "It was begging me to buy it for you."

She reached around to unhook the clasp, slipping the braided gold chain from her neck. Using her fingernail she opened the locket to examine the portraits inside the tiny ovals. The man and woman, who looked very young, stared back at her, the nineteenth century clothing stiff and formal.

The man had a square jaw, sideburns and longish hair, a severe expression in his dark eyes. The woman's round face was surrounded with soft curls, setting off her pointed chin. A lace collar lay around her swan-like neck, this very locket visible in the hollow at her throat. In her eyes was a canny brightness, a look that said, 'I know things'. It was this woman who plagued Rosemary's dreams, as though wearing the locket had linked them forever. And yet for some reason she could not bear to take it off. A looped R H had been etched into the back, followed by the words: Together Forever.

Rosemary re-hooked the locket around her neck, feeling the cool heaviness settle against her over-heated skin. She picked up the glass and took a sip, thinking back on the day. The forgotten bottle of wine was nearly the only thing that hadn't been taken by the family, or rather 'looters', as she now called them. She let out a long sigh, her gaze moving to the fading purple blooms on the Wisteria vines crisscrossing the wooden arbor. The structure and plantings had been done when the house was first built back at the beginning of the twentieth century. John Russell Pope was the architect her father had employed to design the Georgian mansion, and it was a house she had loved since the first time she was able to recognize its magnificence.

The trying day was finally coming to an end—the chattering and greed of her family that had interrupted her deep personal musings about her father's death. They pawed through his possessions, claiming whatever they could get their hands on. The furniture, china and knick-knacks had been picked over and decided on. But this was what the will stipulated—divide it all up amongst the immediate family, her one aunt and her two obnoxious daughters, her sister, her sister's current husband and the four children accumulated from marriage one and two. They had drawn straws to see who went first and then divided everything piece by piece, her father's legacy marching out the door in the arms of those strong enough to carry it. Professional movers would pick up the heavier pieces that now stood abandoned in the middle of the enormous entry hall.

Her aunt Cecilia had been the only bright spot, her arms coming around Rosemary to hold her close. "Don't let them take away your joy along with the furnishings," she'd whispered. "You have your father's memory and his love. He will always be with you."

"Thank you, Aunt Cecelia. I'll try and keep it in mind. When will you visit me? You haven't been in a long time."

"I've had many things on my mind," she'd said enigmatically. "But as soon as they're sorted we'll come for a weekend."

Her aunt was her mother's younger sister, a woman who had consistently been there when Rosemary and Amanda were young. Unlike Rosemary's petite mother, Cecilia was large boned with an attitude to match. She was involved with women's rights and belonged to several organizations that spoke out about equal rights, encouraging women to get into the labor force. She'd lost her husband the year before Rosemary's mother had committed suicide, her own grief fresh as she sought to comfort her two bereft nieces. She'd recently remarried, her new husband and his family taking up a lot of her time. Rosemary had yet to meet the new man in her life. The two daughters from her previous marriage, now grown, had arrived at the house with their husbands, who seemed in awe of the antiques and china and glassware that were up for grabs. Rosemary had made sure to strip her father's roll top desk of personal writings and legal documents before everyone arrived.

Before today it had been months since Rosemary had last seen her aunt. The mention of 'we' in terms of a trip to see her, did not appeal. Apparently a quiet visit with just the two of them was not to be.

Rosemary put her glass down and stood, walking barefoot along the packed earth paths, letting her gaze wander across the fountain shaped like an urn, the pleasant gurgle of water soothing her overwrought nerves. Her gaze went to the bright pansies planted around the base, their lion-like faces turned to the now-fading sun. The shadows had grown long, the day nearly done.

"Rosie?"

The male voice wafted out of the growing dusk, the sound like a distant memory. She turned. "Dylan?"

A man appeared, striding toward her, restless hands running through his thick salt and pepper hair. "I heard this was the day. I'm sorry I didn't get here earlier to support you. What a terrible burden."

Rosemary met the hazel eyes of her husband, Dylan Hughes, a man she rarely saw these days. He hadn't changed much, his square-jawed face just as handsome as it had ever been. She smiled. "Thank you for your concern, Dylan. It went as I suspected it would, the younger ones clamoring for what could bring them a buck."

He came close, but instead of embracing her, he placed a hand on her shoulder. "I should have been here."

She let out a laugh tempered with exasperation. "It wouldn't have helped, and frankly your appearance would have set them off. None of them like you, you know."

"That's because I don't tolerate their money-grubbing ways. Can we go get a drink? I have something I need to talk to you about."

"There's an open bottle of wine on the porch."

He shook his head. "When I walked through I noticed how empty the house looks—it's like a beautiful bird that has been plucked of every colorful feather. I'd feel better, and I think you would too, if we went elsewhere."

"I had the dream again."

"Just now?"

"Yes. I fell asleep in the chair on the porch. I was crying when I woke up."

"Were you wearing the locket in the dream?"

"I'm always wearing the locket in the dream. But this time I was walking away from the house and I could see gaslights burning by the front door and inside. I guess that places it in time, doesn't it?"

Dylan nodded. "Early eighteen-hundreds, I'd say."

Rosemary and Dylan had been married for nearly twenty years, but the last few had brought an estrangement they hadn't been able to bridge. It was as though the past had intruded between them, creating a rift that neither one could cross. Sometimes she wondered if it was partly the dream that had caused it, a life that had nothing to do with them, and yet seemed important.

"What happened this time?"

Dylan was smiling, but Rosemary knew he took the dream seriously; finding the locket had bordered on the uncanny, her initials and his attraction to the piece of jewelry and its inscription furthering the mystery. "I don't know, but that woman's pain remains long after I wake up."

"Why don't you visit one of those gypsy fortune tellers? I have a friend who knows a reputable one in the city."

Rosemary scoffed. "I don't believe in it. I wouldn't be able to keep a straight face."

"And yet you have these recurring dreams that seem to point to…" Dylan hesitated.

"Seem to point to what?"

Dylan met her gaze. "I'd say it's a past life. I've had the dreams too."

Rosemary felt a twinge of something along her spine. "You have? When?"

"Many times, Rosemary. Ever since I bought the damn thing and gave it to you. Even during prison camp."

"I'll just get my wrap," she said, heading to where she'd left her shawl. Dylan had also had the dreams? And he'd never told her until now, letting her think she was going crazy.

Dylan now lived in Washington while Rosemary remained in Virginia, living in the old farmhouse she'd purchased before he returned from the war. She needed the solitude of the country, while Dylan thrived on Washington politics and culture, his job at Raytheon keeping him busy. Rosemary had only come into D.C. today to carry out her role as executor of her father's will. The estate had been unsettled since her father's death several months before, an event that had torn her apart. Complications with the will and her own grief had prevented her from doing her duty earlier.

Her mother's untimely death when she was barely thirteen had left Rosemary and her younger sister, Amanda, to carry on without her, pitting them against one another in their fight for their father's affections. The jealousy between them had never gone away. Their father had never remarried, although several women had been present at various times, women who attempted to get close to the two daughters, all of them failing.

Following Dylan toward the front door she took one last look around the house, her gaze going to the niche by the stairs where the grandfather clock had stood. She couldn't remember which relative had managed to snag it--maybe one of Cecilia's daughters? The wide stairs looked bare without the Persian carpets, the glass French doors that led out to the garden forlorn without the sheer curtains. For a moment she heard the faint laughter of bygone years when the house had been full of people for one celebration or another. She could almost see the fir boughs decorating the fireplace at Christmas, the red candles on the table, and the maids scurrying here and there with serving trays. She'd grown up here, spent time here when Dylan was held by the Japanese as a POW. Dylan was right. The house felt like an empty shell, its life force gone. Once outside she secured the door behind her and locked it with the key.

As Dylan drove, Rosemary stared out the car window, not surprised when he pulled up in front of the familiar hotel restaurant. So many of their special occasions had taken place here, including their wedding reception. The valet opened the doors and whisked the car away to park it while Dylan guided her inside, his warm hand on the small of her back.

Her family was well known here, her father's years of business turning Rosemary into a minor celebrity. Despite not having a reservation, Sam, the *maître-d*, hurried to seat them. "Welcome Mr. And Mrs. Hughes. It is so good to see you both," he gushed. "I was so sorry to hear of Mr. Hewitt's passing."

Dylan murmured a response while he pulled out the chair for Rosemary, his eyes on his wife. "You look quite exhausted," he said quietly, once they were alone.

"How else would I look? My father just died, a man I adored, and I've had raptors swooping down wanting to scoop up every single thing he owned. It's been a nightmare."

"How is Amanda?"

Rosemary made a face. "Amanda is as she always is, nasty to me and self-serving. She managed to grab that gorgeous set of Limoges china before anyone else had a chance to think about it, and also the hand-carved medieval chest that belonged to my great-grandfather."

"She's always been a touch acquisitive. But think about it this way, Rosie, you were your father's favorite, you're a lot better looking than she is, and you're married to me."

His gaze caught hers, making her laugh. "Hard to call what's going on between us a marriage, but we haven't yet divorced, if that's what you mean."

"Amanda is now on number four, correct?"

"Yes. I don't know him at all, but judging from his behavior today he's looking out for himself. He's never spent much time with me or Daddy, and yet he was the one checking out the most valuable pieces of furniture—he must have been studying the pieces for quite some time to understand their value. I think he's an uneducated social climber."

"You really are a snob, aren't you?"

Rosemary thought of the lifelong guilt she carried about being born into a family like hers, and what she'd done over the years to help those, from no fault of their own, who were less fortunate. It galled her to hear him say this, but instead of telling him, she responded in the way she knew he expected. "Isn't that why you married me?"

Dylan let out a low chuckle. "And did he manage to snag them?"

"Most of them, but we drew straws and went around the circle so that everyone had an equal chance. Can you imagine sitting in a circle on the floor with the smaller items like Mother's jewelry and paperweights and inkwells and gold and silver cufflinks laid out in the middle? So many of those things hold memories for me, especially when I used to sit on my father's lap when he was at his desk. Mostly it was a depressing display of greed that put me into a very bad mood and gave me a roaring headache."

"And brought on the dream," he muttered, looking down. "How did you deal with Amanda's children? Did they get to pick?"

"They did. Daddy wanted it that way."

"How old are they now?"

"Toby is eight, Alex is seventeen and Sandra is eighteen. All from different fathers, of course." She recalled the short conversation she'd had with her sister:

'You never told me what happened with Henry,' she'd said before Amanda gathered her booty up to take home.

She thought of how Amanda's gaze had darkened. 'He was dipping into my trust and gambling it away. Grant would never do anything like that.'

Her answer had not been as cordial as she'd planned, words spilling out of her mouth before she could stop them. 'I'm sorry to hear that. I hope you're right about Grant—your choices when it comes to men have not always been the best.'

'Don't take your sad loveless life out on me, Rosemary,' Amanda had shouted, glaring. 'At least I have a man who cares enough to stick around.'

The words had stung because they were true.

Dylan made a derisive sound in the back of his throat, bringing her back to the present. "Too bad we didn't have children."

She sighed, thinking back on the various conversations they'd had on this topic. "You say that now, but as I remember you were not keen during my child-bearing years."

"I was a prisoner of war, for God's sake. And when I was released we went through that bad patch."

"If you're referring to my affair, say so, Dylan. It doesn't become you to prevaricate. And as we've discussed, I thought you were dead. I never once heard from you."

He stared at the table for a long moment before his eyes met hers. "I wasn't so much thinking about the affair as I was the rest of it—my inability to feel, for instance. That's a time I'd rather not revisit."

"If you remember my father was very insistent that we stay together," she continued, ignoring him. "Now that he's gone we can divorce." She picked up the wine list.

Dylan gazed into the distance, his expression resigned. "I will miss him."

Rosemary nodded and looked up as a waiter approached.

Their food had arrived as well as the excellent bottle of Zinfandel, before Rosemary brought up the subject at the front of her mind. "Can you please explain why you've kept me in the dark about your dreams? I've been sharing mine for years and not once have you mentioned your own. Why, Dylan?"

Dylan frowned, his fingers running through his hair nervously. "This was what I wanted to talk to you about. I've been planning to tell you for a while, but we've barely seen each other. I didn't want to bring it up on the phone. And having the visitations felt like an embarrassment somehow, as though I had no control over my life, especially after prison camp. The dreams still bother me, coming when I'm not prepared and leaving before I can get a proper read on them."

"Tell me about it. Mostly they're vague and sort of foggy."

Dylan nodded. "Same for me. I find them frustrating and disturbing, as though my life is being taken over by supernatural forces. And I do not like the person I become. There's no one other than you that I can talk to about this. Anyone else would think I'm insane."

"Do you see a dark-haired man and a woman with brown curls and a pointed chin?"

Dylan nodded. "The ones in the locket. They love each other and yet there are insurmountable obstacles between them. I think he betrayed her in some way." He put his fork down and took a sip of wine. "We should spend time together and compare notes. Figure out why this is going on—we both seem to be caught up in it, whatever it is. And besides that, I miss you. "

She shook her head and smirked. "You don't miss me, you miss some fantasy woman you conjured during those years of imprisonment. I cannot be your Penelope, or some goddess on a pedestal. I thought you understood that."

He frowned. "And you weren't, were you? Penelope remained faithful while Ulysses was absent, despite having many suitors."

20

"You really are the limit, Dylan. Your preoccupation with heroines who stand by their men through thick and thin is quite extraordinary."

He scoffed, his dark expression lightening. "I'm well over that now. It was a device I used unconsciously to get me through the worst of it. Those years in prison camp were harrowing. I honestly never expected to see you again."

She met his gaze. "I know they were, and we did talk to the psychiatrist about all that, but in the end you went back to your old self. You told me you wanted to grow things, to be close to the earth, and now you're pursuing another career that has to do with the military."

"I didn't want to be dependent on your money. When you purchased the farm I wasn't here, wasn't part of the decision. I thought working for an innovative company and securing government contracts for life saving equipment might help me feel better about myself. The pay's great."

She put her wine glass down. "If you felt that way why haven't you said? You could have contributed to the farm, you know. Your military retirement should be enough to support you. Why do you insist on making this about me?"

"When did I say it was about you? I only said I didn't want to depend on you."

"What I'm trying to say is that you said one thing and did another. Don't you think I see who you are? It would be impossible for you to live on the farm, to raise horses, or goats or whatever. You're ambitious and driven. I am not."

"That's because you don't need to be. I was brought up differently. For me getting ahead was everything. I had to get out of that shanty town and make something of my life."

"And you did. Why isn't your army career enough? Why must you work so hard at something that has no meaning?"

"Why do we always end up at the same place every single time we have this conversation?"

Rosemary pushed her half finished dinner away and signaled the waiter. "Can I have a brandy, please?"

"Make that two," Dylan added.

It was late when they left the restaurant, both of them a bit drunk. "Where do you plan to sleep tonight?" Dylan asked once they were in the car.

"I had planned to drive home, but it's too late now."

"I wouldn't let you make that long drive after all the alcohol you consumed."

"And how would you stop me?" she asked belligerently.

"Never did like what alcohol does to you," he muttered, turning the key. "You're staying with me tonight, whether you like it or not."

Rosemary put her head back and closed her eyes, making no comment.

CHAPTER TWO

Washington, D.C.
August 1939

The wedding was the talk of the town, society page headlines reading: **Rosemary Hewitt, society daughter of wealthy businessman, Boyd Hewitt, to marry Captain Dylan Hughes in National Cathedral!** A picture of Rosemary and Dylan at the Junior league ball, showed the two of them dancing together, their smiling faces turned toward the camera. The papers were full of it, mainly because of the looming threat of war and the desire to think of more pleasant things. But the guest list did include several senators and *crème de la crème* of Washington society.

Rosemary stood in front of the gilt mirror, examining herself as though from afar. She didn't recognize the woman encased in yards of satin, the look of confusion in her eyes. What was she doing? Captain Dylan Hughes had swept her off her feet, his romantic overtures overriding her good sense. And there was also her father, who was smitten by him almost as much as she was. Boyd Hewitt had always hoped for a son, and this man fit the bill perfectly. Dylan was a charmer, there was no doubt about that, but did he truly love her? Or was this a charade that fit some hero and heroine he'd read about, a fantasy that he hoped to make real? She loved him, but there was a part of her that worried. He seemed almost too good to be true with his dreamy vision of their future, the way he doted on her. He was on a career path in the army during an unsettled time. What would their future hold? Their backgrounds were so different.

She sighed and fastened her veil into place, taking one last look at the stranger dressed in white before she left the room.

"Hurry!" Amanda called out as Rosemary carefully descended the wide staircase, trying not to step on her long train or her hem. It wouldn't do to tumble down and break an ankle.

In the hallway her sister stood with hands on hips, her face pink, her small hairpiece already coming loose. The chartreuse dress did not suit her rosy coloring and light brown hair. Amanda was one of her five bridesmaids. The other four, friends of Rosemary's from school, would meet them at the church.

"We should have had the wedding here," her father grumbled when she climbed into the car. "A church is the last place I want to spend my time."

Rosemary's immediate family were atheists, but the implacable insistence of Dylan's religious mother had forced them to agree to the church wedding. "It will all be over soon enough," Rosemary said, adjusting the tiara that held her veil in place. "One event won't kill us."

"I suppose you're right. I just hope I don't catch fire when I cross the threshold."

Rosemary laughed, gazing fondly on her father. "If you do, we all do."

❧❦❧

Dylan Hughes and his best man Jack were *en route* to the National Cathedral, Boyd Hewitt's concession to a church wedding. One had to be up high up in Washington society to be allowed to have a wedding *there*, Dylan thought, smiling to himself.

As they careened around the corner onto Wisconsin Avenue, Jack finally took his foot off the gas pedal. "We're almost there and it's only 14:10," he said proudly, looking at his watch.

"I told you we had plenty of time." Dylan lit a cigarette and inhaled deeply, trying to quell his nerves.

"How are you doing, old man?" Jack asked, sliding the car into a small parking space behind the cathedral.

"I'm doing quite well," he said, looking over at his fair-haired friend. "Marrying into a family like this is a dream come true."

Jack laughed. "You do love Rosemary, don't you?"

"Oh I love her, all right. She's everything I'd ever hoped for. My only worry is how she'll take to army life. She's been sheltered and brought up like a hothouse flower. After her life of luxury how will she cope in army housing on my salary?"

"Does she have money of her own?"

"Her father set up a trust fund that she and her sister draw from, but she's promised me that she'll leave it alone once we're married. I think she's afraid that her being independently wealthy might emasculate me."

"What do you think?"

Dylan thought of the *soirées* he'd attended at the Hewitt house, the celebrities he'd met, including the throaty voiced actress, Tallulah Bankhead, as well as Margaret Sanger, the infamous proponent of birth control. There was definitely something to be said for moving up in society. "I think that having some extra money around to dine out at the best restaurants, shop at the best stores and take trips to resort areas will only enhance our lives."

"You are a lucky bastard. I hope you appreciate what you have."

Dylan grinned and stubbed out his cigarette in the ashtray. "We'd better get a move on," he said, opening the car door.

While the two men walked toward the cathedral Dylan's mind drifted back to all the drab years he'd spent in the down-at-the-heels house of his youth. His parents rarely entertained, the only social gatherings happening around religious holidays and filled with distant relatives that left him cold. But without his father's membership in the Masons and their perseverance, he wouldn't have been accepted into West Point. He had to give them credit where credit was due.

Dylan entered the cathedral, Jack on his heels. He let thoughts of the past drift away as he gazed into the cavernous interior where hundreds of people had gathered to watch the ceremony. Soon he would be married to a wealthy heiress, a beautiful woman who loved him as much as he loved her. He *was* a lucky bastard.

The wedding vows seemed to happen in a sort of dream-like haze, Dylan's awe at now being married to this beautiful girl making him suddenly shy. "What is it, Dylan?" Rosemary whispered as they walked into the sunshine. "You aren't having second thoughts, are you?"

He took hold of her arm, helping her negotiate the steps in her long gown and into the waiting limousine. "Quite the contrary—I feel like the luckiest man alive." Inside the car he turned to her, his intense kiss reiterating his words.

"Careful," she said, pulling away. "My lipstick needs to remain intact until I can touch it up. Photos will be taken at the reception."

He laughed, running a hand through his thick hair. "You look stunning with or without lipstick, Mrs. Hughes."

CHAPTER THREE

Fort Myer, Virginia
July 1940

Rosemary was surrounded with boxes, her hands on her hips. This minuscule living room and small house would never accommodate all their things. "How am I to deal with all this without any help?"

"You are perfectly capable of unpacking, Rosemary. And when the movers arrive you can certainly give them directions. I told you how things would be on base. Just tell the men where to place the furniture and get out of their way."

"Easy for you to say," she grumped, pulling her hair back and securing it with bobby pins. "I have half a mind to head home until all of this is completed."

"Don't you dare. You're my wife now and as such I expect a competent helpmate. Have you even looked at the list of protocols I brought home?"

Rosemary narrowed her eyes. "I have an art class this afternoon, and I refuse to miss it because of this."

Dylan frowned. "Learning what is expected of you as an army wife is a lot more important than your damned art class.

You're on the list to give a tea in three days. You need to get up to speed and stop behaving like you're above all this. For God's sake, Rosemary!"

Rosemary didn't reply, watching him pick up a file folder and march out of the apartment toward a car that had just pulled up. So far they'd been holed up in a two room hotel room for six months waiting for housing. "And this isn't much better," she muttered, gazing around the tiny living room, the galley kitchen with old appliances and no counter space. The one bedroom was like a closet. Would the beautiful canopied antique bed her father had given them as a wedding present even fit? There was no way she'd invite any of their friends here for drinks.

Dylan's stringent schedule, and his impatience and expectations, were beginning to wear thin. Even their physical connection, always there in times of stress, had disappeared in the past weeks. Her ability to cope with life as an army wife was growing slimmer by the day. The bloom was definitely off the rose.

The three days went by in a whirl of unpacking and arguments. Rosemary was seriously fed up by the time the tea rolled around, feeling that she'd made a mistake in marrying this man. He arrived home from work with a sheaf of papers, hardly acknowledging her other than complaining about something she'd done or hadn't done. Her dinners were not appreciated, her attempt at conversation ignored.

There was no putting of the inevitable, she thought when the doorbell rang. Maybe having the tea go well would put her back in Dylan's good graces.

"Please come in and make yourselves comfortable," Rosemary invited, holding the door wide. As the women filed past, she glanced around the living room to make sure everything was in place. Her hard work had paid off. It looked perfect.

"What lovely furniture you have!" Sara Roberts said, gazing around at the antiques. She removed her gloves and hat and then settled into one of two upholstered chairs. Candace Martin, Marcela Bartlett and Barbara Campbell settled on the couch, their wide eyes wandering the room.

"Wonderful rugs," Candace said. "Where on earth did you find these?"

"My father gave them to us for an engagement present," Rosemary confessed, an uncomfortable feeling moving thorough her mid-section. The paintings on her walls were all originals; the rugs and furniture were the best money could buy. "I'll fetch the coffee," she said, her nose picking up the scent of burning. Rushing into the kitchen she pulled open the oven door to find her molasses cookies thoroughly blackened around the edges. "Damn!"

Sara appeared in the doorway. "Can I help?"

"It's fine. I'll just be a minute." Rosemary stared at the ruined cookies, wondering if there was something, anything, she could offer in their place. She poured the coffee into the silver pot and placed the creamer and sugar dish next to it. Sighing she picked up the tray, heading out of the kitchen, but on the way toward the coffee table her foot caught on the edge of the rug, pitching her forward, tray and all. She watched in horror as the coffee pot flew through the air, landing with a sickening crash on the other side of the seating area. The creamer didn't fare any better, landing on the rug and leaving a trail of white liquid. By now all the women were on their feet, expressions of dismay across their features. From her ignoble position on the floor Rosemary heard exclamations of 'oh my goodness, oh dear, and oh my', as she struggled to stand.

"I'll fetch a rag," Candace said, hurrying into the kitchen. Sara was now on her hands and knees picking up sugar cubes.

"I'm so sorry," Rosemary managed to say. She was very close to tears and hoped to keep them at bay.

"These things happen," Sara answered. "If you have more coffee I can refill the pot."

"It's on the stove." While Sara was in the kitchen Rosemary mopped up the cream, using the rag Candace had found beneath the sink.

Sara brought in coffee and cups, placing them on the table. "Today we'll dispense with etiquette in favor of relaxation." She poured herself a cup, gesturing to Candace and the others to do the same. "This is Rosemary's first time at this, and although it began awkwardly, let's try to enjoy one another's company."

"What a disaster," Rosemary said, and then she was laughing, all the others joining in.

"Now, ladies, here's your homework," Sara told them an hour later, handing around the printed material. "Read these instructions carefully and we'll go over them next time. At the end of next month we'll be joining the colonels' and generals' wives, and my role will be usurped by Mrs. Porter." Sara laughed, her hand going to her hair that had come loose from the chignon.

Once they'd gone Rosemary cleaned up the kitchen and called her father. "Will you be around this afternoon?"

"For you? Always."

"I'll be there for luncheon."

Two hours later she was in the paneled dining room, sitting at the oak table with her father, watching Ingrid bring in a tray of cucumber and cream cheese sandwiches. As soon as the German maid was out of hearing she turned to Boyd Hewitt. "Father, I'm miserably unhappy."

Boyd turned to her. He ran a hand over his graying hair. "What has happened?"

"Aside from being expected to make friends with a bunch of social climbing women, give teas and become the perfect wife to an army officer?"

Boyd smiled sympathetically. "I'm sure it will take some getting used to. But you were brought up to understand how these things work, Rosie. It's politics."

"Dylan wants me to give up my painting." She took a bite of her sandwich.

"I seriously doubt that. He's a reasonable person who I highly respect. And you, my dear girl, have been spoiled. It's time to grow up."

Rosemary gazed at her father in disbelief. "You think I'm spoiled?"

"Your life has been worry free and indulged, and now you're faced with a reality you were never aware of. I know you can rise to the occasion. I never would have approved the marriage had I not thought that. Now take yourself home and take care of him. He needs you to be strong."

"I wish he'd prepared me. I can't talk to him—he's like a different person now that we're married."

Boyd gazed into the distance. "If I remember correctly he did prepare you, Rosie. He was adamant that you should understand before you agreed to marry him. When he confided in me I told him you were certainly up to the task.

And you are. Now go." Boyd stood. "I must get back to work."

"But Daddy, I…"

"Don't let the man down, Rosemary. He's under considerable strain right now. This is an unsettled time in the world and he's in the thick of it."

Boyd exited the dining room, leaving her there to mull things over. Instead of heading back to the base Rosemary went into the garden and wandered the paths, letting her thoughts meander along their shaded trails. She sat on a bench under a cherry tree, watching a robin pull a worm from the grass. She and Dylan had sat in this exact spot, his protestations of love like a romantic passage from a book. Kneeling in front of her he had asked for her hand in marriage, promising to do everything in his power to keep her happy. They had been married for less than a year, and already those promises had been dismissed in lieu of his career and his obsession with how she should behave in her new role. And she was failing miserably. If they were unable to work this out there was no future for them.

❧

"I'm planning on my art class tomorrow, whether you approve or not," she told Dylan later that evening, ignoring her father's suggestions.

"Please, Rosemary, can you refrain from using that tone? My day was not the best and I would appreciate a warmer greeting."

"A warmer greeting? Oh, do you mean the drink I haven't yet provided, the cigarette case that isn't full? Or should dinner already be on the stove? I gave a tea this morning, not that you've even thought to ask." Rosemary heard her strident voice echo in the room, horrified by what she'd just said.

Dylan flopped into the overstuffed chair. "I would like a drink before we get into another argument. Why are you always so angry and sarcastic?"

Rosemary stared at the floor before getting up to make drinks. "I...I don't know what gets into me. I was perfectly happy and then I was screaming like a fishwife. I do feel somewhat put upon by my duties, as you call them, but the tea wasn't so bad." She laughed, handing him a glass filled with bourbon, ice cubes and branch water, just as he liked it. "I made a complete mess of things, but it seemed to lighten the mood. I like the women who were here today."

"I'm glad to hear it. I've noticed a pattern to these moods of yours."

Rosemary stared at him. "What are you suggesting?"

His eyebrows lifted. "Isn't there something you can take to smooth things out?"

She shrugged, embarrassed for a moment. "I don't know of anything. Perhaps I can ask Amanda." She sat across from him. "Now that you mention it I've been up and down for three days now. This move has put me off balance as well. I shouldn't have expected that all our things in storage would fit. The place is too small."

"I'm sorry, Rosie. Until I'm promoted this will have to do."

She glanced at his face, noticing the strained expression. "I'm not blaming you, Dylan. I just wasn't quite prepared. I hope I can get used to this life."

His dark eyebrows pulled together. "You signed up for it."

"Did I? I don't remember you telling me I had to be a gourmet cook, a perfect hostess, and a housemaid."

Dylan let out a sigh. "As I've said a million times, the wife of an officer can make or break a career. I thought I made that clear. And I also mentioned that if you need to hire help, it's fine with me. If you really feel you can't manage then perhaps we should live apart."

Rosemary stared at him in surprise. "You would do that?"

"Rosie, if you can't cope with this life, I don't want to force you. My work is hard enough without worrying about whether you're happy or not."

"I suppose I could get a cleaning service, that might help."

"Do it."

By bedtime Rosemary had had several drinks, her worries dissolving when Dylan pulled her close.

"I would hate to live apart," he murmured, moving her hair back to kiss her neck.

She shivered as his hands roamed across her body. "I don't think I could stand to live without you."

He pulled back, gazing at her. "Shall we make an agreement?"

"What kind of agreement?"

"That you will do your best and I will have patience when you feel out of your depth. I love you , Rosie. You're my sun, moon and stars."

"You're drunk."

"Not that drunk," Dylan laughed, picking her up and carrying her into the bedroom.

Dylan was gone when she woke in the morning, a headache brewing as she picked up her hastily removed clothing and straightened the bed. The night came back to her in hazy indistinct images, the two of them entangled, heavy breathing and moaning as they coupled. She had not used her diaphragm, and if her calculations were correct she was at the point in her cycle when pregnancy could occur. Was that why she'd been so out of sorts? She let out a groan and headed to the kitchen for coffee. A pregnancy now would not be good, especially after the news Dylan had imparted after they made love. He'd received his orders. They were heading to the Philippines in one month's time. Her father's prophetic words came back to her: *"Don't let the man down, Rosemary. He's under considerable strain right now. This is an unsettled time in the world and he's in the thick of it."* Her father must have known before she did. No wonder Dylan had been so somber the night before.

CHAPTER FOUR

Manila, Philippines
August 1940

The boat docked just before sunset on August seventeenth, 1940. A forest of coconut palms filled in the landscape behind long empty beaches, and in the far distance, cloud shadows raced across a range of dark mountains. The smell of the sea coupled with the sweet perfume of flowers wafted by on the warm breeze.

Rosemary and Dylan stood on the deck watching the sun disappear until there was only a faint line of orange remaining on the horizon. Here so close to the equator there was no twilight, and night fell suddenly, a velvet curtain coming down. They spent that night packing what they'd brought along on the ship, and it wasn't until the next morning that Rosemary noticed the ominous array of naval ships in the harbor. Sunlight glinted off their otherwise dull metallic surfaces. Sailors, like tiny ants, raced back and forth across the decks. Ten thousand U.S. troops and twenty thousand Philippine Army soldiers were here on this island. For the first time she registered just how far from home they were and what it might mean. She shivered despite the warm morning sun.

Carts pulled by water buffalo and donkeys came into view as she and Dylan left the ship. The Spanish city of Intramuros was not far, the mellow, sand colored buildings covered with bright bougainvillea and surrounded with mimosa trees in full flower. The Philippines had been in the hands of the Spanish from the 1500's until the late 1800's, when it was fought over in the Spanish-American war. In the far distance beyond the city, deep emerald rice paddies were visible along the lower slopes of Mt. Mayon, a still active volcano. Clouds were building over the mountains with a promise of rain. Around the harbor the din of foreign voices echoed, calling out to hawk their wares, a cacophony mixed with alien birdcalls, engine noise from motorcycles, jeeps, and a few cars adding to the general chaos.

The commanding officer and his wife were on the dock greeting the new intelligence officer, Dylan's role of aide-de-camp forgotten for the moment. General MacArthur was not in attendance but there was to be a meeting held at his penthouse for later in the day. A short ceremony was held before Rosemary and Dylan were shown to a jeep driven by a Filipino soldier who would take them to their temporary quarters outside of Ft. McKinley, seven miles south of Manila.

They bumped in and out of ruts on the dirt road, swerving around water buffalo, children on bicycles, chickens, donkeys, and dogs, sometimes narrowly missing them. The wind whipped Rosemary's hair into a tangle and she was sweating profusely by the time they reached their destination.

Rosemary stared at the line of rustic cottages with sloping metal roofs. For some reason she had expected colonial architecture, whitewashed walls and cool tiled interiors. She followed Dylan up the dilapidated stairs to a covered porch littered with weathered rattan furniture.

"This is our quarters, at least until we find a place to rent."

When Dylan's eyes met hers she could see the strain there and curbed the remark that had been on the tip of her tongue.

"The driver will get the luggage. Why don't you go in and have a look around? I need to see what the plan is."

A sharp musty odor assaulted her senses as soon as she walked through the door. But despite the stale air the place looked clean. The dark wood floor had been polished to a high shine, large casement windows open to let in the fragrant flower-laden breeze. The kitchen was small and old-fashioned, with a chipped porcelain sink and electric stovetop, but the wood floors sparkled and the cabinets had been freshly painted. The living room was another matter, and she immediately intuited that the mustiness came from the forlorn fabric that covered the bamboo couch and two armchairs. She examined the cheap fabric in disgust; there were areas where the material had been stained and almost worn through. When was their container arriving? It wouldn't be soon enough.

At the back of the house two small bedrooms connected with a bathroom. The same unremarkable bamboo furniture prevailed, reminding her of a 'down in the heels' hotel room. She sighed heavily, lifting the damp hair off her neck. Next to the porcelain sink in the bathroom was a stack of towels on a white rattan table. At least the towels were thick and looked clean.

The back porch held an ancient washing machine, a sagging clothesline suspended between two posts behind it. She had a vision of her hair tied up in a scarf, working to hang up clothes as sweat poured off her brow. She started to laugh and then stopped herself with an intake of breath. Was it her job to do their laundry? In this heat ironing would be nearly unbearable.

Beyond the row of houses was a small forest of enormous Dipterocarp trees, interspersed with date palms and banana trees, all of them new to her. She could hear raucous birdcalls, but the canopy was too dense to see them.

By now the driver had brought in the luggage and placed it in the middle of the living room floor. After he left she walked slowly along the porch, examining the parched red dirt around the house. Entering the front door for the second time the acrid odor of mold seemed even stronger. Trying to let go of a rising panic, she grabbed one of the heavy bags and dragged it into the bedroom and hoisted it onto the bed. First she peeled her stockings down and threw them into a corner. There would be no more of those. Once free of the rest of her damp clothing she threw open the casement window, letting the light breeze blow on her naked body.

The tap in the shower sputtered and then let loose a foul- smelling brown sludge before running semi-clear. She fought the urge to cry, concentrating instead on washing with the thin sliver of soap she found.

By the time she had dressed and unpacked her suitcase she heard the screen door slam, Dylan appearing in the bedroom looking hot and irritated. "You could use a shower," she told him.

"I don't have time for that. It seems we are to be *presented* to the 'big man' in exactly one hour."

"What does that mean? Are you talking about General MacArthur?"

"Yes, MacArthur! And it means the man is a pompous ass! The CO is trying his best to maintain a good attitude but I can see the strain on his face."

"What is the meeting about?"

"That's just it. It isn't that kind of a meeting. He, I mean MacArthur, is not planning to communicate with us at all. It'll be more like some sort of ceremony."

"Maybe that's a blessing in disguise."

"I don't like being left out of the loop and I'm sure General W is in agreement. This is no longer the man's purview."

"Shouldn't you reserve judgment until after the meeting? After all, he's been here a long time. How many years has it been?"

"He's been in the Philippines off and on for years, but he's retired now. I think he's taken on a kinglike proprietary attitude toward this place, as though it belongs to him."

"From what I've read, this is his home. And he's a new father. You know how these events can shape our behavior."

Dylan looked toward her, his brows furrowed. "He needs to learn how to turn over the reins."

"Not an easy task, judging from the little I've heard about the man." It would not do Dylan's career any good if he didn't get along with the officers in charge, and especially MacArthur, who wielded tremendous power here. "I do hope there's a cleaning service because I do not want to be ironing your shirts in this heat."

"Of course there is," Dylan muttered under his breath. "I wouldn't expect you to do it. Now where did you say I could find a clean shirt?"

"I'll get it for you."

Dylan ran his hand over his face. "I might shower after all." He grabbed the shirt out of her hands and headed into the bathroom. A minute later she heard the squeak of the taps being turned. "Jesus Christ!" he bellowed.

Rosemary waited for a moment and then opened the door a crack. "Do you know if they supplied us with any booze?"

"Check the kitchen, but I'm sure they did."

"I'll make drinks for when you get back."

"Don't bother. I'll be heading to the Army-Navy Club after the meeting."

"When will you be back?"

"No idea."

He came out, dressed in a clean uniform, and headed toward the door without a backward glance. He hadn't asked her what she thought about their quarters, probably because he knew what she would say. Manila was not what she had envisioned, and her future life here was an unknown. In the rush to leave Washington her painting supplies had been left behind.

She drew a bath and sank into the lukewarm water, her hands going to her flat belly. No baby had come from their one time of unprotected sex, and that was a good thing. But despite knowing this, she was sad, a heavy feeling coming over her as she sank deeper into the water.

After her bath she pulled on a robe and went to search for a drink. The whiskey bottle was on the top shelf over the sink and she dragged over a chair to stand on in order to reach it. She poured herself a finger of the amber liquid and filled the glass to the top with ice and water and took a small sip. Carrying her glass into the living room she sat on the couch, resisting the urge to cover the fabric with a clean towel. She lit a cigarette from the open pack Dylan had left on the coffee table, inhaling deeply. The smoke felt cool as it went down her throat. They'd had a lot of time to talk on the boat over, and she'd promised him she would try to be a good wife. But now that they were here in the unbearable heat and humidity, she wondered—should she have stuck to her plan to remain in Washington with her father? There was a palpable energy here that made her nervous, as though everyone was on tenterhooks due to the possibility of war.

Placing her drink on the table next to her she leaned back and closed her eyes.

When Dylan entered the cottage an hour and a half later, she woke up, surprised to find herself in the unfamiliar surroundings.

"You look exhausted. Let's get you to bed."

She let him help her to her feet and tuck her in, his kiss soft against her cheek. But she didn't sleep, instead lying awake and listening to his snores as she contemplated her life.

CHAPTER FIVE

Manila
September 1940

Rosemary reached through the mosquito netting for the cup her husband had placed on the bedside table. Dylan, newly promoted to major, had left at first light, heading to the base and thankfully leaving her to sleep; the heat kept her up most nights, the only rest coming in the wee hours. The coffee was cold now, but the coolness on her tongue was welcome. It had been unbearably hot for many days, the sun nearly invisible through the moisture-laden air. The monsoons were late this year the natives had told her, and without the cooling rains the heat was unrelenting.

She sighed, leaning back against the soft pillows, her mind going to her family in Washington, D.C. and her decision to accompany Dylan to this remote island in the south Pacific. Being so far from her friends and family was wearing thin, letters received and sent not enough. Her gaze went to the large casement windows, opened wide to let in the cooler night air. Above the Dipterocarp trees the sky was charcoal. It was eerily silent, without the usual call of birds or even the buzz and chirp of insects. Suddenly she was fully awake, her senses alive with disparate scents riding on the breeze—animal dung mixed with the cloying scent of flowers, and the odor of rotting fruit--the familiar bouquet of the jungle surrounding the cottage where they had lived for the past month. But today something else stirred.

Pulling the mosquito netting out of her way she stepped out of bed, moving to the window to breathe in the distinctive fragrance of coming rain. The wind came up, causing her thin cotton nightgown to billow and swirl. An instant later the sky opened up and a million dancing hooves raced across the tin roof above her. Climbing over the sill onto the porch, she watched the heavy curtain of silver pour onto the parched ground, turning it into cinnamon pudding. Her heart lifted as the temperature dropped; this was the moment she'd been waiting for.

As rain pounded the leaves of the Dipterocarp trees some broke free and fell, floating away like small boats in the quickly forming streams. Closer to the house, chartreuse leaves, black twigs and cream-colored flower petals twisted and turned in the rush of water, a dress parade in the race for lower ground. An intense longing went through her to paint the enormous trees with their leaves sodden with rain. The dark green held a bright shine of light--maybe a bit of Payne's gray and cerulean blue, she thought, mixing the oils in her mind. Bright green vines twisted through their limbs, silvery gray raindrops pooling on the smaller leaves. Where the trunks met the earth, roots stood out like flying buttresses. Banana trees swayed in the wind, turning from yellow-green to almost purple as the light shifted--lush, saturated colors. But her paints, like the rest of her life, had been left behind.

Rain soaked her nightgown as she made her way down the porch steps. Water ran down her face, her hair in limp strands that she pushed behind her ears. Opening her mouth to the sky, she drank in the fresh coolness. The path around the cottage had turned to mud and she pushed her bare toes into the squishy red clay feeling like a naughty child. Behind the Dipterocarp trees, the bananas tempted—bright yellow, they jutted from a curved green stalk, a dark purple flower unfurled at its end.

From her sheltered spot beneath the wide banana leaves she regarded the steady curtain of rain. She twisted off a small banana, peeling back the thick skin to reveal the pale succulent fruit. As she bit into the soft flesh, the tangy sweetness satisfied some inner craving. Her mind scattered backward to the first days in Manila, the shock of the alien culture and language, the unrelenting humidity. By now she was used to the bright malongs of the natives, the staccato beat of the Tagalog language, and the customs so different from her own. But if she had known what Dylan would expect of her she might not have agreed to come along.

Nearly every day brought unwelcome social responsibilities—organizing teas, bridge, cocktail parties, classes to learn the never-ending protocols required of an officer's wife. Organizing was not a talent of hers, nor was the social chitchat—her shy, artistic nature did not do well in these situations. But she felt the pressure of Dylan's dependence on her. Promotions were made and broken by the wives. And so she kept her chin up, trying to overcome her anxiety.

She glanced down at her mud-streaked legs, the wet, transparent nightgown. What would Dylan think if he could see her now, sitting in the mud eating bananas like an animal? A giggle worked its way out of her throat and then she began to laugh, giddy and hysterical. Luckily there were no witnesses to this act of complete abandon.

Leaving the bananas behind she fought her way through the wind and mud back to the cottage, worried about her husband's imminent arrival. But before she could take a shower and wash away the evidence, he had jumped from the jeep just arrived, his eyes widening when he saw her standing on the porch. The jeep drove away as he came toward her.

Instead of chastising her, his eyes were alight with desire. He removed his jacket, threw it over a chair and took her in his arms. "You look like a water nymph," he whispered, his breath warm against her neck.

He picked her up and carried her inside to the shower, placing her on the floor in order to strip off his freshly pressed trousers and shirt. He flung them aside, his eyes never leaving her. "Hold your arms up," he ordered, sliding the wet nightgown over her head until she was free of it. He turned on the shower waiting for the water to warm as he examined her body with the look of a predatory animal.

She shivered with anticipation, her own desire rising until she could barely stand to wait. "Dylan," she moaned, reaching for him.

He gazed at her, his eyes at half mast. A moment later she was in the shower and pressed up against the shower wall. The water slid down her body, taking the red mud along with it as he did things to her that he'd never done before. The long awaited rains had loosened something in him as well, as he kissed and caressed her until she thought she might faint from pleasure.

When it was over he stared at her. "Did you do this on purpose to distract me from my duties?"

Rosemary smiled. "It's the monsoons, Dylan, the monsoons seduced us both."

It was several days later and Rosemary was in the kitchen, the whine of the jeep sliding up the mud-slick road alerting her to his arrival. It was after five and she was dressed in a cotton skirt and peasant blouse, her hair dry and styled. Her cheeks were powdered, her lips painted the vermillion that Dylan favored. A few moments later the engine shut off, and the car door slammed, followed by a string of curses. By the time he reached the door she had it open, holding out a glass filled with ice cubes and bourbon. "Here, dearest. I'm sure you're tired after a long day."

"That blasted mud has ruined my last clean uniform." Dylan frowned, shaking his pant legs. He didn't look at her as he took the glass and went to sit on the couch. His irritation took up all the air in the room.

She sat next to him, her hand on his arm. "I'm sorry you had a bad day, but you're here now with me. Let's not let it spoil what we have together."

Dylan turned, his expression softening. "You're right. Another ruined uniform is nothing in the grand scheme of things."

"Tell me about what happened and I will try and listen like a dutiful wife."

Dylan laughed and lit a cigarette. "You would not believe what goes on over there. What a bunch of idiots. I've been trying to tell them for a week that we needed to drill the horses, and now the rains have started." He sighed and leaned back, blowing a plume of smoke into the air. "Even the Filipino soldiers haven't been listening to me. They must have known the monsoons were on the way. For God's sake, it happens around the same time every year."

"We certainly made use of the monsoons, didn't we?" Rosemary asked innocently.

Dylan gazed at her. "Something came over me that day, seeing you standing there soaking wet, rain streaming down, that diaphanous material clinging to your body. God's, woman, I couldn't control myself at all."

"You were like a wild animal."

"You seemed to enjoy it."

"I did, very much."

Rosemary went to the kitchen and poured herself a drink. Through the window the trees moved back and forth in the wind as rain lashed the branches. She imagined herself walking barefoot along rain-drenched paths—she could almost feel the mat of leaves and detritus massaging the bottoms of her feet. There were places under that dense canopy that remained dry no matter how long it rained; she envisioned herself curled up next to a massive trunk breathing in the heady smells and feeling the power of the storm tearing through the tree limbs above her. Into this vision Dylan appeared, his arms around her as the rain lashed above them. They kissed as they had in the shower and she felt the same desire rise up.

"Rosie?"

Dylan's voice cut into her reverie. She pulled her gaze from the window and picked up her drink, heading into the living room. "I was caught up in a fantasy about the two of us…"

He raised his eyebrows. "The two of us…what?"

"The two of us out in the jungle together."

"Making love?"

"We could be, I guess." She smirked.

"You have a one track mind."

"And you hate that one track, I suppose?"

"I adore that one track. Come over here and I'll show you just how much."

But the days that followed brought more and more tension and worry, Dylan's moods turning dark and brooding. He was exhausted when he got home, many nights falling into bed right after the evening meal. Rosemary remembered their courtship, the hours passed lying under trees on blankets, a picnic spread around them, smoking cigarettes and discussing art and feelings they shared about the world and each other. His cheerful demeanor and droll sense of humor had made her laugh. Now he was obsessed, consumed with what was happening here, leaving little room for her needs.

Her father's words came back to her, the meaning quite clear. She had to grow up and stop acting like a spoiled child. This was the life she chose, the man she loved. It was her job to support him.

She forgave him because she knew what he worried about. Dylan was overworked and out of his depth in his new position. This posting to the Philippines was organized to train the Filipino soldiers in fighting techniques in the possibility of war with Japan. Japan had already invaded China. Japanese warships moved through the South China Sea. War was coming—there was no doubt about it.

As the days and weeks went by she forgot about that first wild day of rain and what happened between them. She knew he needed a helpmate and strove to do the best she could to lighten his load, organizing clothing drives for the poorer natives, as well as hosting cocktail parties for Dylan's fellow officers and their wives. Despite the threat of war, there was a festive atmosphere in the city of Manila, with legalized gambling and fancy dress balls at the officer's club that went on until dawn. After living in the Philippines for five years, General MacArthur had been referred to as a *Dhobie* soldier, a term that meant 'gone native'. And this devil-may-care attitude was pervasive among most of the men stationed here.

Rosemary enjoyed dressing up in taffeta and pearls, making the rounds on Dylan's arm; and the socializing was agreeable after a couple of cocktails. But sometimes late at night she would wake to hear the rain and the chirp of tree frogs, sitting up to breathe in the primordial scents of rotting vegetation and wet earth, remembering the passion that had flared between them. She'd been taken elsewhere that day, the two of them traveling to another time. Where it was seemed right on the edge of her consciousness, but she could never quite bring it into the light.

Rosemary's days included meeting the locals, her trips into town to organize the clothing drives bringing her face to face with many native women. Ahgoo, a dark-haired woman in her late thirties, had befriended her, answering Rosemary's endless questions about the life and culture here. As they sorted through donated clothing Ahgoo told her that the less fortunate native people were supported by their families and the church, that true poverty was not high in the Philippines; what people needed and wanted most was work. She went on to say that the people had lost a lot of self-respect as a result of being colonized for so many years by the Spanish. She added that many good things had also happened during those years, such as a much higher standard of living and access to education and modern medicine, but it all came with a price. There was an undercurrent of resentment that any country occupied by another was bound to have.

After the revolution against Spain in the late 1800's, the Filipinos had wanted to take their country back, but then the Americans arrived. Ahgoo looked apologetic before she continued, saying that *of course* the Americans had brought a lot of good things to the country, building schools and the introduction of democracy, but still...

Rosemary listened, marveling at her intelligence and clarity. Although not wealthy, she was obviously well educated and from a good family. Rosemary's mind opened to a new vision of what life here was all about, making her want to know more. Her knowledge of foreign countries was minimal, to say the least.

Working side by side, Ahgoo and Rosemary had conversations on topics that were conspicuously missing from other relationships—subjects like women's rights, (women in the Philippines still did not have the right to vote) and comparisons with the U.S.—(Ahgoo was very interested in all aspects of life there.) Also they discussed the religious practices here and what the native beliefs were before Catholicism was introduced. Rosemary learned that Islam had come to the Philippines as early as 1300 from Indonesia, and was still the most prevalent religion in the south. Before that time the people worshipped a variety of spirits and gods that guarded the mountains, forests, and streams and even houses. Bathala, who created man and earth, was the most important of these gods. Shamans and priests were in every small village helping the people placate these spirits, some of whom were good and some not so good. What happened in the afterlife depended on behavior in this life.

The Filipino woman also questioned Rosemary about her family. Did she have sisters and brothers? Did they go to church? Rosemary told her that in the U.S., a lot of people didn't believe in God, explaining that her husband's family was deeply religious and members of the Episcopal Church, but that her family thought that organized religion was a farce. "And Dylan agrees."

Ahgoo was shocked by this. "You go against your husband's family?"

Rosemary smiled. "We don't see them much. His mother wasn't happy with our choices, but she accepts it now." In reality Caroline and Samuel Hughes had not accepted the atheism. And army life had kept them from visiting Dylan's parents as much as they would have otherwise. Dylan had adopted her family, leaving his own behind.

Her life before the Philippines seemed so remote now, as though she'd seen it all in a dream. The people she loved were so very far away. Her heart contracted at the thought of them. How long would it be before she saw them again?

CHAPTER SIX

Ft. McKinley
November 1940

When Dylan reached his office and opened the door, a putrid wave of heat poured out. Damn it all to hell! Why hadn't someone thought to leave a window open? He left the door ajar and walked across the room, roughly pulling up the window on the other side before he searched for a fan. He was really sick of this infernal heat and humidity. It made work in the office feel like a living hell. Who could get anything accomplished in these conditions? The rains had cooled it down for a few days, but it was back again with a vengeance.

On his desk a stack of memos had been placed, filled with the newest intelligence coming out of Washington. There was one regarding the recent trip of King Leopold of Belgium to Berchtesgaden, asking Hitler to release Belgium prisoners and to provide better provisions. The king had raised enmity with several leaders earlier in the year when he surrendered his country instead of holding fast. The French Prime Minister, Paul Renaud, as well as Lloyd George, who considered the king to be a double-dealing reprobate, vilified him at the time. Dylan was not up on all the scuttlebutt about this particular situation and had more pressing things on his mind, for instance the letter recently received by Roosevelt from Winston Churchill. Leafing through the various *communiqués* he was able to come up with the summation of their recent correspondence, as well as the army's take on what was coming down the pike. Things were heating up on the western front and he longed to be in the thick of it. He sighed in frustration, scanning down the list of countries that were now in the hands of the Germans. If Roosevelt didn't do something soon there would be nothing left to save.

He lit his first cigarette of the day, inhaling deeply. No one had arrived yet, but soon the room would be filled with fellow officers trying to bring order out of chaos. His thoughts spilled into the past again, his mind going to his wife and how little they saw of each other these days. In army terms, she had turned into a model wife, but in personal dealings their love life had stalled. He was too tired at night to do anything but fall asleep. They were socializing a lot, which seemed to help, but he needed the closeness that came with intimacy. He needed a fucking day off. He knew Rosemary's moods were affected. She seemed distracted and remote. They'd discussed it once or twice and she'd assured him that she understood. But did she? He certainly didn't.

He had arranged for his driver to find her some art supplies, hoping that would help her through his lengthy absences. Surprisingly she'd begun doing portraits of the wives, giving her a chance to get to know the other women one at a time. She was spoken of highly now and he was proud of her. And, he had to admit, her notoriety was helping him too. A wife like that was an asset in this political game he played, her popularity bringing him the kudos he needed. He longed to hold her in his arms again, to enter that world they'd visited together on the first day of the monsoons. He had to get some time off.

He glanced out the window, not happy to see several of his fellow officers approaching, their heads together in conference. It would be a long day.

"So, Dylan, what's the latest from HQ?"

Dylan looked up at Major Carter. "I haven't had a chance to go over today's memos. Is the general around?"

"I saw him over at the mess hall. He's not in a good mood. He's heard something, but he did not share it with the likes of us," he gestured expansively to the other men walking toward the office.

Dylan heard the irritation in the man's tone, knowing it was because of Dylan's standing with the general. "I am his aide, Carter, I can't do much about that."

"Not your fault, Hughes. I understand, but it tends to get under my skin, especially since I outrank you."

Dylan chuckled. "As soon as I find out anything of interest, you'll be the first to know."

"Hey, how is that gorgeous wife of yours? Annie showed me the portrait she did—Rosemary is a talented lady."

Dylan smiled. "I don't spend enough time with her. I'm hoping to get a day off sometime soon."

"According to Annie, she seems to be taking care of herself."

"I think she loves her art more than me," Dylan said with a laugh. The image of Rosemary, naked, her body pressed up against the wall of the shower, arrived unbidden in his mind. Blood rushed into his face, making him hotter than he already was. He loosened his tie and shook the image away, putting his mind on organizing the scattered memos on his desk. But that image lingered at the corner of his mind, distracting him and making him long for her even more.

CHAPTER SEVEN

Manila
April 1941

The news came in April. All civilians were to be evacuated in May. As a result, the trip Dylan arranged to the mountains to get out of the heat was bittersweet, their frenzied love-making and talks lasting deep into the nights. Now that their time was to be cut short they were both overcome with a sadness they could hardly express.

The April days in the mountain town of Baguio were filled with sun and the sweet scents of the many blooming flowers. Bougainvillea covered the crumbling walls above the Spanish city center and climbed into the trees, filling the green depths with their bright pink and red blossoms. Birdsong filled the silence as they walked up the road out of town hand in hand.

"I don't understand why I have to leave. Nothing dangerous has happened."

"I don't have any control over it. For whatever reason they are insisting that civilians leave now. I'm heartbroken, but we must be strong."

They climbed over a low stone wall and found a place to sit where they had a view of the city below. They sun was about midway down the western sky, and above them stretched a cobalt dome filled with white puffy clouds moving slowly by. After the heat and humidity in Manila the weather in the higher elevations was heavenly.

Dylan reached into the wicker picnic basket and pulled out a bottle of Spanish wine they'd purchased in town. He opened it and poured red wine into two glasses, handing one to his wife. He placed his on the ground beside him and lit a cigarette, drawing the smoke deeply into his lungs. "We knew this day was coming."

"But now that it's here I just can't believe it."

Dylan stubbed out his cigarette and wrapped his arms around her. As her head came to rest against his chest she began to sob.

"Let's try to enjoy our remaining time together. I'll take you to dinner tonight at our favorite place, how does that sound?" A few moments later he pulled out the ever present camera he'd purchased in Manila, taking endless pictures of her, his hands on her shoulders to turn her slightly, or position her shawl and hair. "You look like a goddess," he told her, snapping away.

Their nights left little time for sleep, their arms tight around each other as they tried to make up for the parting to come. In the mornings they woke to the sounds of birds, the heady scents of flowers wafting through the open casement windows.

On their last morning when Rosemary reached for her robe, he pulled her back. "I want to remember you just as you are now—your eyes sleepy, your body unclothed, tangled hair strewn across the pillow," he murmured, kissing her. She did not complain. But later when he reached for his camera she turned her head away. "Even more delectable," he laughed, "with your shadowed profile, half closed eyes and strands of hair across your cheek. Sultry chiaroscuro."

She sat up, pulling the sheet over her body. "Did you take a picture of my exposed breast?"

He grinned.

"Dylan, you have to have those developed. What about the man who...?"

He placed his camera down and leaned over her. "It's a tasteful photo, Rosie, an art shot." When his mouth met hers she was instantly plunged into a world of sensation, the camera forgotten as she let herself go.

Driving down the mountain later Rosemary moved close, running her fingers through his hair. "If you get yourself killed I will never forgive you."

He turned and smiled, but the light in his eyes had dimmed.

༺◎༻

Rosemary suspected she might be pregnant before she left Manila, but decided not to mention it. It was too early to be sure and she didn't want Dylan to get his hopes up for nothing. The parting was terrible, both of them in tears before she boarded the ship. She kept her eyes on his form as it grew smaller and smaller until she could no longer see him, and then hurried into her cabin where she could sob without witnesses.

The first few days of the ocean trip were the hardest, tears catching her unawares and sending her into a despair she couldn't shake. The closeness they'd achieved before she was evacuated had made up for every cross word and argument they'd engaged in. She loved him, and couldn't imagine being without him.

The locket Dylan had given her hung heavily around her neck, as though the people inside it grieved for her. And in her grief and sadness she opened it to gaze on them, hoping she would be comforted by their familiar faces. But instead, the cabin where she sat began to shimmer and fade, her current reality disappearing as she fell backward in time...

"What shall we have for our evening meal?" Rebecca asked, pondering the larder with the kitchen maid. Her father was in his study working—he would be no help with decisions of this nature. She glanced down at her well-mended dress, thinking about silk and lace, fabrics to buy in the local mercantile to take to her dressmaker. It would not do to be dressed so shabbily when Edgar introduced her to his parents. She thought of her future, smiling in anticipation, but then the premonition came, the dark one about his future. She was plagued with visions, dismissing most as foolish. But there were others that frightened her and kept her awake at night. Was she a witch? It scared her to think these blasphemous thoughts, to know the future before it happened. She had been this way since she was a small child, her parents laughing at her when she spoke of the need to go around a rock strewn path or to avoid a tree due to a branch that would soon break and fall.

On the way to market she walked close to the cliff, heading across the grassy windswept fields that she so loved. If ever she could paint it would be this wild scene she would do first. But women were not artists; it was the men who honed their skills, the men who were given commissions by the most prominent and influential families. She'd dabbled a bit with egg tempera and pastel, but her father had not encouraged her to continue, despite her burgeoning talent.

She turned her thoughts away from the frustrations of her life, her mind going to the man she loved. She would see him tonight—he would come for dinner. Edgar Hathaway. Why hadn't he yet asked for her hand? Did he really love her as he said he did? He was so congenial, so full of himself, and yet he had captivated her heart. She gazed out to sea, the salt air filling her nostrils. Gulls were wheeling and shrieking above the rough surf. One day soon she would walk the steep path to collect the mollusks her father so enjoyed to eat. She envisioned her bare feet, her skirts hiked up as she waded, her head bare of the usual bonnet and warmed by the sun. It was a place where no one went where she could behave as she wished. She was tired of the restraints of the day, the heavy fabrics covering every part of her even when it was hot. She thought of another time in the future when women did not have to wear bonnets, when skirts were short and feet could be seen. If only she were there now. How she knew all this was a mystery, but she accepted what she saw, knowing it to be true. It was her gift.

Edgar would be scandalized if she mentioned her wayward thoughts. His family members were staid and deeply religious. A moment of misgiving went through her, turning her joyful mood into worry. She would need to keep her thoughts well hidden for fear they would turn Edgar against her. But a moment later she skipped across the field, letting her natural exuberance return as a laugh bubbled up and was released into the misty air.

When Rosemary woke her heart was racing, as though she'd been running. She opened the porthole and let the fresh sea breeze blow in. She tried to make sense of it. Had she been in the past? It certainly felt that way, although it could just be a daydream run amok. Maybe time had merely intersected for a moment. She'd read stories about such things—H.G. Wells, Jules Vern, and others.

By the time Rosemary arrived home in Washington a month later there was no more doubt that she was carrying

Dylan's child. Conceived on the trip to the mountains, the baby would be born in late January. She was sad that she hadn't mentioned the possibility to him before she left. He would be thrilled, just as her father had been when he heard the news.

As summer approached her thoughts centered on Dylan and what was coming down the pike. She had heard nothing from him, despite having written several letters. But with ship travel curtailed the post was iffy at best. Nonetheless, she worried.

When she hadn't heard anything by the end of July she had serious concerns. The Japanese had announced their war plans. The newspapers were full of stories. All the islands, including the Philippines, were on their list for take-over. Her hands went to her belly where new life was beginning. She wanted to share it with him. What if…but she stopped the thought before it could take root. No. She would remain positive despite the constant anxiety in the pit of her stomach.

By September Rosemary was frantic for news. Her nights consisted of thrashing around in between nightmares, anxiety a permanent fixture. Dylan was in a vulnerable position as aide to the general in charge, and from what little she could glean, the Filipinos were in no condition to hold back the Japanese forces. Dylan had worked with them for months, drilling with the horses and trying to make them combat ready, but he'd told her that the Filipinos were simply not the fighting type. It would be up to the American troops to hold back the tide.

In October she woke to terrible cramping and a lot of blood. Her trip to the hospital was fraught with tears and recriminations. Amanda accompanied her, trying to soothe her sister and having no luck whatsoever.

"I should have used birth control," Rosemary managed to mutter, embarrassed to be seen in such a vulnerable position. "I'm such a fool."

"Maybe they can save the baby," Amanda said hopefully, squeezing her hand.

But Rosemary knew they couldn't. And later, when her own life nearly went too, she mentally careened into a dark tunnel. The doctors kept her in the hospital for over a week before they allowed her to go home. From that moment on Rosemary pulled away from her friends and her family, her need to be alone stronger than it had ever been. She cried nearly every day, sure that if she'd only done this, or hadn't done that, she wouldn't have miscarried. Dylan's face arrived in her mind, making her cry even harder. Was he safe?

When Pearl Harbor was attacked in December, there was news soon afterward of Japan's move against the Philippines. "Is he still alive?" she asked her father one January morning in 1942, fully aware that Boyd Hewitt would not be able to answer the question.

He smiled sadly, reaching for her hand. "I certainly hope so, for all our sakes, but the news out of Manila is spotty at best. I only know what the newspapers print, and it isn't enough to go on."

Her thoughts went to the baby who would have been born this month, her hand coming to rest on her empty womb.

As time went on, Rosemary's art, the only thing holding her together, was put aside in her obsession with the war. She perused every newspaper she could find for details of what was happening. MacArthur was pictured in nearly every article, his swaggering stance beyond annoying in the face of what she knew of the man. In March of 1942 Roosevelt had ordered him out of the Philippines amid worry that the islands were about to fall. He'd promised to come back with help. In Rosemary's mind MacArthur had hung the troops out to dry. If the island was taken, her husband and all the others would be killed or taken as prisoners of war. She sank even further into despair.

CHAPTER EIGHT

Journal entries

<u>*December 1941*</u>

*D*earest angel, from this moment on this little book becomes not only a recital of events, but also a dissertation with you. The fall of Manila is a matter of hours, and I know now that my letters written since the war will never reach you. This has been a sad year—first because we have been denied our only pleasure in this world—that of being always together, and second because I know you are terribly worried about me. I think of nothing but you—all of this hate and killing has come to my door—yet my mind is miles away where only the noises of nature exist. I am yours alone. Neither of us has been religious, although we've both had our way of worshipping God. Nevertheless, three days ago I prayed that God help our side if he felt it the right side.

We have been quartered in an old church in Bacalor for three days now, and it is here that I asked God to help our cause. I say this because I sometimes wonder whether the United States isn't just as responsible for this war as Japan. We have attempted to freeze her economically and left her no avenue of retreat—put her in a position of a cornered rat. However, who started it is a sideline—my reason for relating my prayer is to tell you that suddenly I found myself awestricken when I entered this *antique place, and I wanted to break from the fetters which keep me from believing in a life hereafter. I have had that feeling ever since, and though my thinking mind tells me that the idea is fantastic, nevertheless something within me keeps saying it's so. Not that I want a life hereafter for selfish reasons, but a love like ours cannot die—it will forever remain as fresh and beautiful as the bougainvillea which grows so luxuriantly around these old buildings.*

The locket appeared in Dylan's mind, the one that he'd given Rosemary on the day he proposed, the one she now wore around her neck. He'd bought it because the initials inside were Rosemary's initials. RH. Somehow that piece of jewelry represented what he'd written here—an eternal love. He did not know why. He longed for her in a way that clutched at his heart.

January 3, 1942

The New Year has come and gone, my thoughts of you crowding out everything here for a few hours. We continue to fall back and have almost reached Bataan. Manila has been uncovered and is under Japanese control. This is to spare the civilian population. Our only hope is in holding the enemy at bay until more troops and air support arrive. We have had no air from the outset. Nichols and the big chiefs or our air force have left for Australia, having lost most of their planes on the ground. As we have no air support whatsoever, our troops are at the mercy of hostile aviation. We must conceal ourselves like moles. Hostile planes are forever overhead either scouting or dropping bombs. How long we can last on the peninsula of Bataan is a matter of conjecture—certainly as long as our ammunition holds out. After that I do not know! Only in the last extremity were we to withdraw into Bataan, and here we are on our way.

January 10, 1942

General MacArthur left Corregidor today and visited our besieged troops of Bataan. He was so optimistic about the whole situation, and so enthusiastic that I suddenly found myself feeling a part of momentous events. He stated that the enemy's temporary superiority of the air would soon be a thing of the past, and if events proceeded as expected, a counter attack was in the offing. He further stated that our defense had caught the imagination of the American people, and plans for immediate help by way of Australia are in the mill.

The General cited me in orders today with a Silver Star citation for my trip up to Demortis. I feel rather ashamed receiving an award for such a little service when so many others have done so much more, but I shall be worthy of it and even greater awards.

January 16, 1942

The hot breath of the enemy is close upon us. Our forces still hold the pre-arranged main battle position in Bataan—the Abucay-Moron line. Several times in the last four days the line has been dented, but has been straightened out again. Gen. MacArthur has dispatched a message to all troops in part as follows: "Help is on its way from the U.S. Thousands of troops and hundreds of planes are being dispatched. It is imperative that our troops hold until these reinforcements arrive. I call upon every soldier in Bataan to fight in his assigned position, resisting every attack. If we will fight, we will win; if we retreat, we will be destroyed."

The Filipino, even though trained, is not a fighter; the Philippine army generally speaking is not trained. Most adept are they, both officers and men, in getting into civilian clothes after fleeing to the rear. I have observed soldiers in the front lines before contact has been gained, leisurely talking to girls, picking fruit, lazing in the sun. Thousands of troops and hundreds of planes from the States are necessary, and when they arrive, there will be an end to this punch-less force, which Gen. MacArthur now commands.

January 19, 1942

The long awaited arrived yesterday. Three small ships destroyer size, one cruiser, and a troop transport resembling the Washington in size and make-up appeared off Moron. The three small ships entered Port Binanga, the other two lying outside. Their position was at the extreme range of our 155's, but nevertheless we opened on them, and so hot was our fire that by evening they withdrew. Air reconnaissance this morning indicates no ships along the west coast between Subic Bay and Corregidor.

General W. and I personally watched activities of vessels sighted from the vicinity of Moron, and personally fired upon Japs hiding in a haystack just south of Moron. I have never enjoyed hunting of any game, but this is the greatest game-hunt any soldier has ever been privileged to engage in. This barbarian horde has violated every rule of mankind, has invaded this peace-loving nation, has raped the Filipino girls, has sacked their homes. The day of recompense is I hope not far off.

This morning about 8 a.m., a dogfight between 3 of our P40's and 4 Jap fighter planes was fought over our C.P. One American plane was definitely shot down. It fell in Bagac and exploded upon impact. Its pilot, Lt. Anderson, bailed out and was followed by a Jap who riddled pilot and parachute, then strafed the dead pilot on the ground. This action was observed by Thorpe, our corps Provost Marshall. Anderson fell 100 yards from where he stood. Another example of the sporting Jap! Two Japs are believed to have been shot down, one pilot bailing out in the China Sea.

January 22, 1942

Situation, if anything, worse. Tokyo broadcasts, which we hear most often, because San Francisco news reports are usually jammed by the enemy, indicate that Japan is fighting against the tyranny of the U.S. Before the war they indicated that the U.S. was building an iron ring around them. Results prove that the U.S. is not even prepared to defend her own interests in the Far East, let alone go on the offensive. In listening to Tokyo broadcasts I sometimes wonder whether Japan did attack Hawaii without warning, seize Wake and Guam, then jump on the P.I., Hong Kong, Singapore and the N.E.I. Perhaps it's all a bad dream. Nevertheless I've seen and fired on the Japs, so they must be here. This conclusion might also be drawn by our presence on the peninsula of Bataan.

January 23, 1942

Darling wife; I live from day to day, thankful when I am permitted to live another. However, I live not with the expectancy for the new day, but for the comparatively quiet night, which follows the day. It is then that I am able to think of the happy days, which we have had together; it is then—when I am permitted to sleep—that my dreams bring us together. Sleep has become my only pleasure.

Our situation becomes more precarious. Our 1ˢᵗ Division is still cut off; landings are being made south of us in the service area. I expect our C.P. to be swarming with Japs at any time. The west road has been under constant bombing all day, bombs falling a km. or so from our location. Aircraft carrier reported off Bagac, probably softening us with bombs in preparation for another major landing. Our 155's are the only obstacle to such an attempt. The line on the beaches is a thin one which will break on the least provocation.

January 27, 1942

This has been one of the blackest days since the beginning of the war. The enemy made another small landing on our rear early this morning. This makes three in all. These people get hidden in the jungle and all hell won't blast them loose. Their absolute control of the air makes it impossible for us to contain them and starve them out. General W is very disturbed about the situation—believes these landings a prelude to much larger ones. We cannot take men from our front line; it will be a miracle if it holds with the number of men now there. If we stay where we are I have no doubt that the whole Corps will be cut off. Gen. W recommended to Usaffe today that we consolidate all our means further south where our beach defenses will not be so thinly spread. Otherwise this is the beginning of the end.

February 1, 1942

Life becomes an ever-increasing burden; if it was not for you my dearest wife, and my desire to see the complete annihilation of the Japanese who have brought much misery and sadness to the Far East, I would not care about my personal safety at all. These Japs are fanatics, made so by their Government, whose only desire is to kill; the only way to stop them is to treat them in a like manner.

When an enormous explosion went off Dylan put the pen down. What the hell? It was the middle of the night, for God's sake! Oh how he wished he'd sent these damn journals, or letters, or whatever they were, back with the last courier. It was becoming near impossible to get anything out now. He'd had no word from Rosemary nor had he been able to send her the smallest note. He heard a bloodcurdling yell and rushed into the darkness to see what the latest catastrophe might be. But things were quiet, no one hurt. *This time,* he thought as horrific images arrived in lurid detail. He'd experienced enough of this for a life time, and yet he knew that this was only the beginning. There would be a lot more death and pain before it was over.

If only seemed to be the first words on his lips in the morning and the last before he drifted to sleep, that is when he had a moment to rest. Everyone was exhausted, their eyes red-rimmed and hollow. If this kept up much longer they would all lose their minds. Was that the intent of the Japanese troops—to keep them awake so long they couldn't think or even hold up their weapons to fire back? He picked up the pen and continued, despite his shaking hands.

You may not know me when I come back, dearest. The sight I am seeing will haunt me forever as I have no taste for the kill as some do; thus I may be reluctant to discuss this phase of my life, and too, my hair becomes a little grayer around the temples each day. I shall try to 'sparkle' the way you want, but it may be dimmer than before. My love for you is the food which makes it possible for me to face the new day.

March 29, 1942

This is the sixth day in a row the enemy has kept us under continual air raids. We live in tunnels which will take a lot of bombing before it goes. I have seen many victims with legs amputated above the knees, punctured internal organs bringing about slow painful death—too horrible to discuss. I have tried not to hate the foe, to view the war impersonally as a mighty struggle of governments, but the sight of the war's results in the maiming of human beings, brings to me a fanatical hatred of the treacherous greedy Jap. When a bomb shook our tunnels today and your wedding picture fell, landing face up on the cot, I stared into your sad eyes, and you seemed almost alive. I had the feeling you knew what was happening here. We have reached the stars together and will find them again and they will be even brighter.

April 12, 1942

4 months and 4 days of war—it seems a lifetime. Last year we were preparing for our never to be forgotten trip to the mountains. With your departure imminent we were both under a cloud but none so dark as this one, which now covers the entire world.

I am amused at the Tokyo broadcasts. You must have had a vivid picture of Gen. W. and me fleeing to Corregidor from Bataan in spite of the might of the Japanese fleet. General W. was ordered to Corregidor 3 weeks ago when he took command of all forces in the P.I. It is such lies that make wars possible; without them many difficult situations could be easily solved. It appears now that the Japanese are attempting to incite the Filipinos against the Americans so that the task of reconquering the P.I. will be made more difficult. Should Corregidor also fall (which it must not) I doubt whether there will be more fighting in Luzon. The P.I. will simply enter into the peace treaty...

...I plan to send this diary to you tonight, my dearest, so today's entry will be the last. The situation is serious; we have been under

continuous air and artillery pounding for days. Corregidor is so small that any hit on the island strikes something. ..we are attempting to get out the official records of this war by plane tonight, and as all of the North Luzon Force and 1ˢᵗ Phil. Corps records have been destroyed, it is imperative that this book of personal and official data be preserved. As you can see it is uncensored, so the need for secrecy as to its contents is indicated. It will throw a bomb-shell I know into the MacArthur story of the war, but I wrote nothing in criticism of any individual or any group. I simply wrote the truth as it appeared to me at the time. The fall of Bataan has saddened me more than I can say, for no end of work was done there. For months we continually improved our positions; every inch of our front line was walked by Gen. W.; and it is prophetic that when the break came it was in Gen. Parker's 2ⁿᵈ Corps. The right flank of Gen. W.'s old Corps was first struck just west of the Pantingen River, failing there they moved the force of their attack to the east, folding up in order the 41ˢᵗ, 21ˢᵗ, and 51ˢᵗ. the Phil. Div. moving up to fill the gap found such chaos that the avalanche could not be stopped. As the line folded from west to east, panic reigned until the whole 2ⁿᵈ Corps line was gone, enabling tanks to drive into our rear areas. Actually there was little infantry action except by elements of the Phil. Div. as the front lines had been so bombed, strafed and shelled that the line gave way on first contact. It was inevitable, however, that these lines should go, and it is a tribute to Gen.W. that the lines of his old Corps held in spite of the debacle on the east side. However, they were unable to attack as ordered by Gen.W. and so found themselves pocketed. No doubt in spite of Gen. K.'s capitulation many preferred to fight guerrilla warfare in the mountains....

On May 6ᵗʰ, 1942 General Wainwright unconditionally surrendered all U.S. and Filipino forces to the Japanese. On

May 12th the last troops holding out in the Philippines surrendered on Mindanao. It was over.

May 14, 1942

The year just past has been <u>long</u>*, dreary and sad. If and when I return, my life will be devoted to her; I do nothing without her consent, military duties included.*

CHAPTER NINE

Washington
October 1942

The dream was upon her again, Rosemary's reality disappearing as she slipped into the past...

"Edgar, no! You must listen to me. Do you not trust me? I thought you believed in my premonitions. Something will happen today. I do not know the details, only that it will happen suddenly and take you unawares. Please, Edgar! Do not leave!"

Rebecca followed Edgar on foot to where he would board the carriage for London, her only hope to stop whatever it was before it happened. He was minding his own business, waiting for the carriage, when she noticed a dark haired man standing in the shadows. A carriage approached, a private one that had no intention of stopping here, the horses in a full canter when the dark haired man ran from his hiding place and shoved Edgar from behind, sending him sprawling in the direct path of the carriage. "No!" she screamed, running headlong toward where he lay. She heard the driver call out, saw the dust rising on the roadway as she scrambled toward Edgar, her heart in her throat. The driver could not bring the horses to a stop quickly enough to avoid him, nor was there a way to go around with the trees that narrowed the roadway.

She pulled up her skirts and flung herself into the path of the carriage, barely managing to pull Edgar out of harm's way before it rolled past. "Are you daft?" the driver shouted at her over his shoulder.

How she managed it she didn't know. She sat there helpless, wondering what to do, when Edgar opened his eyes. "Becca? I was just dreaming about you." He smiled up at her, his eyes dreamy before he registered his surroundings. "Where are we?"

"Someone tried to kill you, Edgar."

"What?"

"Can you sit up?"

He took her proffered hand and pulled himself to sitting. "I have no memory of what happened," he said, his hand going to the back of his head where a lump had formed. He looked around. "This is not the route I chose."

"No, it is not," Rebecca agreed. "You were on your way to a meeting with J&J Printers on the High Road, but the proper coach does not travel this way."

He stared into the distance. "Now I remember. I was on my way to catch the one that comes by at noon. Why are you here? I'm certain I would not have brought you along on a trip like this."

Rebecca looked up as another carriage approached, the driver pulling the horses to a stop beside them. "Can I help you?" the whiskered man asked, looking down worriedly.

"Yes, you can. This man needs to be taken to J&J Printers. Is that on your route?"

"It is not, but since you are obviously upstanding citizens who are in need of help, I will take you. Climb in."

Rebecca helped Edgar stand, supporting him into the carriage. Once they were settled he turned to her. "Tell me again what happened?"

"I followed you, Edgar. I had a premonition that something like this was going to happen."

Edgar frowned. "I thought I strictly forbade you to continue with this silliness."

She laughed. "Strictly forbade me? Your memory has most certainly deserted you. I am not your wife, nor am I your daughter. I am a free and independent woman who thinks for herself."

"Now look here, Rebecca. Apparently the accident you predicted has happened. Time for you to take yourself home."

"Did you not hear my words, Edgar? Someone just tried to murder you. I saw it with my own two eyes. If I saw him again I would know him. Now who would do such a thing?"

Edgar shook his head, frowning. "No one that I know of. You must be mistaken. I do wish you would stay out of my business, Rebecca. This obsession with me and my life cannot go on."

"Obession? I am merely looking out for the man I love. If you would but listen to..."

Edgar put his hand over her mouth. "You will not speak of this again. And if you have some other idea of future events I do not want ot hear of it. Do you understand me?"

Rebecca clutched at the fingers that were keeping her from breathing properly. When he removed them she gasped in air. "You are not in your right mind," she whispered, straightening her hat. "That bump on your head has addled your wits."

Edgar ignored her, his gaze going to the scene rushing by outside the carriage. Once they reached the High Road he called out to the driver, "Please let me off here and then take this woman back to where you found us." When the coach came to a stop Edgar stepped down. Rebecca watched him hand the man a wad of bills, his dark gaze on her before he strode away.

Rosemary woke in her bed on the third floor, surprised by the clarity of the dream. It was like a song she had heard, a distant memory that rose up from time to time. It must be from the book she was reading; Daphne Du Maurier's *Rebecca* was an eerie story. That Rebecca's life was similar in a way to the Rebecca Rosemary seemed to become, both of them controlled by men. In the bath she forgot about it, her mind already on her art class and getting out of her father's house for a while.

"Where are you off to?"

Rosemary turned from her laborious trek across the marble tiled hallway carrying her easel, a sheaf of paper and a box of pastels. "Art class."

Her father smiled. "It's good to see you up and about again."

"I have to get on with things. I haven't heard one word since the day I left Manila."

"That doesn't mean he's gone, Rosemary. Have a little faith."

Rosemary sighed. "If you say so, but those words sound odd coming from your mouth."

"Can you imagine the chaos over there? Maybe you should speak with the wives who came back on the boat with you, see if they've heard anything."

"I did that back in July. Sara has had two letters and Candace three."

"But surely not since the surrender in May."

"No, not since then. What do they do with prisoners of war?"

"The Geneva Convention rules apply. He will not be tortured."

"You say that now in this house with all our finery around us. Can you imagine the conditions over there?"

Boyd frowned. "I'm afraid I can, my dear."

"Sorry, father. I'd forgotten."

"I put it all behind me long ago. Your birth brought the light back to my eyes."

Rosemary thought of Ilise, her mother, the fair-haired woman who had loved her father and raised two girls with him. It still made her sad to think of her despair and subsequent suicide. No one had ever understood what drove her to slit her wrists. It had taken her father a year to recover, his horror and sadness keeping him hidden away from his two girls. She and Amanda had bickered and fought, vying for his attention and not getting it. And now, years later, she hardly had any memory of the woman who gave birth to her. "I'll be back around four," she told him, adjusting her heavy load.

Outside the car waited, the chauffeur taking the supplies from her to stow in the boot. It was a beautiful fall day, crisp and clear, but her mood was not in keeping with the weather.

As the car sped toward Georgetown she thought of Dylan and the war. Living with her father had been a good thing to begin with, his support helping her in the early days after the miscarriage. But now…was it time for her to get a place of her own? Other wives had housing on the base, something she'd shunned. Why live there when her father wanted her close? Maybe she would speak to Amanda about it. Her sister was about to marry for the second time and would surely have an opinion on the subject.

"Why don't you rent an apartment, Rosemary? That way when Dylan comes home you won't be tied into anything. He'll surely expect you to live on the base again, won't he?"

Amanda had come by for a visit, the two of them together in the living room in front of a roaring fire.

December had brought a snow storm, stopping traffic in its tracks and bringing gusts of cold wind down from the north. Today the sun had melted a lot of it, and the roadways were clear again, at least until the next storm arrived.

"You make it sound like a done deal that he'll come through the war unscathed. I can barely think beyond today. But maybe you're right. Father won't like it, but I really feel I must have my own space now."

Amanda smiled. "I know just the place. How about we take a drive over there this afternoon? And afterward you can help me pick out a wedding dress."

"Surely not white again?"

Amanda scoffed. "No, not white. I'm going with cream this time. Gretchen will be in the ceremony as my bridesmaid."

"Is it proper to have your daughter in your wedding?"

Amanda frowned, her lips pursing. "I don't really care if it is or isn't. Henry and I have dispensed with protocol, something you should applaud."

"I'm only concerned with Father's reaction."

"No you're not! You're being your disapproving self, as always. Why don't you mind your own business? Surely you have enough on your mind to think about without concerning yourself with how I'm conducting my affairs. Henry isn't Father's golden boy like your husband."

"That's uncalled for, Amanda, especially now. We may never see him again."

Amanda's expression softened. "I'm sorry. I'm nervous about the upcoming wedding. I shouldn't tell you, but…I'm pregnant. We have to do this quickly or…"

"Everyone will know."

Amanda turned bright red. "You are so judgmental!"

"I'm only stating the obvious. I don't care whether you and Henry have slept together. It isn't as though you're a virgin. Now stop taking offense at everything I say and let's go look at the apartment."

Amanda looked mollified, a smile hovering around her full mouth. "I'm so excited about the baby," she gushed. "And Henry is positively ecstatic!"

Rosemary's stomach clenched, envy snaking up her spine. If she hadn't lost the baby she would have a part of Dylan here with her. She rushed from the room, hurrying up the wide stairs to fetch her coat. She didn't want Amanda to see her sudden tears.

✵

The apartment was in Georgetown, close to the studio where Rosemary took art classes. The street was tree-lined and shady, red brick apartments a nice contrast against the green. Rosemary spent many pleasant days furnishing her new digs with antiques, and perusing shops for dishes, glasses and silverware. She loved the light that filtered in through the tall windows, thinking the living room would make a wonderful studio. But it was only a rental and if she began using her oils here the dark wood floor was bound to be ruined.

She thought of the belongings she'd left behind in Manila, wondering what had happened to it all. A bleak vision filled her mind, the small house where they lived lying in rubble, the enormous trees scorched and toppled. She thought of Ahgoo and the other brightly dressed Filipinos, their smiling faces, the babies the women carried on their hips, wondering if any of them still lived.

It was only a week before she was settled in, wondering why it had taken her so long to move out of her father's house. Boyd had been disappointed, but he understood. "You need your own life," he told her.

And when she and Charles, her art teacher, began to spend more time together, she had a place to bring him where no questions would be asked.

As the months went by her art flourished and her social engagements grew as she made the rounds with Charles. He knew the art scene, taking her here and there to openings and exhibits she would never have known about. So far her landscapes and still life's were not good enough to be shown…but soon, he told her.

At first when he asked to stay over at her apartment after a night of wine and dinner, she refused him, but it wasn't long before she gave in. He was a nice man who obviously enjoyed her company. It wasn't long before her weekends revolved around Charles, his courtly attentions giving her a reason to live again. With his love of food she had a renewed interest in cooking, making exotic dishes she'd never have thought of without a person who appreciated eating. Two years had gone by without any word, and by now she was positive her husband was dead. She tried not to think about him, putting her mind firmly in the present whenever her thoughts wandered.

The dreams she'd attributed to her choice of books persisted, taking her into the past and leaving her wondering why…

"You will not be mollified at all, will you?"

"Why should I accept your apology when I know you are not sincere? I love my art. Why should I have to give it up once we are married?"

"Because ladies of wealth and standing do not do such things. Your father agrees with me, Rebecca. Would you go against him too? You are the most stubborn woman I have ever met."

"In that case maybe we should postpone the wedding. I am in the middle of my pastel studies and I am loath to give it up."

Edgar stared at her. "You would put off our marriage because of a pastel class?"

"Why not? We spend nearly every day together. What difference does it make?"

His eyes went soft as he gazed at her. "There are other benefits to being married, Becca. Have you considered those?"

"I suppose you are referring to the marriage bed. If you would like to begin before our vows I am not averse to the idea."

"Rebecca! I am scandalized! How can you be so brash and wanton? Of course we will wait. What if I got you with child?"

"There are ways around that, Edgar. I know several midwives who are versed in herbal lore."

Edgar shook his head, his eyes narrowed. "I hope sincerely that this attitude of yours does not mean you are no longer unspoiled."

"What? I would never...I only mentioned this because we have plans and I know you love me. How could you even think such a thing?"

"Because your ideas are so outlandish, that is why. You scare me sometimes with your free-thinking ways. Most women are afraid of the wedding night, but you seem to be perfectly fine with it. That in itself makes me suspicious."

She reached up on tiptoes and kissed his chin. "But you love that part of me—you've told me so. Why so stuffy?"

"I have a reputation to uphold. It is one thing to be stepping out with a woman who speaks her mind, but to marry one? Worrisome, Rebecca. Very worrisome. I need a good wife, one who enhances my standing in the town. You do understand that, do you not?"

Rebecca scoffed. "Fiddlesticks, Edgar."

Rosemary came back to herself, wondering how she had ended up sitting in the grass outside her apartment. She laughed, thinking about the relationship between these two people, but she also had a feeling that something disturbing was on the way. They did not seem suited to one another. Rebecca's vision of Edgar was skewed. Possibly he'd been one way when they met, but he was stuffy and pretentious now.

When she was in the past she *was* Rebecca, her thoughts belonging to this other woman, her sense of the past era where she lived clear in her mind. The times were repressive for women. It was all so real, as though she had lived that life. But she knew that was impossible.

Charles arrived, his brows furrowing when he spotted her. "Communing with the trees?"

She laughed, letting him pull her to her feet. "I had the funniest dream," she told him, dismissing it as she put her focus on Charles.

✧❦✧

"I'd like to move in with you," Charles announced the next morning over coffee. He adjusted his paisley robe over his bulk, staring at her with an intense expression.

"I can't do that, Charles. My father would find out, my sister would be horrified. And I'm still a married woman. You know how society loves a good scandal."

"How long will you wait, Rosemary? He's been gone for over two years."

"And the war is not over."

"You've told me you believe him to be dead."

"And so I do. But I can't get on with my life until I know for sure."

Charles pushed his straggly hair back off his forehead. Although somewhat heavy around the middle, he was handsome, his gray hair thick like a lion's mane. He was fifteen years her senior, but he had the energy of a much younger man. "What if you never find out?"

She turned to the stove. "I can't discuss this. I've said no."

"I want to marry you. Will you ever be free enough to do that?"

Rosemary turned, too shocked to speak. "Charles, I…we…I thought we had an arrangement. Even if Dylan is gone for good I'm not sure I would want to marry again."

Charles stood, his tall frame slightly stooped from his time bent over an easel. "I love you, Rosemary. I want a child."

This declaration was too much. The thought of giving up on Dylan and marrying this man—having a child? It was preposterous. Her feelings for him were limited to their time together—she wasn't in love with him. "No, Charles. I'm very fond of you, but…that will never happen."

"So, you've been leading me on all this time?"

"Of course not. I had no idea you felt this way. I thought you were happy with how things are."

Charles let out a long sigh. "At first I was. But the more time I spent with you the more I wished…well, I'm older now, but I wanted a child. I've never married. I would love to have an heir."

Rosemary felt sick for a second. He suddenly seemed repugnant to her. "I'm sorry, Charles. I am not the person to give you an heir."

It was in the weeks after this conversation that Rosemary began to come somewhat unglued. She'd had a letter from a friend, delivered to her father's house, that intimated that Dylan was still alive. "He's in the hands of the Japanese along with my husband," Sara had written. "He hasn't been able to get a letter out."

Rosemary had promptly written back, asking for more details. But Sara's next letter hadn't been so hopeful. In the meantime Charles was becoming overbearing, expecting her to be with him every moment. When she'd finally had enough, he shouted at her and hit her. Thankfully he'd left after that, giving her the opportunity to consult with her sister.

"He hit you?"

Rosemary nodded, showing the bruises. "I don't want to give up the apartment, but I'm afraid I might have to."

"Move home. Henry and I will take care of things here."

Rosemary gazed at her very pregnant sister, smiling despite herself. "Henry is good for you."

"I agree," Amanda said cheerfully, her hands going to her enormous belly. "If I can keep this one inside for another month I'll be out of the woods."

Rosemary laughed. "You can always say the baby came early, you know."

"That's what they all say."

"Don't worry about it, Amanda. Who really cares?"

"Well, listen to you! I guess the affair with Charles changed your holier- than-thou position."

"Did I really have that attitude?"

Amanda smirked. "What do you hear from your friend—the one who said Dylan is alive?"

"She said he *might* be alive. But the last letter I got talked about several officers who've died, including Jack, Dylan's best man in our wedding."

"Oh, I liked Jack. How does she know?"

"Someone must have gotten a letter out."

"It must be maddening not to know! I feel sorry for you, especially now with Charles and everything. You need to let us take care of things. Pack a bag and move home."

It was the next day when Rosemary confronted Charles. "Please remove your things from my apartment."

Charles didn't say a word, his systematic removal of his clothing, and his shaving equipment, tooth powder and toothbrush from the bathroom taking more time than it should. He gave her one last lingering look as he left the apartment. "I didn't mean to hit you," he said. "You have an uncanny way of driving a man to violence."

Rosemary didn't answer as she held the door open. Once he was gone she cleaned and scrubbed the apartment from top to bottom, stripping the sheets from the bed and rearranging furniture. It was four in the afternoon before she finished. She poured herself a glass of wine and settled into a cozy chair to watch the sunset through the window, glad to know he was no longer in her life. When she closed her eyes Dylan rose up in her memory, a sad expression on his drawn features. Could he still be alive? She barely remembered him.

CHAPTER TEN

Journal entries

<u>*4 January 1943*</u>

W*e were taken to a wind-swept plain about one mile north of our enclosure this morning and there commenced breaking ground for another garden. Although I wore a shirt constructed from a blanket, a Japanese enlisted man's work shirt, a blue jumper made of hemp—sold to us since arrival here, and a Navy raincoat—lent to me for the day by Gen. W., I was chilled to the bone. Both a.m. and p.m. consumed in this work; I was unable to give any time (except watering) to my own piece of ground. I say my own—it has been assigned to five of us...*

Our animal farm, with the addition of the goats, which arrived today, now numbers 20 pigs, 22 goats and approximately 90 chickens. These last are being cared for by the Japanese members of the garrison. They come to us soon.

<u>*10 January 1943*</u>

How my system craves grease! A slice of bread and hog fat would be pure gold.

NIKKI BROADWELL

11 January 1943

Bitter cold again. There is no fire within my body; I cannot keep warm. Weeded garden east of enclosure. Temperature 49* within our squad room.

17 January 1943

Sun. brought squad room inspection and much needed bath. Hearts, livers, lungs and stomach of cattle, which are being slaughtered for canning, are to be brought to us every other day until end of month.

19 January 1943

Approx. 25 kg. tripe and lights in soup tonight. It was marvelous.

23 January 1943

A.M. worked on hill. We learned through the camp authorities that Domei has announced to American nation the presence on Taiwan of Gen. W and other American generals.

30 January 1943

On hill a.m. Plot slightly increased. Tea and tobacco are god-sends from the camp authorities, but eternal hope for freedom, food cooked by you, an open fire with you as scenery, and together (we two) living, laughing, and loving kindles the dim lamp which burns forever within my heart.

8 February 1943

Cold weather again. Temperature in squad room 48*. Hearts, lungs, etc. (approx. 25 lbs. every other day) which terminated Feb 1st are sorely missed. My cravings for certain foods have passed through the following stages: 1st, scrambled eggs and toast; 2nd, hot stewed figs; 3rd, oatmeal with cream and sugar; 4th, buckwheat cakes with buckwheat honey or maple syrup; and now cheese (any kind) with toast or bread. (over 6 month period)

10 February 1943

Throat still raw. Did not go to work in p.m. as did others. Have yet to see sun during Feb. One of our best men died late this p.m.

12 February 1943

Burial services in the antique cemetery. He was only 27 years old. His complication was Ludwig's angina followed by pneumonia. As he was a Catholic, in accordance with Gen. W's request, the Nipponese authorities permitted him to be buried without cremation. Gen. W included me in group attending the funeral. How good life is and how fragile! Death is not a subject for fear, but it is so terrible when loved ones are not present at the end. I must go on, my love, until our reunion. There are so many important things I must tell you, most important of which is my eternal, undying love. And when the time arrives when we too must cross over the river, I hope our ashes may repose, mingled in one urn.

13 February 1943

Day of continuous rain, spent with my morbid companion, "Crime and Punishment". Pleasure derived from reading is God-sent, but I must be careful, for my eyes bother me considerably. (Vitamin A soluble in fat for assimilation.)

Dylan was suddenly overcome, his head going down onto his arms. He was crying without making a sound. He had to take a break from writing, had to let his eyes recover, had to stop thinking anything would ever change.

6 June 1943

Moving again. Dismantling rabbit cages and readying

11 June 1943

It appears we have arrived here in the midst of the rainy season, for ever since our arrival on the 8th, the rain has come down silently and steadily. Fortunately it was intermittent during our trip on the open sugar cane RR cars and subsequent march, so we arrived here comparatively dry. The camp is in a vale, high ground on all sides. The bamboo fence surrounding us defines an area of about 40,000 yds.(200x200 no more) thus far the mud has been so heavy that I haven't strayed more than a few yards from our barracks. A sea of mud intervenes between barracks and the wash rack and benjo. The water resembles weak coffee, but an analysis of it discloses no dysentery or typhoid germs. Three long buildings quarter the Generals, the American and British Colonels, the Dutch and hospital. Buildings are of construction similar to our C.C.C. camps, beds of slatted bamboo, ticks (if and when issued) filled with straw. Partitions between rooms do not go to the roof (as rafters substitute for ceiling) but a certain amount of cloth screening helps keep down the fly menace. Food, as heretofore, means rice and soup 3 times a day. We've had some bananas, some meat in the supper soup the first day, and several new vegetables, including bean sprouts, squash, and a watery vegetable (not as bitter as the Karenko daikon) referred to as chayote. Our R.C. supplies dwindle and an oz. or so of corned beef a day seems to soon be a luxury of the past. The ants are quite a nuisance and hard to cope with. We plan to hinder them with water traps when containers become available. They are especially fond of R.C. sugar, bananas, and parts (both exposed and unexposed) of sleeping P.O.W.'s

12 June 1943

Our animals came through in good shape. We now have 19 chickens, 24 goats, and 66 rabbits (including several litters of young). The egg production (for the hospital) has dropped to 1/3 (approximately 12 eggs/day to 4), probably due to lack of a runway and consequent loss of exercise. The goats pass the nights in an empty benjo, meander about during the day in the rain, which they don't like, so when possible, they climb under and walk in the barracks. The rabbits appear to be faring best; they don't mind close confinement in their hutches, for many of them have young to care for.

29 June 1943

Malaria is spreading itself in the camp. I have 4 in hospital and 2 sick in quarters. Of the 336 members in camp, 21 are in the hospital, 13 sick in quarters. Sick exceed 10%.

91

"Stone walls do not a prison make
Nor iron bars a cage;
Minds innocent and quiet take
That for a hermitage.
If I have freedom in my love,
And in my soul am free,
Angels alone that soar above
Enjoy such liberty."

Thursday, July 22 1943

I rise and mechanically perform my chores drugged with sleep and dreams of you. The long day passes. In a short time I shall return to those dreams, so real, so beautiful, so necessary. Exquisite, tender, understanding, long-suffering little wife, I hope that you are well.

Friday, 23 July 1943

I am in good health. Please do not worry. I send my love to all.

Saturday, 24 July 1943

We get a heavy rain almost every afternoon making walking on our one and only path almost impossible. Yesterday it rained so hard and for so prolonged a period that for a time our building stood on a small island—the drainage ditches could not carry the water away fast enough. Opportune slackening prevented any damage to the buildings, and a wonderful outdoor bath was provided for all who desired one. Tom and I did!

Sunday, 25 July 1943

Meat in the soup and one half pineapple promised per prisoner of war (so it was rumored yesterday by one in our midst) and it's materialized.

July, 1943

By means of the inadequate medium of our language, I shall try to jot down some ideas on love, war, religion, and government, not because I think these ideas are profound, but because I desire to view them in retrospect when I leave this life of close confinement.

Love It can be limitless, climbing as it sometimes does from the physical, to the spiritual, to the intellectual. Upon reaching its pinnacle, it is the mind which caresses the body.

War It is inevitable. All life is a war—a war between individuals, between classes and creeds, between nations. An examination of the animal world reveals a similar situation, the strong devouring the weak, spiders ensnaring flies, bats ranging miles to eat night-flying insects, hawks pouncing on pigeons. Might does not make right, but nevertheless in enforcing right, might is of paramount importance.

Religion It has been shown through history that a personal God and personal immortality are necessary to the bulk of humanity. Having sprung from members of the Christian religion, and having been brought up from childhood in the Episcopalian (Church of England) faith, I find its ritual most beautiful. I feel thus about the ritual of the Catholic faith also. The latter is more ornate, more barbaric, and appeals even more forcibly to the imagination. The principles of Christianity are most admirable and could easily serve as a code of ethics. However, though I enjoy the beauty of the service, and appreciate the high principles, I have not been able to reconcile as yet the existence of a personal God and personal life after death, though undoubtedly there is a master-force which maintains a cosmic universe.

Government A government by the wisest and best (as I believe the framers of our government, George Washington, Benjamin Franklin, Thomas Jefferson, etc., favored.) A cross between democracy and autocracy. A government in which all have equal opportunities of education, which can be solved (I believe) by State and Federal subsidized Universities. Authorized birth control to prevent criminals and insane from propagating.

By a cross between democracy and autocracy, I mean particularly the right to vote, which should be restricted. By so doing, unscrupulous politicians will not be able to secure the votes of the ignorant by bribe, as those given a vote will realize the value of their vote and will do their best to cast it toward better government.

Wednesday, 28 July 1943

More malaria....there have been 67 cases since our arrival in this camp.

Tuesday, 3 August 1943

Policing, carrying of bricks, etc. I am having trouble with a few men who are willing to have the balance of the squad do their share of the work, which we are ordered to do by the camp authorities. After consulting with my assistant, I have decided they shall not share in the next issue of rice issued to workers. The amount of work-rice is negligible, but as most of these old men think of their stomachs above all else, failure to receive this extra spoonful will probably make them see the light.

Thursday, 5 August 1943

Many prisoners, I among them, are afflicted with itching skins. Harold says he believes the lack of vitamins, particularly B, responsible. In some cases, by scratching, the skin has been broken and open sores have resulted. Many are covered with these blisters and present a hideous appearance.

Friday, 6 August 1943

We have gotten a heavy rain in the late afternoon almost every day. Today it rained off and on all day, making exercise impossible. Our library of pooled books is a blessing.

If I ever get out of here I will live only in your reflected light.

Dylan was surprised as always by how writing took him away from where he was—writing and reading, and his thoughts of Rosemary were the only things that kept him sane. His writing had become more flowery and sentimental of late, traits he had never recognized in himself. Too bad these missives weren't being read by Rosemary—she would laugh to see what a romantic he'd become.

CHAPTER ELEVEN

Washington, D.C.
late January 1943

The war raged on while Rosemary tried to sort out her life. She had to accept that she was now a single woman and act accordingly. Lunch with her friend, Sara Roberts, from Ft. Myer days, revealed disturbing news.

"I had a letter from my husband three months ago but I've heard nothing from him since then. He mentioned that malaria was rampant in the camp and that several officers had succumbed. It is not a pretty picture over there." She wiped her eyes with a napkin.

"Did he mention Dylan?"

She shook her head. "He only said that some of his closest friends are dead now, and I think Dylan falls into category."

"Oh God." Rosemary tried hard to control her tears, but a few slipped out. "I've had the sense that he's gone for some time now, but hearing this is difficult, nonetheless."

"Do not take my word for it, Rosemary. There's still hope."

But Rosemary had no more hope, her mood dropping into a black hole. During her affair she'd been able to keep her spirits high, settling into her art and her time with Charles. But now, here at her childhood home with nothing much to occupy her, she was not able to keep the depression at bay. Without Dylan in her life what would she do?

The dream arrived while she was on the third floor dozing on the bed. She'd been crying, falling into a stuporous sleep that seemed to shift into the past. Her consciousness fell away as she became Rebecca, the woman in the locket…

"You lied to me!" Rebecca tied on her bonnet and straightened the dark wool cape around her shoulders. "I must go to the market before it closes, but we need to have a long discussion. I never knew you to be so secretive!"

"Rebecca, for goodness sake. Just because I kept my plans from you does not mean I am secretive. Husbands and wives do not share all. If they did all hell would break loose."

"So I am expected to carry on alone for the next month without a cross word, is that it? How can you be so utterly selfish?"

"Are not all men selfish?" Edgar smiled.

Rebecca shook her head, dislodging her bonnet. She pulled it off and threw it on the floor. "Blast these things, anyway! I have a mind to go to the market hatless today."

"Do not be rash, Rebecca. You will incur the wrath of the parish ladies for sure." He bent to pick it up. "Now put it on again and act your part."

She grabbed it out of his hands. "I really do hate you, Edgar."

He laughed, grabbing her around the waist. "You love me, Rebecca. Now say it or I will not release you."

She wriggled but couldn't move from his grip. "Stop it! I have to go."

"Give us a kiss, Mrs. Hathaway, and tell me you love me."

Rebecca laughed, lifting her mouth to his. "You are truly a horrible man," she told him, "but for some odd reason I do love you."

He grinned, releasing her. "You will get used to my absence, my love, and when I return you will take me into your bed and make me happy to be home."

She made a little moue, fixing him with her most annoyed frown before heading down the lane toward town. "Please pen the chickens before they eat up all my pea shoots!" she called without turning.

By now she had to admit that these dips into the past were more than dreams. Her consciousness as Rosemary was gone when she was there, Rebecca's needs, wants and ways of looking at the world as clear as could be. Rebecca was light-hearted and loving but Edgar did not appreciate her. Rebecca knew this but chose to ignore it. Looking at it from Rosemary's perspective in the present Edgar's attitude infuriated her. He was off on a trip on his own, having failed to mention it. He took her for granted. Why were relationships so complicated? Shouldn't love carry you through? But love hadn't kept the war from separating her from Dylan, and love would not keep him alive.

CHAPTER TWELVE

Journal entries

<u>*Monday, 30 August 1943*</u>

*I*n compliance with the following instructions, I wrote the following article for transmittal to Headquarters:

"Future of the World War II to be written frankly, neither taking into consideration of your present situation nor the interest of Japan and your country, leaving our fate to Heaven, as the victory solely depends on God's will.

Presenter: Commandant Sazawa

Date of submit: Aug. 30th

<u>*Future of the World War II*</u>

I must of necessity preface any statements made in the following short discussion by advising that I am unspeakably ill-informed concerning the current events of the day. Therefore, statements made by me concerning the outcome of a giant fracas between the greatest powers of the world—opposed almost equally---would be a presumption which I cannot afford. However, the FUTURE of World War II is within my ken. No doubt all nations participating in this war will find themselves losers. Their youth, their culture, their wealth will have been expended in a conflict in which principles for which they fight will have changed before the conflict is complete. The FUTURE of this war, I hope, will be international tolerance of all races for one another, all creeds for one another, and redistribution of the world's wealth to prevent gigantic monopolies. Great men—noble men—wise men—unselfish men will be needed to decide such momentous questions. In their hands will be the FUTURE of World War II. May they be able to rise to the task which faces them!

Wednesday, 1 September 1943

I awakened this morning to find that I couldn't open my right eye—either an insect bite or poison from the grass I was cutting yesterday.

A Japanese artist, whose name the interpreter informs me is Mr. Niyamoto, did pastels of Gen. B, several others as well as me. Mine was in profile as my eye was still half closed.

Saturday, 4 September 1943

I was permitted to write a letter to you for transmittal—it's number 57, in detail as follows:

Dear, dear Rosemary:

First I must tell you that I am well. Do not worry, please. You must remain young. I long for word of you.

The latter part of July, I was permitted to write 35 words which were to be broadcast. I look forward to an answer.

God bless and keep you, dear wife. If my loyalty, constancy, and love are of value, you are rich indeed, for these feed the undying fire which has maintained me since your departure.

Forever your devoted, Dylan

Tuesday, 12 October 1943

Spent the entire day exercising ducks in the new pond, returning them to their runs, etc., etc. It is simple, childish pleasure, I suppose, but I do get a kick out of their pleasure in seeing me, even though I know it is hunger which creates those cute little faces, which look up at me expectantly. I am everything they have in the world in the way of father, mother, and so forth.

Thursday, 21 October 1943

In a speech before breakfast, we were informed by the camp commandant that many P.O.W.'s believe there will be peace in the near future. P.O.W.'s must disabuse their minds of such thoughts as events in Europe will affect in no way the War in the Far East. Japan has the will to win---even the women and children feel this. Thus we must plan ahead for six months at least, and we must cooperate in work on the farm. Carrying fertilizer (human) is part of this scheme. In Japan this system has been carried on for centuries...

Friday, 22 October 1943

Air-raid practices, blackouts! P.O.W.'s remain inside the buildings during the real thing.

Wednesday, 17 November 1943

Information received indicates that exchange ship reached Yokohama on Nov. 14th and that Nipponese papers blare forth cruel treatment internees received in U.S. Our papers undoubtedly contain similar headlines as Manila internees were taken out by this ship. It is regrettable that lies, near lies, and fanciful tales are necessary in human intercourse. In many cases, enlargements of cruel treatment are made for self-aggrandizement. Then, of course, there is the rabble-rousing propaganda fabricated by the leaders themselves for hate purposes. But when the propaganda takes the form (as the Nipponese does) of cruel treatment personified by rising at 4:30 a.m. to cook one's own eggs, it appears rather silly to us who would rise at any hour to boil and eat the unknown egg.

Saturday, 20 November 1943

...I have been 'puny' for the past three days. I believe a Post Exchange issue of a small jar of pickled papaya is responsible. It may have been slightly fermented—its effect has been devastating. Periodic pains and numerous trips! I have been able to swallow a little of our

60% rice, 40% barley combination, but even this brings on the pain. The sun-less days are especially depressing, when the slightest movement makes the stomach rumble. I write not in complaint; I write the meanderings of a P.O.W.'s introspective mind. I fear this life is slow decay mentally and physically, but I have been and hope to continue to combat such action. Dearest love, there can be no gangrene of the heart, I left it with you.

Dylan paused, rereading his words. He'd sent so many letters out, but had had no response from her. Others in camp had received dozens of letters. Had she decided to forsake him for another? He felt sick for a moment imagining her in another man's arms. He couldn't think like this. He probably wouldn't make it out anyway.

Wednesday, 1 December 1943

Old ennui has me by the tail once more. I sicken of banal conversation, flies, the smell of benjo. I try to control myself; I do not want to complain of my lot, but I long for you with surges of feeling mighty as the tidal wave.

Thursday, 2 December 1943

Still referring to yesterday's entry, I should say as mighty as the surge of the earthquake (jishin). I was shepherding my ducks to the feeding ground when there came a shock greater in magnitude than the numerous ones which have preceded it. Not only could I feel, but could see the ground shaking beneath me, and I was dizzy for minutes after its conclusion. No buildings came down, as they are all of one story, beams jointed with T and L-irons, sides braced with leaning poles.

Friday, 3 December 1943

There is no denying the fact that dreams have become the stuff by which I live. Surely I was with my Rosemary last night, so vivid the subconscious, arm in arm we were, I telling of events now happening…All so real, so wonderful, making awakening repugnant.

Saturday, 4 December 1943

Approximately a dozen guitars have arrived in camp. I got one as did many others. There is a Dutch E.M. who has promised to give lessons—it remains to be seen whether same will materialize. Mexico is known as the land of manana, but this fact gives it no priority over the East, land of (in the present ruling tongue) hashita. The E.M. is half-Malay as are many of the Dutch E.M.

Tuesday, 7 December 1943

Our camp Commandant, Capt. Imamura, left a few days ago— yesterday there arrived the new—1ˢᵗ Lt. Wakayama... He addressed us in the vein of the previous Commander. He informed us in addition that ennui indicated lack of cooperation and improper contact with the spiritual. Being happy is in the mind and so forth...Quite true but prosaic, are my sentiments. Try as I may to blend with the (so-called) spiritual, my mind constantly brings me back to earth and says, "You have loved ones at home."

Tuesday, 14 December 1943

The soup today (consisting of greens as usual) was so full of dirt that I couldn't eat it, save at breakfast when it contained some miso. Our kitchen crew do not overwork. Perhaps, however, it is not entirely their fault. The water shortage may have something to do with it.

Wednesday, 15 December 1943

It is difficult to realize that another Christmas is almost here. (It will be the 3ʳᵈ in a row without you, my dearest wife.) However, carols are being sung by our carol group...and so in spite of the comparatively warm weather, fog, and rain, the realization that Christmas is near grows in the minds of all.

Thursday, 16 December 1943

Strange the fads which start even in a prison camp. This time last year it was menus; now it's star-gazing.

Friday, 17 December 1943

Col. R. received a package from California today containing 100 Lucky Strike cigarettes, razor blades, bouillon cubes, dried fruits, and cheese. With the exception of a package of candy received by Col. F. some weeks ago, this is the first package received by anyone in the camp.

Sunday, 19 December 1943

It's been a beautiful, warm, cloudless day. I spent a delightful morning in the park. Near me the Protestant service was held; the familiar hymns bored into my heart as did the welcome sun. The Sunday supper brought pork-fat in the soup. Truly a wonderful day!

Wednesday, 22 December 1943

Sixty ducks arrived for Christmas. We also had a bun at supper.

Thursday, 23 December 1943

Dearest Rosie, I'm afraid that I must admit that the thought of Christmas without you once again has made me feel dull, numb, and apathetic. I cannot describe to you how I long for you—words are without meaning.

Saturday, December 25 1943

Excepting the fact that our loved ones are far away, this has been a Merry Christmas and feeling has run high. With the rice, we had pork broth for breakfast, fried pork, tomatoes, and cabbage for lunch (85 kg. pork for 500), and 51 ducks cooked in the soup for supper.

This afternoon athletic events, including a 3-legged race, sack race, spoon race, etc., were held, followed by a sing-song. The British 10th Squad produced a short melodrama, "King Arthur's Court 20th Century", which was excellent. They also provided a band consisting of a mandolin, guitar, tin cans, mouth-organ, and bamboo-wax paper trombone. All day long this same squad held open house; hours having been spent decorating, horse races were held and games like pinning the tail on a water buffalo were played.

Prizes of bananas were given to those participating in the athletic games, and everyone received approx.. 4 oz. of bread.

I managed to keep smiling throughout the day, but my thoughts were by a fireside on the other side of the world.

<u>*Friday, 31 December 1943*</u>

…As the year rolls out, I find that I have read 78 good books, which is at least something constructive. In addition, I've read parts of Epictetus—Moral Discourses, H.G. Wells—Outline of History, and Van Loon—Geography. These I could not finish due to unavailability.

I believe I've learned something this past year. Certainly I've learned to keep silent when the impulse has been to say something, which, once said, cannot be retracted. I've learned that there are many schools of thought, and although they may not agree with mine, they, nevertheless, may have merit. I've learned to live frugally without complaint. I've learned that separation from one's loved ones can be made tolerable when nights are blessed with dreams of them. I've learned that prejudices and hates must be fought against—with them, power and strength are useless. The things I want in the future are not all material. I want a little room, yes, a room filled with the books I like, a room where my wife and I can be together—our fortress, a room with an open fireplace; I want a hot bath, yes; I want some clean old clothes and a healthy body to put them on; I want some faithful dogs; I want a child, a son to embody the best in his mother and father, and more besides; I want to be myself with no ostentatious show; I want the love, admiration, interest, and respect of those I love. I want to grow old gracefully, admired by my friends. And finally, I want my ashes to mingle with those of my dearest creature, my own most dear wife.

May 1944 blot out the prejudices of the past; may it bring peace and understanding to the world. May I be a better inhabitant thereof—I shall do my very best to be!

To be happy

Excite no envy by ostentatious show.

In general, keep your thoughts to yourself.

Never (under any circumstances) dispute concerning religion and politics.

Live within your income.

October 1, 1943-December 31, 1943

To my beloved:

Upon completion, this journal of daily events (which I have kept as a reflection of my mind for you and for you alone) seems commonplace and trivial. For this reason, I add that no attempt has been made to dwell on profound subjects (no doubt the same result would have been obtained if I had)—I have written the simple little incidents which have occurred in this simple life and the thoughts which have emanated from the mind of one for whom the West is calling.

12 January 1944

Last night an hour or so before midnight three heavy explosions (each explosion resembling a string of bombs) took place. One observer (it was not I, for I was half-asleep on my canvas pallet) stated that 50 seconds separated the flash and the third string of explosions, indicating that the center of attraction was approximately 10 miles away.

14 January 1944

Between 400 and 500 letters arrived for Prisoners of War—all British. None for Americans! Recently we received the Nippon Times to include Nov. 28th. These papers were full of stories telling of brutal treatment meted out by Yankees in our internment camps. This world seems full of schemers and liars. The practice extends throughout the globe. We read what our (so-called) betters want us to read. We think as they want us to think. We fight for ideals, yet the ideals we fight for (according to the controlled press both sides) are the same for both antagonists. Sometimes I think that I never want to hear of politics again. It (and its companion-piece, religion) are used to justify actions— actions which need justification a-plenty.

15 January

There have been quite a few air-raid alarms lately (though I've neither heard or seen planes), and today the acting camp Commandant, told the engineer in charge of camp improvements, that the situation is serious and fox-holes must be dug. A few were constructed this afternoon—only sufficient to house the guard.

17 January 1944

Morning and evening roll calls at 7 a.m. and 8 p.m., respectively, are held in the same amount of gloom. In the morning Venus is in the eastern sky, Jupiter overhead; in the evening Mars and Saturn are slightly to the east of overhead. Usually, however, even these can't be seen due to the low hanging clouds, so we live in a world of our own in more than one way—beings whose bodies are here under the thick blanket of gloom, but whose minds are on the other side, which we hope is bright. Many men have become victims to this war—our numbers dwindle.

18 January 1944

Our library, subscribed to by almost all, is one means we have to dispel gloom. As I say, almost all have subscribed, having donated their books. In addition, the Tokyo Y.M.C.A. has donated some books. We have with us, however, one Pigdon, Australian Dr. (Col.), who has in his possession Well's "Outline of History", much in demand, which has not graced the library shelves. There are others---

19 January 1944

I came to the end of R.L. Stevenson's favorite, Sir Walter Scott's "Rob Roy", today. I'm afraid that in spite of the fact that H.G. Wells criticizes lovers of Scott as incurable romanticists, I am nevertheless one of them. In my present state, I find them an excellent anodyne, and the closer the heroines resemble my own wife, the more engrossed I become in them. Diana Vernon, beauteous horse-woman, lover of masculine pursuits, uncomplaining during periods of adversity, exhibiting loyalty to her religion and politics, fidelity to her beloved, made up a character not unlike my paragon.

20 January 1944

The camp received another T.B. patient today.

21 January 1944

My recommendation that we kill 30 of our stunted ducks for use at the hospital for T.B.'s has been approved. These ducks (stunted due to lack of food in the early stages of their growth) have pecked each other clean of feathers, making them very susceptible to the moderate cold spells, which we've had.

26 January 1944

I had a row with enlisted man who has been taking care of rabbits today. Since Brig. M put me in charge of the rabbits on the 11th, I've prescribed boiled vegetable (or at least vegetable dipped in boiling water). Cooper has his own ideas, and it has been only with the utmost supervision that I've been able to carry out my dictates. Two days ago, uncooked potato vines were fed, and since that time, three rabbits have died.

27 January 1944

I write this tonight to show how important a place dreams assume in this life of constant anticipation of going home. When the 6:30 bugle awakened me, I was in the midst of a plea—a plea unanswered—leaving me throughout the day sub-consciously depressed. In my dream, I had evidently returned to find my wife remarried. However, undaunted, I walked boldly into her bath (unbidden) where I found her radiant, beautiful, covered in soapsuds. She seemed undisturbed by my intrusion, but to my plea that she return to me, she was non-committal. I threw myself on the floor before her, grasping her knees with my arms, bowing my head in her lap, only to be returned from Heaven by consciousness.

28 January 1944

I am spending all of my day every day trying to improve conditions on my rabbit farm in order to produce for the camp. This includes watching diet carefully, disinfecting with means available, etc., etc. Smith now helps me with the young litters.

30 January 1944

T. C. prepared a delicious soup using the rabbits, 1 gallon cooking oil, 10 kg. beans, sweet potatoes from our garden, and large string beans which came in on the daily cart. Our fare for several days (aside from the miso soup in the morning) has been greens and the water they are cooked in, so tonight's soup was doubly delicious. If it brings me sleep filled with dreams of my wife, I can ask for no more.

31 January 1944

One of our pigs was slaughtered today. Wt. 63 kg. before being killed, 47 dressed. We get 40 kg. including bone, intestines, feet, and other viscera.

My dearest Rosemary, I fear that I will not come out of this alive. I wish fervently that I had given you a child before I got mixed up in this mess. Now it may be that the thread of this part of the Hughes name will be gone forever, lost in the fog of war.

Dylan realized that his former hope of an end to the war and rescue were slowly being mangled under the heels of the Japanese. His body was weak, his mind filled with a despair he'd never felt before. Rosemary's face loomed up in his mind, but even that had now become hazy and indistinct. They had spent less time together than his stint in prison camp.

Of late his dreams had been filled with another life, one that bore no relation to Rosemary—it took place in a past before cars had been invented, where clothing was formal. In them he was in love with a woman very similar to Rosemary in her sensibilities. They were to be married very soon. But even here in this other time and place a war loomed on the horizon, one in which he would surely serve. The man's selfishness and disdain of his wife bothered him. Dylan did not want to be that person, but he was, whether he liked it or not. And when he was back there he was happy enough as

Edgar, a smugness about himself overriding any guilt related to his behavior. He was a man at a time when men ruled. It was his duty to reprimand his wife and keep her in line.

CHAPTER THIRTEEN

Washington, D.C.
July 1943

The dreams were coming nearly every day now. Why was this happening to her? She asked her father about them but he waved her off with a laugh.

"Perhaps your mind wants to be free of this mortal coil for a while, Rosemary. Think of them like a good book you're reading. I know it's been enervating waiting for Dylan to come home, but the war is turning in our favor now. It shouldn't be long."

"You're quite the optimist. What makes you think he's still alive?"

Boyd Hewitt shrugged. "I will reserve judgment until the moment he does not return. I believe him to be a resilient young man. I have the sense that he will pull through."

Rosemary was in the garden, enjoying the sunshine when she felt the shimmer come over her. She tried to hang on to the present, but a moment later she was inside a dark house with the stink of paraffin and the aroma of roses.

"Why do you refuse to heed my warning?" Rebecca asked Edgar, one gloved hand resting on his forearm. *"I've seen the future. Why will you not trust me?"*

Edgar didn't speak for a moment, a frown appearing on his even features. His eyes darkened. *"If I took everything you told me at face value, I'd be relegated to my house and never accomplish anything."*

"What have I ever said that did not occur? It will come suddenly and you will not be prepared."

Edgar scoffed, gently removing her hand from his arm. He pulled down his vest, a personal habit he seemed unaware of, before checking his pocket watch. *"If you could be more specific perhaps I'd listen, Becca. But this vague uneasiness that comes over you is not enough to prevent me from going on a business trip. I have an appointment—how would I explain my absence? You have already saved me from one such disaster. How many of these are to befall me?"*

Rebecca fiddled with the strings of her hat, finally pulling it off altogether. A mass of brown curls tumbled to her shoulders. It was a hot day and they were standing very close to the forest trail. No one would see her act of indiscretion. *"You could say you were sick."*

He shook his head, wavy hair practically the same shade as hers falling across his smooth forehead. He ran agitated fingers through it and let out a heavy sigh. *"I do love you, but this has to stop. I cannot live my life with a woman who is constantly predicting one disaster after another."*

She gazed into the green-brown eyes, feeling a pressure in her chest. Could she keep her visions to herself? Of course not. They were part and parcel of her, gifts that came from the unknown. *"Please, Edgar. This one is strong. If you go I fear I will lose you."*

"No, Becca. I will go as planned and nothing untoward will occur. You will see." He smiled and grabbed her hand, pressing his lips to the inside of her wrist where her pulse beat.

Rosemary came to with a start. Someone had called her name. "Dylan? Is that you?"

"Rosemary, are you all right?"

She looked up to see her father bent over her.

"You just called out for Dylan."

"I did?"

"Yes, you did. Were you dreaming?"

"I was in the past—the 1800's, I think. But I can't remember much of the details. An argument? I don't know."

"Well, it's time for lunch. Your sister is here to see you. Sadly she has three children in tow."

Rosemary peered into her father's eyes, letting out a laugh. "You don't enjoy them at all, do you?"

Boyd scoffed. "Not even one tiny bit, I'm sorry to say."

Rosemary let him pull her up before following him into the house where shrieking high-pitched voices echoed. When she glanced at her father he shook his head and rolled his eyes, his expression resigned.

CHAPTER FOURTEEN

Journal entries

... O nce I sought glory, prestige, increased rank, and power, thinking these would bring happiness. Now I seek happiness, but in a different way. I feel much closer to nature. I want to wake up in the morning and be glad that I am a vigorous healthy animal, because the day will bring me into contact with other healthy animals, also glad that they are alive. I want the respect, admiration and love of my wife. If I ever get out of here I will do everything in my power to achieve these things.

March, 1944

I long for the March winds of my native land in my hair and the soft April rain on my cheek. Dear almighty, if you exist actually as you do in the minds of men, teach me to be patient and teach me to be grateful for the blessings I have had. I see you, God, through one I long for steadily, the center of my humble orbit.

April, 1944

A dreary life. It is impossible not to have fits of despondency, but I tell myself that soon we will be reunited, despite my bouts of sickness and the very real possibility that I will die before we are rescued. In my private world behind the mosquito netting, time and space mean nothing, and we are together once more.

Dylan put down his pen, wondering why he was unable to write in his journals about the persistent dreams. It was as though he was living two lives, one in some distant past and one here in this horrible place that he wondered if he'd ever get away from. And in between the past and here were the thoughts and visions he had of his wife that had become more and more indistinct; he couldn't even remember what she looked like. The wedding picture he'd carried with him had been taken, a cruelty he didn't understand. What he did remember was the feel of her skin and the way she smelled. He wanted to hold her in his arms again—please God, he thought, let this war end. It had been nearly three and half years since he'd seen her. She, at least, had pictures of him; any other pictures he'd once had were long gone, destroyed in the early bombing or during one of the many moves. When he remembered looking through his camera lens, seeing her in an artful pose, the curve of her cheek, dark eyelashes against pale skin, the hollow of her neck, he wanted to scream. Those photos were long gone, and his memory of them as indistinct as all the rest of his past.

The ones who remained clear were the two portraits in the locket, as though their life was more important than his and Rosemary's. He wished he'd never found that damned locket. Was Rosemary plagued as he was with a life that had long since been over? Was he losing his mind? He hated that man, hated the way he felt when he was Edgar. But the hate only came once he returned to himself. Edgar was perfectly happy to behave like a bastard. What did this have to do with his life—was this some lunacy brought on by deprivation?

The only thing good about it was his escape from this life he was leading, if even for a few moments.

May, 1944

We've been under a continuous blanket of rain for three days. Needless to say, the hollow which we occupy is a sea of mud and filth. Our black lotus root soup, with which we wet the rice before force feeding ourselves, continues with a vengeance. Our sow farrowed and nine young are alive and strong. Apparently there is some concern among our captors that when and if we are rescued that we do not look starved. Hence the rabbits I'm raising, and the chickens. We are to write letters saying that are being well-treated. Why have I not heard from you, my sweet? Others here receive letters with alarming regularity. I try not to worry when I picture you with another man, hoping that my Penelope, has not forsaken her Ulysses.

June, 1944

Emergency roll calls during hours of darkness; no visiting between huts; no talking among prisoners; no reading on benjo guard; no newspapers; no cablegrams. A captain, sixty-one years old placed in solitary for having in his possession a silver-bladed fish knife; a British soldier, three days in solitary for having in his possession a pair of shoes; a Dutch Colonel, in solitary for lying on his bed during daylight hours. Rain is relentless. I am sick with a flu that has entered the camp. My hand is not steady as I write. It has been discovered that I have jaundice too, which accounted for why I have not been interested in eating.

July, 1944

It would be difficult to give you a true picture of this odious life which we are leading—a few watery vegetables a day, over-crowded huts, malarial mosquitoes, ubiquitous sentries demanding salutes at every turn, the rain coming slowly down. Roll calls come at odd hours all night long and when they happen we must dress fully which allows more mosquitoes under the netting. We are being driven mad with interrupted sleep, most of us already slightly deranged from what we've had to endure.

August, 1944

8:30 roll call, then the battle with the mosquitoes awaiting 9:30 p.m., so that retirement under the netting can at least become an actuality; then the noises of the two kittens under the hut and the cries of the sentries engaging in establishing contact with one another by voice; then fitful sleep; then the cry of 'tenko, tenko', roll call once more at 11:25 p.m.; return to the small area of my canvas bed; gradual diminishing of sounds; incomplete sleep again; wild dreams; more shoutings; noises of squads other than own to answer the insistent, often repeated cry of 'tenko tenko', wakefulness in anticipation of further risings; then drowsiness once again; deep sleep at last; 6 a.m. bugle; movement of humanity again—a typical night.

Back problems due to loss of muscle. Have you ever felt you'd come to the end of the road—that you've come as far as you can—that there's a huge blank wall in front of you?

September, 1944

Our numbers diminish as men succumb to illness—TB, diphtheria, and this latest was heart failure as were several others. We buried him in the little cemetery. Typhoid has appeared in the camp. Our gardens are no longer to be tolerated—all plantings to be dug up, leaving us with rice and what we are given. Rice alone is what we live on now. I feel lifeless and weak, a perfect candidate for illness.

January, 1945

Sick and nothing to say. Less food now. Some eggplant and lettuce greens. Rice. Air raids. Many planes flying over now but we are kept inside with blackout curtains. No one will know of our presence in Shira Kawa. Bombs falling to our north. Rabbits have died from the cold but we have a few pigs now and chickens—unfortunately there is little food for them to eat. Another patient dies. There are twenty-four crosses and the most recent bear nothing but dried wreaths. They seem so pathetic with their sprigs of leaves and flowers. They last but a few hours and seem another reminder of the transitoriness of this life and the short memory of the human mind. I live expecting that the next day may bring my departure from this camp. I cannot describe the feeling; it is something approaching the supernatural.

February, 1945

In a few days I shall be off on a great adventure, one which I am glad you do not have to share with me. Through-out this period without you, which now amounts to all out four years, you have lived in my heart just as if you were beside me. I believe I am en-route to Manchuria via Japan, but of course I do not know. What we shall travel on I cannot imagine. We wait and wait as air raids blast our sleep apart. We are to travel by sea, it seems, but how this will occur is beyond me.

March, 1945

It is most difficult to put down on paper the thoughts which have been running through my head and the events that have taken place during the last 30 days. I am sure I have crossed the river Styx, met Cerberus on the other side, for Hell itself can hold no horrors any longer. For ten days I've been in a new camp somewhere between Moji and Nagasaki in the heart of the Japanese coal mining district. Since our arrival we've been strictly regimented, heads clipped, drilled, placed in an old abandoned mine shaft during raids, perpetually cold, but even this is Heaven compared to what has gone on before. We left Shira Kawa on February 19th. We marched to Kagi that afternoon, a distance of about 18 km., I should imagine, arriving sometime after dark. A train was commandeered and we were all jammed into two day coaches all seats filled and aisles jammed until any movement to the toilet at the end of the car was impossible.

In the morning we arrived in Taihoku where we detrained, and after a great deal of standing around in the rain, marched to the camp which was 3 or 4 miles away. We were wet through and spent the night in wet blankets and clothes leaving at dawn the next day for Kilung.

Again hours in the rain, then a tightly packed lighter trip we found ourselves on the Melbourne Maru. It seemed like hours before we got under cover on that ship. A long queue extended to the forward hold, and it moved very slowly. When I reached the ladder I discovered why. A hot fetid breath reached me at the top, and as I passed into that hold I found myself in an inferno. At the dock other prisoners had joined us, and we were now 700 in number. When I arrived my comrades were being bamboo sticked into shelves which extended around a 30' by 30' pit of blackness. It was my first taste of events to follow. There was sitting room only. Later our baggage was hurled down and sitting room became standing room. There was no going on deck except in small numbers during the day; at night wooden tubs for relieving ourselves were placed in the hold with us. How space was cleared for them is beyond me; before their arrival it was impossible to move without walking on fellow human beings.

The ship got under way on Feb 21-22. It seemed there was no air for breathing. I wondered how much I could stand. Later I discovered I could stand much. There is no limit to human endurance. Death is the end and it in most cases comes on little cat feet...six of us were to go. If I had known what was in store for us I would have said there would have been more. On the 22nd while waiting in the tub queue I came within a fraction of fainting due to lack of air and prolonged waiting. Knowing that I was going to fall if I lingered one more minute in that putrid air with the mob clambering on all sides of me, and knowing that I should be trampled unknowingly, I fought my way up the ladder, sightless, and like a tiger cat, at the top throwing myself on the deck where fresh air and running sea brought me back to complete consciousness. It was later that same day when our ship struck bottom.

March 22, 1945

If anyone had told me I could lie in the hold of a ship in Kilung Harbor for almost a week and live to tell the tale, I would have said, "No, it can't be done." We did not have enough water and fights broke out because of it. Dirty water from the tarpaulins dripped down and was collected. Diarrhea was on the rise. There was no time night or day when there wasn't a long line to the wooden tubs used for toilets. Men lay inches from those tubs. But no one could stretch out. The noise was nerve-wracking; the heat intense; the smell nauseating. The air and heat in the hold was like the foul breath of some predatory reptile of prehistoric days. I have not mentioned the lice. That hold was filled with them and when we were trans-shipped, thousands left with us. The toilet tubs at night were again a nightmare. Pitch black as it was, it was difficult to locate them at best; many of the men, who had become more animal than human, did not try.

Our first death occurred on or around March 2nd. It is believed he had spinal meningitis. He was buried at sea. On March 4th we weighed anchor. Some said we were off the coast of Shanghai. A second man was buried at sea. Two more dead men accompanied us to the empty warehouse near the quay. I cannot describe the filth and degradation of our group of 752 unwashed for almost three weeks. We filled the warehouse. Our group of 164 officers left Moji early afternoon on Mar 10 and arrived at Miata about 6 p.m the same day. I have seen ice flurries and snow. Most of us have little heat in our bodies to draw from.

Dylan had to stop writing. He was shaking with cold, his teeth chattering. Every day he woke to draw breath felt like a miracle now. If they weren't rescued soon he was sure his body would quit on him.

CHAPTER FIFTEEN

Washington, D.C.
early May 1945

"There is good news, Rosemary."

Rosemary turned from her place at the dining table as her father arrived holding a newspaper.

"The war is definitely drawing to a close," he continued. "The Germans have surrendered, Mussolini has been captured. The atrocities the Germans wrought have finally been revealed. It's all over the headlines this morning." He handed her the paper, the headline reading, **Nazi concentration camps exposed!**

She skimmed through the article feeling sick as she read what the monsters had done. "How could any human being do these things?" She picked up her cup and took a sip of coffee trying to dispel the terrible imagery that had arrived in her mind.

Boyd shook his head. "I do not know. But it's nearly over. The fighting has been brutal these last weeks but now it's all coming to a close."

"And the Pacific front? What of them?"

"The allied forces are winning."

"But the prisoners—has there been any..."

"No, Rosie. You know they've been moved from place to place. You must trust in the Geneva Convention rules. The prisoners must be fed and kept alive as best as possible. It is a shame FDR isn't here to see this."

Rosemary thought of the president's sudden collapse and death the month before. People were devastated, the entire city seeming to go quiet for a while. "He would have been happy. I can almost hear his voice. He was such a good orator."

"But Truman is a good man, even if it was his decision to drop those goddamned bombs. I was not in favor of it."

Rosemary swiveled to stare at her father. He never used language like that. "They stopped the war though."

"At the expense of a great many people. The repercussions will be felt for years to come."

"As usual the innocent are the ones who suffer." She turned back to her breakfast of eggs and toast which had turned cold. When her father left the room she took a tiny bite of toast, but it did not sit well. She read through the paper, finished her coffee and left the room.

Rosemary had just taken up with a new beau, one who seemed more her type. He was an exceptional artist, younger than she was by five years and quite good-looking. So far they had only spoken during classes and gone out to dinner a few times. This news had her questioning her decision to continue seeing him. Maybe her husband *would* come home after all. But the idea seemed remote, despite her father's continuing optimism.

For one moment her heart soared, but in the next it felt like a bird that had been shot out of the sky. She ran up the stairs, taking them two at a time. Alone in her room she tried to picture Dylan in her mind. She couldn't see him at all. Searching through her belongings she found a picture of the two of them, her gaze on the man she married nearly six years before. He would no longer resemble this joyful person who wore a huge smile. Was he alive?

It was later that day that she called her new friend, William. "I'm afraid I have to cancel tonight. I received news today that my husband might possibly be alive."

"That's wonderful news, Rosie," he said. "What did you hear?"

"Only that the war is ending and the allies are flying over the islands attempting to find the camps."

"So nothing definite, in other words."

"Nothing definite, but until I know for sure I would not want to continue what we've begun. Would you be willing to put it on hold?"

"Of course. I understand completely and I hope for your sake he returns home. I know how much you loved him."

"Yes, I did…I do. And thank you for understanding."

"Let me know either way. I'm not going anywhere."

She hung up the phone, her eyes filling with tears. Should she allow herself to hope, or would it be better to expect the worst? The dream came on with such force that Rosemary was unable to prepare. She was overcome with dizziness, her legs giving away. She was so immersed in the dream that she barely felt the impact when she landed on the floor.

"You cannot go, Edgar! I have a terrible premonition that you will not return!"

Edgar took her hand and brought it to his lips. "My dear sweet girl, I cannot let your fanciful meanderings rule my life! I have told you this over and over. If I had known how you would fret, I would have reconsidered our marriage. If you continue in this vein I will be forced to lock you up somewhere. There are institutions for hysterics who pretend to know the future."

Rebecca pulled away, glaring. "How dare you! You know about my abilities. I have saved you from yourself more than once, Edgar. I have half a mind to move back to my father's house."

"Your father would not have you. He is as disturbed as I am by what you term 'your abilities'. Now please let us talk of other things. I will be off soon and I would enjoy some special time with my wife before I go. You do know how much I adore you, do you not? I would do anything for you, but this is not possible." He smiled his most winning smile. "I have been called upon to do my duty. There is nothing for it but to go. Now take my hand and come with me into the garden. The roses are in full bloom."

Rebecca felt chastised and hurt. Edgar had always applauded her foreknowledge. Why had he suddenly decided she was an hysterical woman? She knew of the place he spoke of, knew of women who had been taken there and never seen again. She was not deranged. She loved her husband, but if it came to being shut away she would not hesitate to run away. But where could she go? Married women were not free, and the ones who were free were not in trades she wanted to think about. Perhaps she might take up nursing. That way she could accompany him to war and watch over him. But it was too late for that. He would be gone in only a few days.

"Remove that unpleasant expression from your face," he said tilting up her chin. "Now tell me how much you love me and we will forget this conversation ever happened."

"Why are you being like this, Edgar? You know me better than anyone. From what you have always said, I am a special person. I thought you appreciated who I am."

"Who you are is the wife of a soldier, and as such you will do as I say. I rule this house, Rebecca, not you. Do you understand that fact? I care for you but I will not be bullied by a woman."

When Rebecca began to cry he pulled a handkerchief out of his breast pocket and handed it to her. "It is time to dry your tears and make the best of things. You are a very lucky woman with a lovely house and a beautiful garden. You have a servant to help you in the kitchen and a husband who does not beat you. What more could you ask of life?"

"I would ask you to treat me as an equal, Edgar, as you did before we married. Where is that man?"

He scoffed. "That man is a figment of your wild imagination. Women are not equal to men, nor will they ever be. I treat you with the utmost respect, Rebecca, but society would frown on it if I offered you the same equality as a man. How would that look?"

"You would set an example for others."

He laughed and put his arm around her waist. "You are such a delight, my dear. You entertain me with each surprising remark that comes from that pretty little pouting mouth of yours." When he bent to kiss her Rebecca wanted to pull away, but his arms held her firmly against him. And in the end she kissed him back because she knew he was right. Society was not ready for women with her sensibilities. What bothered her was how Edgar had treated her before their marriage and how he treated her now. He had lied to her, wooing her with his false promises.

"Rosemary? What happened?"

Rosemary came back suddenly, a sick feeling in her stomach. She was lying on the marble floor of the hallway, her skirt askew. She rose to her knees, her hand going to her head. "I may have fainted," she explained, rubbing the bump on the back of her head.

"This is the second time this has happened; you need to eat more. You simply must stop worrying about Dylan. Please believe me when I tell you he will come back to you."

She tried to smile. "Are you a fortune teller now?"

"I am no fortune teller, but I do know that man. If anyone could survive prison camp it would be him." He helped her to her feet. "Why don't you go into the living room and sit next to the fire. I'll ask Ingrid to bring you some soup. You're as pale as the marble."

It was May and the flowers were blooming, but a cold front had come through, dipping daytime temperatures into the forties. She wobbled into the living room and sat on the couch, pondering the trip into the past. The fire burned merrily in opposition to her mood.

Was this to be her fate as well—a husband who would not return from war? At least she had good memories. Rebecca had to live with the memory of the condescending bastard Edgar had turned into. Were all men at that time such beasts? The uncertainty of her own life was enough—why did she need Rebecca's as well? Her fingers went to the necklace, wishing Dylan had never discovered it.

CHAPTER SIXTEEN

Journal entries

April, 1945

I have thought of eating as a pleasure, but perhaps it is more accurate not to include it as such. There is a continuous gnawing which never seems to be appeased. Meals are looked forward to, yes, but when a meal is finished, the same amount of rice could be consumed all over again. The bath is most certainly a pleasure, washing away the dirt of the hillside where I work, and the night and sleep is the greatest pleasure now extant—the time I no longer know I am a prisoner and I am able to soar to the land of my own where hazy images of another life hold me fast. I know it is you who hold me fast, even if I no longer can see your face.

Another death, the eighth since our group left Taiwan. I miss Shira Kawa, our garden and animals there. Now there is nothing to look forward to but our freedom.

May, 1945

Much has happened in the past month. We left Miata on April 25, a series of short train rides taking us to Fukuoka, Kyushu, where we arrived in early afternoon. There next morning we boarded a packet ship and landed around 4 at a Korean port. Two days later we were in

Mukden Manchuria. It was the most comfortable trip I have taken in many a moon.

We've been here exactly a week today, still in quarantine, still unbathed, still with our lice. Amoebic dysentery has shown up in profusion among us and it may be that our quarantine will be extended three more weeks. Some Red Cross has made its appearance during the past week in the form of a package of American cigarettes, 3 oz. of butter, 3 oz. of chopped ham, 2 lumps of sugar, 4 oz. of soluble coffee.

I've been in the hospital since the 19th and have not felt like writing. The headaches which I had in Miata were continuing along with some fever. They appear to have been sinus headaches. I have no amoebic, no malaria. My heart and lungs are normal. Blood pressure 100 over 70. Some anemia in red corpuscles.

June, 1945

Left hospital—feeling much improved. This is probably the ugliest bit of ground in the world; beyond that there is little to be said. The days pass slowly and miserably. We live surrounded by a ring of human feces, and we have a fly problem, the equal of which I've never seen. They are abominable and there is no way to rid ourselves of them until the cold weather lulls them to everlasting sleep.

The fly situation is fast becoming worse. The benjo of barracks #2 has overflowed on the ground, and the overflow of the hospital has formed a small lake. Millions of flies. We receive no help. It is a pitiful situation. My back begins to bother me again. The air is black with flies. They are like a plague. We have taken cuts in rations and many complain of hunger. Three men died yesterday—one had a brain tumor.

July, 1945

The fly menace continues. Fleas and mosquitoes increase daily. Stealing of clothes, towels, blankets or anything placed on the drying racks appears to be the rule. Another cut in food has taken place. We receive two buns a day and beans every other day. No meat of course. The corn meal is never completely cooked and is often musty, thus many are sour when removed from the oven. Rumors of release are rampant. We have one bare open space pockmarked with foxholes, beyond them a dusty grey wall and beyond the wall tall factory chimneys, smoke, pylons, water tanks, tops of higher buildings, wire. No green no water. Best not to think about it. It must soon end. It is a divine thought. Another birthday. I am appalled by my age. It is unreal. All of my nice unassailable theories, so good at 32 have been blasted. At times I am assailed by an overwhelming claustrophobia, which brings on fits of depression. We lie like cordwood, overcrowded in double bays. The air is stale, the night pregnant with animals sounds of breathing, snoring coughing and anal retorts. I am a trapped animal.

August, 1945

The rumor that the war is over circulates. It appears that an armistice was given to the Japanese 4 days ago after 2 bombings of 2 new types, (atomic). One bomb was dropped in a named city of 300,000, killing 180,000 people, the second dropped in the outskirts of Nagasaki, destroying a large part of that city. Some of the sick here are to be flown out. When I saw the insignia on a plane flying over and dropping leaflets I burst into tears.

Dylan put down his pen. I may make it home after all, he thought suddenly, his heart lifting. He lifted his pen and began to write again.

Tonight Nip soldiers occupy the guardhouse, cell block. They are guarded by Americans. All the hatred built up during these long years under the 'vermin Nip' seems to have left me. I cannot but feel sorry for them, having been through such a vile experience myself. Several of them have been good to the American P.O.W.s. We have just inspected them and they lay in a line under the mosquito bar just as we did in Manila over three years ago. I will try and send these journals ahead in order to give you a preview of the life I've been leading. Many are censored but are written in such a way that I may recall many unpleasant events. These I plan to enlarge upon should I ever find sufficient ability latent.

By my continuing dream forays into the past it seems that these events have not come to a close. Despite being a free man Edgar and Rebecca still haunt me. Their life is nearly as real to me as yours and mine, dear Rosemary.' Dylan closed the notebook, reveling in his freedom. Dreams of another life were nothing in comparison to the idea of seeing his flesh and blood wife again. He thought of her skin, her hair, and the feel of her body against his. He could hardly wait.

CHAPTER SEVENTEEN

Washington, D.C.
October 1945

The reunion with Rosemary brought on a depression he'd thought he'd left far behind. She was standoffish and cold, his own feelings not what he'd hoped. They did as they were expected, greeting each other with affection, but underneath it he could feel her reticence, noticing the wary look in the corner of her eye. And for his part, this was not the woman he'd lain awake thinking about during his darker days. He felt completely numb.

"You'll like the place I purchased, Dylan, " she said as she drove him away from Washington. They crossed the Potomac River heading north.

He didn't reply, his gaze on the familiar scenery, the bright leaves that had turned color. The army had given him a month off to recover, but he was due back after that to resume his life on base. He was finally home and yet he felt as though he'd left some essential part of himself back in prison camp.

"Dylan? Are you all right?"

He turned in his seat. "I suppose I'm tired. The flight back was long and I haven't slept well for quite a while."

"Once we get to the farm you can rest and recuperate." She turned back to the road. "You'll be right as rain in a week or two."

He doubted that, but it was a nice thought. "How long have you had the place?" he asked an hour later as they drove down the long gravel driveway.

"I bought it a year ago. I needed a place of my own."

"You could have moved into the base housing. Many of the wives did, you know. Have you seen any of them?"

She shook her head. "I've been busy with my art," she answered vaguely.

The house came into view, plaster white-washed walls, a dark sloping metal roof. It was nestled into the side of a hill, a small pond to the right. A barn appeared behind it as they came closer. "How old is the house?"

"Mid seventeen-hundred's is what the agent told me. It's lovely, isn't it?"

Dylan had no feeling about the house, in fact he had no feelings about anything. "Yes," he replied. He followed her inside, listening to her chatter about the house.

"Our bedroom is up here," she said, opening a door off the kitchen to reveal an enclosed stairway. He followed her up, carrying his suitcase. The bedroom lay beneath a sloping roof, their marriage bed against the wall. It was a good thing they'd left it behind when they traveled to Manila. All their other belongings were long gone now. He placed his suitcase on the floor and looked around.

"The view from here is wonderful," she told him, gesturing for him to join her at the dormer window.

In the distance the land sloped off, a dark fence enclosing a field filled with grass.

"That's where the horses will go," she said, turning to him with a bright expression.

He knew she was putting it all on, trying hard to be cheerful and upbeat. "How many acres is it?"

"Only ten."

"Sounds like plenty to me."

She shrugged and turned away, fussing with the bedspread. "Why don't you have a wash and a rest while I fix us something to eat."

Dylan unpacked, pulling out the journals he'd kept. Should he share them with her? It might help her understand what he went through. He carried them down to the kitchen.

"I kept a diary while I was in the camp, Rosemary. If you want to read them, I'll leave them on your desk."

"Of course I want to read them." She reached for the loosely bound legal sized document. "Are you hungry?"

"I'm always hungry." He sat at the little kitchen table. "What do you have?"

"Sandwiches—soup. Will that be enough?"

"After the meager meals I've had the last few years I'm sure it'll be plenty."

She placed his document on the counter and brought over what she'd prepared, sitting next to him. "You're so thin, Dylan. I'm not sure I've ever seen a man so thin."

"Eating your food will put the weight back on, I'm sure." He bit into a sandwich, bright flavors of cheese, cucumbers and tomato lighting up his taste buds. "Delicious," he mumbled, looking at her. She smiled.

It was evening before he saw her again. He'd rested after lunch and when he came down the stairs he couldn't find her. He wandered the rooms, happy to see a few familiar items they'd left behind when they went to Manila. When he went outside she was sitting on the fence that enclosed the garden, gazing into the distance.

She turned when she heard him approach. "I read a bit of your diary, Dylan. It made me cry."

"I didn't want to make you cry. I just hoped it might help bridge this gap between us."

She sighed and jumped down. "Were you serious about growing things, raising animals? I've been thinking about horses. I could buy us a couple if that would make you smile again."

"I don't need horses, I need time. It will take a while to realize I'm really here, really home."

"I'm sure that's true. But in your diary you said you wanted to feel the earth under your fingernails, to grow things. There's a garden," she said, pointing to the turned earth in front of the fence. "We could plant vegetables, have horses. I could get more chickens. What do you say?"

"I say it's too early to be asking me these questions. Let me settle in for a week or two, at least. And then let's revisit this topic." He stared at the garden, remembering the animals he'd raised, the problems and ill health of the ducks and rabbits, the sheer futility of it all. Yes, they'd had some meat, but mostly it had been a lot of work to feed the guards. When he caught her eye she looked away. Her expression was nervous, almost afraid. He knew he'd changed, both physically and mentally. Right now it was hard to imagine a life here, or a life anywhere, for that matter. And he was too exhausted to fake it.

By the end of his month of leave she'd convinced him to buy two horses, dragging him with her to look at various thoroughbreds before deciding on two. "We can call them Penelope and Ulysses," she said, gazing at him with widened eyes.

He thought of his journal entries, the romanticism that had kept him from losing his mind. "Yes," was all he could manage to say. Somehow she'd managed to keep up her false brightness, a smiled pasted on her face until she didn't think he was looking. It was then that he saw the darkness behind her eyes, her lips pressed together in a grim expression. He had the feeling that she was keeping something from him, but he didn't have the energy to ask. Any emotional upset now would drive him over the cliff.

They slept side by side at night but he didn't have the wherewithal to touch her, and she made no move toward him. He felt remote, cut-off, unable to re-forge the bond they'd once had. He wondered if he ever would.

"Do you think you're up to it?" she asked him the morning he was due to go into Fort Myer.

"Doesn't matter. I have to go."

"Where will you stay?"

"They'll provide an apartment on base. I'll be back down Friday night. And we'd better think about a second car. I don't like you being stuck here without one."

She scoffed. "I'll be fine. I have lots to do now that we have the horses."

"Don't ride until I'm back. You aren't an expert and I don't want you to get hurt."

"I won't, Dylan. Now go, or you'll be late on your first day back."

She accompanied him to the front door and waited with folded arms as he started the car and backed up. He could almost hear her sigh of relief as he drove away.

His first day at the base was just as hellish as he expected. He was treated with disdain, shuffled from one place to the next, and finally put to work in the library. Instead of being a badge of honor, being captured by the enemy and kept in prison camp was a blight on his career.

Mid-week he went by to see Boyd Hewitt.

"How are things with you and Rosemary?"

"We're getting to know one another again. But I wondered, sir, did something happen while I was away? I have the sense that she's keeping things from me."

Boyd Hewitt didn't say anything for a long moment, his stare somewhat disconcerting. "I shouldn't tell you this," he finally said with a sigh, "but she did have a short-lived affair. In all fairness, she was certain you were dead. Did you know she never received any letters from you? And I would imagine you didn't get hers either."

"No, I didn't get any. I worried about that. Not sure why mine didn't reach her. I must have sent several dozen."

"She had another recent beau," he continued, as though anxious to finish the discussion, "but as far as I could tell it wasn't serious. Rosemary is young, Dylan, a desirable woman, you must not take this to heart. As I said, she did not expect to ever see you again."

"Thank you for your candor, sir. It's hard enough without secrets between us. To tell you the truth I feel like a dead man, as though my life force is gone."

Boyd patted his shoulder. "It will come back. Rosemary loves you. She fretted terribly while you were gone. I applauded her social life. I thought it would help. And now that you're back I'm sure she's ecstatic."

Dylan thought of the false brightness in her tone, the way she glanced at him when she thought he wasn't looking. "I'm not so sure about that."

Boyd led the way to the door. "Give her time. Your return has been a shock. You are hardly the man who left here four years ago. And in the meantime I suggest you find someone who can help. I know of a doctor…"

Dylan held up his hand. "I'm not airing my dirty laundry in front of a complete stranger, if that's what you're suggesting. I have to get back to the base now." He shook his father-in-law's hand and left the house, heading to his car.

Once back in the library he called Amanda. "Your father just told me about Rosemary's affair. She hasn't mentioned it. What can you tell me?"

Amanda hesitated. "I think you'd better ask her. My sister doesn't confide in me anymore. I think being alone so long has addled her brain."

CHAPTER EIGHTEEN

Virginia
November 1945

"I cannot believe my father would betray my trust like that!"

"I asked him to tell me what happened. I felt like you were keeping things from me."

Rosemary was fuming. She had planned to tell him in her own time; now they would be forced to hash this out. And they didn't yet have the proper connection to deal with the pain it would cause. "I wanted to wait until we…until we connected again. It was nothing. The man meant nothing to me. It was a dalliance that kept me from going crazy."

"Who he is?"

"He was my art teacher. We broke it off over a year ago, Dylan."

"And this other one—the more recent one?"

"He told you about that too?"

"He felt I had a right to know. How can we go forward with this between us?"

"If you've noticed, there's been very little *going forward*, Dylan. You've walled yourself off and I've been trying to hold steady until you come out of it."

"Is that what you've been doing?" Dylan rose from the dining room table. "I'm going for a walk."

Rosemary watched him go, listening to the slam of the kitchen door as he left the house. Tears filled her eyes. What in the world could they do? Was it time to see a psychiatrist?

She was folding clothes in the bedroom when he came through the doorway, bending to keep from hitting his head.

"Rosemary, we have to talk this out. If you want a divorce please tell me. I'm in a vulnerable place here not knowing what your intentions are."

She placed the pile of clean clothing down on the bed and turned. "I have no intentions other than making it through this...this blankness we have between us. When I talked to Father he suggested a psychiatrist. I hate to say it, but I think we need help."

"Fine. Make the appointment." Dylan turned on his heel and left.

❧

Dylan slept on the couch, nightmares waking him in the middle of the night. His face was wet with tears when he woke, the people who had haunted him for more than a year still there, the troubles between them taunting him. Edgar had married Rebecca knowing full well who she was, and now complained, telling her she had to change. He'd turned into a pompous ass and he was hurting her in the process. Was he supposed to learn something from their relationship? Was he behaving as boorishly as Edgar?

All his ideas about his Penelope had been dashed. Rosemary was no longer his anything. And he knew that her reactions, the lack of intimacy between them, were all his fault. He did not have the physical or the mental strength to deal with it. As much as he didn't want to admit it, maybe seeking help was a good idea.

∾⊙↻

Dylan continued heading off every Monday for work and leaving Rosemary alone. The good thing was they'd bought a second car. They had an appointment with a psychiatrist on Wednesday, which he dreaded. But at least it might clear the air. Rosemary barely spoke to him now.

They met at 1:00 outside the building where Doctor Francis had his office.

"Are you ready for this?" she asked him, reaching up to straighten his tie.

"As ready as I'll ever be." He opened the heavy glass door, waiting as she walked past him.

Doctor Francis looked to be in his late seventies, with white hair and glasses that kept falling down his nose. Rosemary and Dylan sat in chairs facing his desk while he droned on about things that made no sense, using terminology neither of them understood.

Finally he took off his glasses and cleaned them, his gaze going from one to the other. "In order to connect again you must both open up about your feelings," he said, putting his glasses on. "It seems that you're communications have been difficult, if not impossible, so far. "

"I feel nothing," Dylan said.

"You feel, Mr. Hughes, but you are unconsciously afraid that if you delve into those emotions you will lose control. What you went through is a horror, and that horror is right at the surface of your mind. Since you mentioned your diary, I would suggest looking through it and sharing some of what is there with your wife. Slowly, Mr. Hughes, very slowly, you will come back into yourself if you are able to share the pain." He turned to Rosemary. "Are you willing to bear witness, Mrs. Hughes?"

"What do I need to do?"

"You need to support him. You may see a side of him you've never seen before. He may cry, he may rage. He may scare you. I know this is a lot to ask, but from what you have both told me, you were very much in love before the war. The love is there still. The love is what will get you through this." He reached for a notepad. "Do your homework and come see me again in two weeks. I expect things to be quite changed by then." He jotted down a date and time and handed it to Dylan.

Outside the office Dylan turned to Rosemary. "What did you think of him?"

"He seems knowledgeable. Are you willing to do what he suggested?"

Dylan nodded. "Friday when I get home?"

"Maybe a drink first?"

Dylan smiled for the first time. "Definitely."

"Friday it is."

"Call me at the library if you need anything. Otherwise I'll see you in a couple of days."

She nodded. "Goodbye, Dylan." When she headed off in the direction of her car he was still standing there, staring into space.

❧

"Edgar no! I've said it too many times now for you to ignore me. You will not return. I've seen it very clearly in a vision. Please do not take me for a fool."

"I am going, despite your very creative and ingenious tactics to stop me. You will wait for me as a faithful wife should, and be pleased and happy when I return. Now please give me a kiss and say goodbye properly."

Rebecca turned away, afraid for the first time. She could see no further than him not coming home. What would happen to him had not been revealed. "Maybe you won't die, Edgar, but I do not see you coming home to me."

He laughed. "So I shall take up with another woman and make a life in Africa? Is that what you think?"

"I have no predictions other than not seeing your return. Despite how beastly you have been these past weeks I would like to make a life with you."

"Of course we will have a life together. You are as silly as ever." He grabbed hold of her and pressed his mouth to hers, despite her attempts to get away. In the end she relaxed in his arms. She did love him.

After Edgar left on the carriage Rebecca walked the mile to her father's house. She regarded her portly father, suddenly aware of how old he had grown these past months. His face had new lines, his neck jowly with loose skin, his eyes red-rimmed. "Father, you know that I can see into the future. Edgar will not return. I begged him not to go, but he refused to believe it. He was terrible to me before he left, insisting that I was an hysteric and should possibly be locked up!"

Her father gazed down at her, his expression somber. "I am afraid I did not disabuse him of this notion, Rebecca. He's come to me several times asking for advice on how to handle you. He told me you would not *back down no matter what threats he made. I have to say I was quite horrified by his description of your behavior. A well brought up young woman does not behave that way. Women are controlled by their fathers and then their husbands, it is the way of the world. Your actions have been disturbing to me on several levels, especially since I feel personally responsible for allowing it to continue. Your mother suffered from mental illness and now I see you following in her footsteps. She had visions that she could not keep quiet about, strange ghostly visitations that she insisted were there for her alone. Why, one morning she was in the garden in her nightclothes! She told me the fairies had called her out."* He shook his head and frowned. *"I brought her inside before our neighbors could see her."* He let out a sigh. *"I have to say her early death was a blessing for us all."*

Rebecca thought of her mother, an ethereal woman who drifted through life with a smile on her face. She had loved her dearly. Her mother had understood what Rebecca was going through, the clairvoyance that had at first frightened her. *"It is a gift from the goddess,"* her mother told her. *"Never let anyone take that away from you. There will be a future time when women will not be so down-trodden, Rebecca. You will hopefully see it in your lifetime."*

Her mother had drowned in the pond, her long blonde hair full of duckweed, her nightgown torn and covered in weeds and mud. Rebecca had discovered her there, wondering if her father had something to do with it. She had been inconsolable for months afterward, until she had a dream in which her mother came to her. *"Do not mourn my death,"* she'd said. *"Know that I am still around and will be always."*

Her father was talking again and she had missed a sentence or two. She put her attention on him again, wishing he understood her as her mother had.

"For your own sake and mine you must keep your opinions to yourself. If you do not I will be forced to take action. I have a reputation to uphold and having a daughter who exceeds the bounds of propriety

will do nothing to enhance it. I am already on a watch list because of your mother. Now please, get yourself under control and prepare for the upcoming birth."

Tears filled her eyes. "Father, how can you say those things? You know me better than anyone."

He gazed out the window for a moment before he turned to her again, his eyes dark with anger. "I can say them because they are true. The society in which the wealthier members move will not tolerate women who speak out as you have. And I will not be spoken of poorly by the magistrates and others who run things here. Now, please, Rebecca, have a care. You will soon have a baby to take care of. I only hope that event brings you to your senses. It is a momentous responsibility, and if you do not take control of your fanciful thinking I shall be forced to consider taking the baby away from you."

Rebecca stared at him in disbelief. "You would do that?"

"Of course I would if I felt you to be incompetent. After all, this child will be my grandson or granddaughter."

"Your grandson," Rebecca muttered, but he did not seem to hear her.

After this disturbing discussion Rebecca went for a walk, her thoughts whirling. When it came to her, her father and her husband were in complete agreement. Her father had obviously been instrumental in changing Edgar's mind about her. She distinctly remembered how Edgar had delighted in her—he loved her eccentricities, as he called them. He had laughed sometimes, been thoughtful at other times, listening to what she had to say and taking her seriously. But before he left for war he had turned into a controlling tyrant who would brook no argument. Even his lovemaking had turned forceful and angry, leaving her crying into the pillow when he was finished. She did not understand why he treated her the way he did.

In the morning Rosemary woke alone in the bed, her consciousness coming slowly back to her. Rebecca's life swirled in her mind, the woman's unhappiness making her want to do something to help. There must be a reason for this intrusion into her life, but so far she couldn't come up with one. Rebecca's problems were ones she couldn't solve.

She swung her legs out of bed and headed down to make coffee, letting the dream wisps go. Tonight was homework night. Would they get through this without violence? Dylan was not the man she knew. She had no idea what to expect.

❦

They sat together in the sitting room, each holding a glass of wine. The journal lay between them, a dangerous creature to be tamed.

"I've marked a couple of passages," she said, pulling the binder open.

He watched her with narrowed eyes. "I should be the one to choose, Rosemary. After all it is my journal." He placed his glass on the table and reached for the pages, leafing through it. "This was a bleak time," he said, stopping at an entry. "I thought it was curtains." He looked up. "The generals had been taken to another camp. I was in charge of the…" he stopped, choking up. "I can't do this. This isn't about the journals, it's about us. I want to be close again but I can barely feel now…" he let out a sob, his hands covering his face.

Rosemary rose and kneeled in front of him, pulling him to her. He cried into her shoulder for several very long moments until he managed to get control.

"I'm sorry."

"There is nothing to be sorry about. This is exactly what Doctor Francis wanted us to do."

He looked at her with an empty expression. "I want to want you, Rosie, but I can't. I don't know how anymore."

She sat beside him. "Don't force things. We've just managed to make a chink in the wall between us. It will take time to break it down."

He was crying again, his head in his hands. "I want us to be the way we were. When I think of those days in Baguio I see us from afar. I have no sense of what I was feeling."

"You were passionate, romantic, a wonderful lover. I was overcome, immersed in it, Dylan. We were two beings of one mind, lovers who connected on every level." She gazed at him. "My heart has been yours since day one. It isn't going anywhere else now."

He wiped his eyes and looked at her. "Can you be patient with me?"

She smiled. "As long as you come back to me."

"All I can say is I'll try. But must we continue seeing Francis?"

"He's already helped us, Dylan. You broke down, and that's a good thing."

❧

Despite Dylan's reticence they kept their next appointment with Doctor Francis. "Your homework is to give and receive massages," he told them at the end of the hour. "This may seem silly or useless, but I believe it will help break down the barriers between you. You have told me that you had a healthy sexual relationship. Maybe touch will allow you to experience some of those feelings once again."

On Friday night when Dylan arrived at the farm Rosemary had dinner waiting. "Tonight's the night," she told him, in between bites.

Dylan stared at her. "The night for what?"

She scoffed. "Our homework."

"Is there any wine?"

Rosemary rose from the table, returning with a bottle of red. "Dutch courage?"

Dylan smiled. "Maybe."

Two hours later Dylan was lying naked on the bed. She poured oil onto his back and began to knead. He groaned as her hands worked at the taut muscles in his shoulders and down each side of his spine. He was so very thin.

"Am I hurting you?"

Dylan shook his head, his eyes closed. "Keep going. I feel some life returning."

When she got to his calves, he reached around and grabbed her hand. "Isn't it my turn?"

"I thought the massage was for you. Didn't the doctor mention emotions or something?"

Dylan sat up and pulled his shirt on. "Your turn, Mrs. Hughes."

Rosemary stripped off her skirt and sweater and lay down on her stomach.

"What about your underwear?"

She undid her bra and slipped it off. A moment later his hands were on her back, strong and sure as he worked the kinks out. "Oh my God, that feels good."

"Your muscles are bunched and tight." He continued kneading, adding more oil as he moved downward. His thumbs hooked into her underpants and pulled them down before working on her bum. "Your butt muscles are as tight as a drum, Rosie. There are knots everywhere." He worked on the big buttock muscles for a while, his fingers pressing so hard it hurt. "Ow!"

"Sorry. But good God, you definitely need this."

She relaxed under his hands, and when they wandered to other areas she couldn't suppress the moan that came out of her mouth.

When he stopped she rolled over to look up at him. His heavy-lidded eyes held a question. "Yes," she said, "the answer is yes."

He lowered his mouth to hers. And what happened after that broke the wall down completely.

❧❧❧

"I'm so sorry, Dylan. I feel terrible for what I did," she said later, settling back against the pillows.

He reached for his pack of cigarettes, pulling two out and lighting them. He handed her one. "I'm not thinking about that," he said, watching her. "I'm still in the throes of what we just did. I had feared I would never experience this again. God's woman, I feel reborn."

Rosemary laughed, a light sound that lifted into the air like a bell. When she moved closer, he put his arm around her, pulling her against him. There was such a comfort in the feel of her body, the smell of her, the sound of her even breathing.

"I guess the homework paid off," she murmured.

CHAPTER NINETEEN

Virginia
1946-1947

In the summer of 1946 Dylan and Rosemary organized a party at the farm. Dylan invited many of the people he'd been with in prison camp, plus new officers he'd recently met. Rosemary did all the cooking, spending hours in the kitchen making breads, salads and fruit and cheese plates.

They held it on the lawn in front of the house, where they'd placed wicker chairs and tables. It was a beautiful summer day, the rhododendrons in full bloom. A heady scent of jasmine wafted from the fence line where she'd planted the fragrant vines. Rosemary circulated, enjoying talking with some of the wives who she hadn't seen since before the war. But as the alcohol disappeared the noise level rose, stories being touted about prison camp, and wives gathering in clusters to tell their own horror stories.

Rosemary hurried back to the kitchen, only coming out to carry trays around and offer more drinks. She felt the seeping sadness, making her wish they'd never decided to have a party. And when she glanced around she was all too aware of the emaciation and hollow-eyed look of the men.

Dylan appeared better than a lot of them, but he had not regained his sparkle. These men, including her husband, were marred for life. Many of the wives had confided in her that they were considering divorce.

"He isn't the same man," Barbara said, looking around furtively. "I don't recognize him. After work he spends hours alone or heads off to drink with his fellow officers."

Candace nodded her agreement. "I'm hanging in there until he gets back on his feet, but I'm planning to file for. We have no children, no reason to stay together now. I met someone while he was gone and he's agreed to wait."

Rosemary gazed at the three women. "We went to a psychiatrist," she confessed. "Things are better now, but I'm not sure about this gathering. It seems to bring it all up again—how can that be good?"

"According to Pete, it helps to spend time with the men. I've felt left out many times, but I plan to see it through," Sara said, staring at Candace. "I did not have an affair and I still love him."

Candace's cheeks turned pink and she turned away.

"I guess I offended her," Sara whispered. "But honestly, the woman can be so irritating. Doesn't she understand what these men went through?"

"Maybe the love between them isn't strong enough to carry them through. It isn't easy for any of us."

∾◎∾

When the guests left Rosemary took herself off to the guest room and locked herself in. Emotionally she was not equipped to rehash the day. Talking with the wives and learning how many of them were unhappy had filled her with a kind of despair. She and Dylan had worked through a lot of it, but he was still closed off and secretive. He was not the man she married.

When Dylan, drunk, banged on her door she told him to go away. "And don't expect me to do this again anytime soon!" she shouted.

The next day they didn't mention it, the silence going on and on until she'd finally had it. "Why don't you complain? Why don't you yell and tell me what a bad wife I am and how I don't support your friends?"

He gave her a sad look. "I knew it was hard for you, the talk of the war, feeling left out. And the wives weren't much better. You've turned into a recluse here, and this party interrupted it. I'm sorry I put you through it."

"Why must you be so reasonable? I should be supporting you in this."

"I can see them in Washington. That way you won't be forced to participate."

"But I want to support you, Dylan. You went through hell."

He took her by the shoulders. "You support me in other ways; you don't have to give parties for my friends and colleagues. It's all right."

But it wasn't all right when he traveled to Washington without her, coming home the next day hung-over and exhausted. What was it that pulled at him, that made him need to leave her to get drunk with a bunch of men?

❧

The next night the dream came, taking her into the past where Rebecca struggled with the mores of a repressive society...

"He's gone, Papa. I feel it here." Rebecca's hand went to her heart. "What will I do?" It had been four months since Edgar left for Africa and the baby she carried grew inside her. She felt so alone despite how perfectly beastly he had behaved the last few weeks before his departure. Now she carried his child and somehow that fact seemed to make up for it all.

"You will do what is dictated by society. You will carry on, have this child and live your life. I doubt that another man will want you once the child is born, but you have always been self-sufficient. I will help you until you find your way, but after that you must not count on me, aside from sharing this house. I will expect you to work for your keep. There are many chores here to keep you busy."

"But what about our house? I can stay there!"

"The house belongs to Edgar, and if and when he does not return, will go to his family. A wife has no rights to such things unless otherwise stipulated, which he did not."

Rebecca wiped her tears away as she climbed the stairs upward to her room. She was heartbroken. Edgar was not dead as she feared, he was with another woman. She had a clear vision of the two of them together, a rustic hut behind them nestled into trees that resembled umbrellas. They stood together, her skin dark against the paleness of his, her hair tied up in a brightly colored turban. In front of them stretched a flat plain filled with waving grass. But the very worst part about the vision was the sight of her bulging belly straining against the fabric of her dress.

It was late in the night that she woke, feeling a terrible pain deep in her belly, wetness between her legs. The baby, was the last thought she had before she slipped into darkness.

Rosemary woke out of the past, unable to stop the scream that erupted from her mouth.

"What?" Dylan asked, turning on the light. "What happened?"

"The two people in the locket. Rebecca just lost her baby."

Dylan reached for her. "It's not real, Rosemary. What's real is the two of us lying together in this bed."

But to Rosemary it was all too real, her own miscarriage coming back in alarming detail. After he shut off the light she turned her head into the pillow to muffle her sobs.

CHAPTER TWENTY

Virginia
Early winter 1949

It was nearly a year before Dylan fully regained his health. It was obvious he was feeling better when his ire rose at the deck he'd been dealt. His work at the library rankled. He should have been promoted by now. He'd been treated shabbily due to a situation that was out of his control.

"You sound more like your old self," she said one Saturday morning over coffee, listening to his bitter complaints. "Why don't you think about quitting? Remember what you said in the journals, Dylan."

"I remember very well, but working in the garden won't pay the bills."

"Will you be promoted soon and move on from this job?"

"Nothing's been said so far. I have a bad feeling about it."

She put her cup down on the table. "You have enough time in to get a pretty good pension if you retire. And I have money. Why torture yourself?"

He stared moodily out the window at the bare trees. Summer had come and gone, and now it was nearly winter again. "I'll think about it."

In the past months Dylan had vowed to make up for their lost years and to find common ground again. He swore to her that he was finished with the military, with the entire idea of fighting and war. His time in prison camp had given him many hours to contemplate life. His survival had depended on rising above his circumstances, his obsession with her and the life they could have, filling the long hours of his bleak days.

When he was home they shared the chores, his health returning bit by bit as he dug in the dirt and helped her carry heavy bags of feed and compost, and stack bales of hay. His face, arms, and chest were tan from the sun, his muscles strong again. On the weekends during the summer and fall they had ridden across the fields together on Ulysses and Penelope. They shared feeding the chickens, working the vegetable garden, their life filled with simple things. They began to make love the way they had in the past. The health problems acquired from being nearly starved to death, and his mental state, had been restored. Most mornings she woke with a smile on her face, anticipating the day ahead and the night to come. It was a good life and she loved every minute of it.

"This is exactly what I'd envisioned during those horrible days," he'd told her just recently. "Growing things, raising animals, being with you, it's all I've wanted for the past three and a half years."

"Good," she'd told him. "Time to get out of the army then."

And he did, arriving one Friday evening with a wide smile on his face. "I am officially a free man." He promptly grabbed her hand, pulling her behind him up the narrow stairs to their bedroom.

Their life became everything she'd dreamed it could be. When he felt the need to go into Washington for a night she accepted it, never complaining. He was bound to her now, involved with the farm and his role in it. They were happy. Even her dreams seemed to lessen, Rebecca's woes fading into the background as the farm life claimed her more and more.

But the happiness was not to last, Dylan's need for more action taking him into Washington more and more often. At first she chalked it up to a phase he was going through, but when he announced he'd been offered a job she knew this was no phase. It took her a while to absorb his words, to realize what he was proposing.

They were in the sitting room with a fire going when she confronted him. "Why, Dylan? I thought you loved our life."

He ran his fingers through his hair, his agitation clear. "It isn't enough, Rosie. I'm a man of action. I need the city lights occasionally. I'm not you."

"What about what you wrote in the journals?"

"That was then, this is now. I'm getting older and I feel like I'm wasting my life down here. I have a lot to offer the world. I can't just molder my life away."

"Midlife crisis? Is that what this is?"

He shrugged. "Maybe if we had a child…"

"Don't give me that. I talked to you about it several times. You said you weren't ready."

"We talked about it when I first got back, when I couldn't imagine having a responsibility of that magnitude. I could barely take care of myself. "

"Well, I'm not having one now, if that's what you're intimating."

"I'm not intimating that at all. It's your decision." He turned to make drinks. "I've been hired by Raytheon."

"Raytheon. Don't they make rockets and weaponry?"

"That's right. They've offered me a good salary because of my time in the service." He handed her a whiskey sour, his new favorite drink. "I'll come home on weekends."

Rosemary sat heavily, feeling like someone had punched her in the stomach. "I can't manage here without you. There's too much to do now."

"If you hadn't bought more chickens and planted all those trees there wouldn't be."

"You were right beside me when I did those things, Dylan. I can't believe this."

"You're really angry."

"Yes, I'm angry. What did you expect? We have a life together, one that I thought was going pretty well. It would have been nice if you'd mentioned your misgivings. I would have enjoyed knowing your plans before the fact, rather than after. "

"Rosie, it was you who convinced me to retire, it was you who talked me into this place, and it was you who convinced yourself that we had the perfect life. Not once have you asked if I were happy."

She slammed her drink down on the table, sending lemon and whiskey flying. "Why didn't you say something?"

He scoffed. "Do you have any idea what you're like when you're in the throes of a fantasy?"

"You bastard." Rosemary stalked from the room.

He left the next morning, taking many of his clothes from the closet. "I'll be back Friday," were his parting words. Rosemary lay face down on the bed and burst into tears. And when the dream came she was almost happy to sink into the past...

Rebecca wandered into town, her troubled gaze going to the women who carried new babies in their arms. When the tears came she let them run down her face. Nothing mattered now. Edgar was gone, with another woman who obviously pleased him more. The baby she and Edgar had conceived together was no more. He had a child with the African woman he lived with now—she'd seen it in his arms. Her father seemed to hate her, his enmity growing with each passing day. What had she done to deserve this? The tears came faster, a sob escaping before she could stop it.

"Are you all right, Miss?"

She looked into the kind eyes of a young man who stood behind a table covered with vegetables. "I have lost my baby recently," she confessed, "and my husband has taken up with another woman."

His eyes grew wide, his face turning pink. "I am sure it will all sort itself," he mumbled, turning away to help a customer.

Rebecca wandered on, not noticing the critical stares she was receiving. People held their hands up, whispering together as she walked by. She'd neglected to wear her bonnet today and her hair hung untidily around her face. It seemed too difficult to comb it these days.

"Rebecca!" The angry voice broke into her reverie. Her arm was taken in a tight grip. "Why are you here without your cloak and bonnet?"

"Papa. I thought you were at your desk."

158

"I was at my desk, but sadly I was told of your escape from the house. How many times have I warned you?" he hissed, pulling her around to walk the other way.

She let him lead her, an obedient child who was trying to be good. But the angry expression he wore seemed to suggest that she had not achieved her goal.

Rosemary wiped the sudden tears from her face. This woman was distraught and depressed, her behavior not in keeping with the time she lived in. There was a similarity in their emotions even if the reasons were different; she could easily relate to how Rebecca felt. What would become of her?

Her mind went to Dylan and his defection. They'd finally forged a bond—how could he so blithely break it? They'd been apart for over four years and now they were separated again. Yes, he would be back on the weekend, but that was not enough. Not now. Not ever. Through the skylight she and Dylan had so painstakingly installed, stars winked blue, cold and lonely in the vast blackness. She closed her eyes but sleep did not come.

CHAPTER TWENTY-ONE

Virginia
1954-1957

Rosemary had managed to stick out five years of their new life. She wasn't happy about it, but she loved him and didn't want to lose him altogether. She did have to admit that he seemed more energetic and happier.

But one Friday he didn't come home and didn't call to let her know why. At first she worried he'd been in an accident, but after calling around she found no evidence to substantiate her concern. Early Saturday she called his apartment, surprised when a woman answered. "Is Dylan there?" she asked, a sick feeling moving through her body.

"Yes, I'll just get him," the woman answered.

When Dylan came on the line Rosemary was not able to keep the upset out of her voice. "Who's there—who is that? And why didn't you tell me you weren't coming home last night?"

"Sorry, Rosie. Something came up. Gerta is an old friend, someone I knew before the war."

"Are you having an affair?" Rosemary demanded.

There was a heavy sigh. "No, Rosemary. She was married to one of my West Point classmates, but they divorced a few months ago. I ran into her in a bar and we got to talking. Time got away from us."

"And that's the reason you didn't call and didn't come home last night? She obviously spent the night at your apartment."

"Yes, she did stay over. And when I looked at the clock it was too late to call. I'm sorry. I'll be back this afternoon."

"Don't bother." Rosemary slammed the phone down.

June 1957

Rosemary scattered chicken feed on the ground, watching her gray Pekin Bantams, White Silkies, Frizzle Cochins and Lavender Orpington rooster pecking around her feet. It was a warm day and she was dressed in shorts and a halter top, her feet encased in sandals. She'd tied her hair up in a scarf to keep it off her neck.

Her interest in exotic chicken breeds had begun during the time she was positive her husband was dead. Now she'd collected more and they'd interbred to raise even odder looking specimens, all of which delighted her. They circled around her, clucking contentedly as they snapped up the grain. They had their own special chicken house, but not that all of them chose to roost there. The ones who didn't were prey to the foxes that roamed the fields. She'd warned them, but they didn't seem to get the message. So far only one had disappeared, but she feared for them. Each one was special, friends she could talk to without worrying about saying the wrong thing.

Leaving the chickens to their feeding frenzy she moved on to the small barn that housed the two horses. Ulysses and Penelope languished, not exercised enough, their bellies fat, their muscles soft. She pulled the water buckets out to clean and refill and threw them each a flake of hay.

When Dylan began working at Raytheon he rented an apartment in the city where he could stay during the week. But the day she'd hung up on him had signaled another turning point. He had not taken well to her outburst, his anger sending him down to the farm to have it out with her. They had shouted things they couldn't take back, and in the end he'd left, moving into the city for good.

He had a bigger apartment now, one he had purchased that had turned into his permanent residence. It hurt her that his need for excitement and a social life trumped his desire to be with her. After he'd made a comment about a baby, she'd actually considered trying for another child, but once he'd settled into his new job she decided that a child would turn out as everything else had— a responsibility for her to manage alone. She'd never told him about the miscarriage.

She was just walking into the house when her phone rang, Dylan's voice on the other end low pitched and tired. "Why did you leave so early that morning? I was planning to take you out to breakfast. I had hoped I could remove your depression about the feeding frenzy at your father's house. Did I manage at all?"

It had been two weeks since the disbursement of the will and the one night spent in his bed. Why was he bringing this up now? "The dinner was great, Dylan. I appreciated it. But the horses were stuck in the barn, the chickens needed to be let out and fed. I can't be gone that long."

He scoffed. "You and that farm. Why don't you leave the horses in the field? They have plenty to eat and the stream is clean and runs all year. They don't need to be coddled now that we aren't riding them. I wish you'd consider moving in with me, at least on the weekends."

"You're the one who changed our agreement. Living down here was supposed to rekindle our relationship," she added, pointedly. "And now we barely see each other."

There was a long silence before he said, "I do miss you, Rosemary. That night we spent together was...well, it was like it used to be."

Rosemary laughed, thinking about their fumbled attempts in bed. Dylan had managed to seduce her as he always did when they were a little tipsy; the dry spell she'd been in made it a lot easier to succumb to his charms. "Except we were both drunk and didn't know what we were about."

"I certainly knew what I was about. Being celibate is not my favorite state."

Celibate? "If I'd been thinking clearly I wouldn't have done what I did," she interrupted. Was he really intimating that he hadn't taken a lover in the past three years? Women flocked to him, mesmerized by his charm as he held forth on one subject or another. He was a consummate flirt, and it was hard to imagine him going long without sex.

"You have to admit it was good between us, just like old times."

"I don't have to admit any such thing. Now why did you call?"

He let out a sigh. "I have a client I'd like to bring down to the farm. Would you be okay with that?"

"The farm belongs to both of us, but I do appreciate you asking. When would this be?"

"This next weekend. Can you get some help in?"

"Is this someone you need to impress?"

"Well…yes, I suppose it is."

"All weekend?"

"All weekend. And if you don't mind I would like to share your bed so there won't be any awkward questions. I promise to keep my hands off, if that's what you want."

Rosemary's gaze went to a hummingbird outside the kitchen window. He was buzzing her to tell her the feeder was empty. "Schmoozing requires a compliant wife?"

"I'd hardly call sharing a bed, compliant. It's what normal married couples do."

"Except we're not normal. The other night was a mistake. You are welcome to bring down your guest, but I expect you to go along with our house rules. You know what they are."

"Damn it! Why must you be so stiff?"

"If you lived here perhaps I wouldn't be so stiff. But our lives are separate now, and I've come to like it that way."

Dylan hung up without saying goodbye.

Rosemary stared out the window, wondering why she'd agreed. The weekend would be long and tedious. Seeing him always brought her pain; she was unable to keep her desire for more at the back of her mind where it belonged. She knew she wouldn't sleep, his proximity making her crave what she couldn't have. He would expect her to be the hostess, entertaining a man she didn't know. Was he trying to give the impression that he lived here with her? Why? It wasn't as though the acreage and old farmhouse screamed money. She let out an exasperated sigh and went out to weed the vegetable garden.

CHAPTER TWENTY-TWO

Virginia
late June, 1957

Rosemary heard the door slam, the sound of voices in the front hall. Dylan was here with his 'guest'. By the time she reached the front hall the two men had headed upstairs to the guest room. She waited, wondering who this person might be, but nothing could have prepared her for the man who appeared at the top of the stairs to gaze down on her. He was dark-skinned, either Indian or middle-eastern descent, his eyes piercing and bright. His hair was longer than normal and pure white. "You must be Rosemary," he said in an Indian accent as he walked down the stairs toward her.

"Yes. And you are..." Before she'd finished the sentence she realized that Dylan had never told her his name.

"I am Yasir Bukhari." He held out his long-fingered hand, his eyes still holding hers.

"Sorry, Rosemary," Dylan said, hurrying down the stairs. "I had meant to fill you in on Yasir. He's procuring products for his country."

"Which is?" she asked, looking from one to the other.

"I now live in Pakistan, but I was born in India." He glanced at Dylan nervously as though admitting this was not allowed.

Dylan glanced from one to the other. "Yes, well. Why don't we go and have a drink...Rosemary?"

Rosemary met her husband's gaze, his slight nod alerting her to what he had in mind. "I'll have the drinks tray brought down. Please make yourself comfortable," she added, gesturing expansively toward the two couches and chairs set around a large glass coffee table. Without glancing back she hurried toward the kitchen where no 'help' waited. The woman she'd hired would not be coming for another hour.

By the time she wheeled the cart down filled with glasses, ice, whisky and various mixers, the two men were in deep conversation. They looked up when she arrived, her husband's slight frown letting her know that doing this herself was not acceptable. "Sorry, dear. Mary won't be here for another hour or so. I didn't expect you until later."

"Please sit," Yasir said, rising from his place on the couch. "I will make the drinks." And so he did—expertly. "What do you know of the bardo, Rosemary?" he asked, handing her a vodka and tonic.

"The bardo? Nothing."

He nodded, handing another drink to Dylan before making his own. When Rosemary glanced at Dylan his eyebrows were pulled together in an expression of confusion.

"The bardo is the place where souls wait to be reincarnated. Do you believe in reincarnation?"

"Well, I..." Rosemary's hand went to her locket.

"Rosemary is more practical than that," Dylan filled in. "She's had some odd dreams but doesn't see them as having much to do with past lives."

That was a complete lie, but Yasir nodded, taking a sip of his drink as he joined her on the couch.

"There are many who believe that our souls travel in groups like families, that we reincarnate with the same people we've lived with before."

Why is he talking about this? Rosemary asked herself, fingering her locket. When she glanced toward Dylan he looked as shocked as she felt. "Why do you bring up this subject?" she finally asked, picking up her own glass.

"I see in you two souls, Rosemary—one who is living here and now, and another who lived long ago."

"What did you tell him?" she asked Dylan.

Dylan threw up his hands. "I've told him nothing."

"Once in a while I have this ability," Yasir said, smiling. "It is nothing that I cultivate or that I wish for myself, but sometimes it appears. And when it does I must speak out about it." He leaned toward her, his gaze on her locket. "I noticed that when I spoke you touched this necklace around your neck. What is its significance?"

"Dylan found it in an antique shop—and the people inside, the pictures, seem like people I've known before. Maybe they're distant relatives of mine."

"May I?" he asked, reaching to undo the chain.

She turned to make it easier for him, a tingly feeling moving up her arm when he touched her neck. A moment later the locket was in his hands. He clicked it open and stared at the pictures before looking up at her again.

"What is it?"

"This woman is who I saw superimposed over you."

Rosemary laughed nervously. "What are you saying—that I'm being haunted by her?"

"Not haunted, Rosemary. This woman is you in a past life. For some reason your lives are intersecting at the moment. Has there been some trauma lately—some disaster in your life?"

"My father just died, but I've been having dreams about her ever since Dylan gave me this locket." She glanced toward Dylan.

"And we've been discussing our future," Dylan added. "That could be considered trauma, I suppose." He grinned.

"Ah yes," Yasir commented, looking from one to the other as though he knew exactly what was going on between them. "You must discover who this woman is. Perhaps you could be regressed?"

"Regressed? What's that mean."

"There are people who are trained to take you back into past lives. Has your contact with this other life become stronger since your father's death?"

Rosemary thought about her recent trips into Rebecca's life. "I guess it has. The dreams are more vivid now."

"Would you like to know about this other life—this man who loves you?"

"It must be Dylan," Rosemary answered quickly before she could stop herself. "He's the one who found the locket. And here we are again." She smiled, hoping her facile explanation would appease the man.

"And yet you are not."

Rosemary shot a glance at her husband. How did Yasir know all this about them?

"I didn't tell him, I promise."

"It is obvious from the sleeping arrangements, the tension I picked up between you, that things are not as they should be."

Rosemary thought of her husband's overnight bag sitting on the floor of the office where she'd placed a cot. "Are you saying we should be together?"

"I am not saying that at all. But your current life is not in keeping with what you envisioned in the past. This locket says 'together forever', does it not? Now you are apart and estranged. Your inability to forge a life together is causing the past to bleed into the present. Both of you must work to recall this past life, the one that is intruding."

"Mrs. Hughes?"

Rosemary turned to see Mary, her hired gal for the evening, standing in the doorway. "Ah, Mary, perfect timing," she said, moving off the couch. She let out her held breath as she and Mary headed for the kitchen.

As she instructed Mary on the dinner she'd planned, helping her find the formal dishes and chopping up the squash and beans she'd brought in from the garden, she thought about Yasir's words. Why had a man who sought out her husband in order to procure weaponry be interested in a past life—especially hers? And why would the words on her locket carry weight now?

Things had changed between Rosemary and Dylan. He wasn't the person he'd been when he came back from the war, either the lost and traumatized man, or the one he'd become after their visits to the psychiatrist, who had wanted to spend the rest of his life with her. Now he was driven, just as he'd been when she married him, his love for her taking a back seat to his work. If it hadn't been for their closeness in the Philippines, and the ensuing war, they might have divorced early on.

Thankfully the dinner conversation did not revisit the reincarnation topic, Dylan bringing up subjects about the political situations around the world, what it was like to work for Raytheon, and the connections between Pakistan and the United States, a relationship that had been cordial for nearly a decade. They drank wine and ate the creamed shrimp over rice, her grilled squash and green beans as delicious as she'd hoped.

Over brandy the discussions got into tensions between Pakistan and India since the partition created between the two countries—hardly the time for Pakistan to be buying weaponry from the U.S. When she asked about that, and what he was purchasing, Yasir changed the subject. It was classified.

It was only later when Rosemary was getting ready for bed that she began to worry. Despite his knowledge of the bardo and his talk about their marriage, Yasir was a dangerous man. He was about to procure weaponry for Pakistan that could kill thousands, his belief in life after death another reason why lives could be sacrificed in the name of war. Rosemary shivered, snuggling beneath her comforter. Tonight she would have been happy to have Dylan's arms around her.

The next day the two men went hunting, guns slung across their shoulders as they headed out after breakfast. She had a premonition and dismissed it. Dylan would not be shot during the expedition. Dylan had informed her they would expect an early dinner and not to plan on them for lunch. Since Mary was a church goer and could not be here to help her, Rosemary would be responsible for all the cooking.

Busying herself with preparations for dinner number two, salmon, fresh romaine leaves and tomatoes picked from the garden, and scalloped potatoes, she let her mind wander.

The dream had arrived the night before, startling in its clarity. She had been with the man pictured inside her locket, their hands clasped as they wandered dappled trails under massive trees. Apparently this part of their life had come before her last dream in which a very unhappy Rebecca was being hauled off by her father. When she woke she was surprised to find herself in her bed, and felt the two times overlapping in her mind. It reminded her a lot of how she and Dylan had been early on, before their marriage and before the war. When the images faded she felt an inexplicable sadness.

She wondered now about the reincarnation angle Yasir had mentioned. She was an imaginative person, an artist. Her mind was quixotic and quirky. The pictures inside the locket could have triggered some book she'd read or movie she'd seen. But she couldn't dismiss the parallel themes. But why she kept dipping into this past life was a mystery that still needed to be solved. She thought of asking Yasir and quickly dismissed it. She didn't trust him.

The men returned, tired and filthy. Luckily neither one had managed to shoot anything. They went off to take showers while she set the table and prepared the food.

"Beautiful meal," Yasir said once they sat down. "I see that you are a good cook, as well as your many other accomplishments."

"Other accomplishments?" Rosemary looked at Dylan who only shrugged.

"Your paintings in the guest room. They are quite good," Yasir elaborated.

"I should have removed them before you arrived," she mumbled, actually blushing. "Those are early works, done before Dylan and I married."

"I would be delighted to see your more recent work," he said, forking salmon into his mouth.

"She'll show you after dinner," Dylan answered, a look on his face that brooked no argument.

Her studio was a mess and she wished fervently that Dylan had not volunteered this 'showing'. But she did it because her husband seemed to want to give this man everything he asked for. Why Dylan seemed so slavishly devoted to him was a puzzle.

"This one is indicative of your past life bleeds," Yasir said, holding up a half-finished landscape with a dilapidated but once beautiful house in the distance.

"That's just a figment of my imagination," Rosemary answered, taking it from him.

"A house, both in dreams and in art, nearly always represents the foundation, either of a relationship or of a person." He smiled and turned to examine a few others. He picked up a self-portrait she'd done when she was still in the Philippines. "How intricate," he commented, his fingers tracing the curve of her breast and the locket she'd painted hanging around her neck.

She felt his fingers on her own skin, a shudder going through her.

"And still the locket," he muttered. "You were so very lovely, Rosemary, and just as lovely now," he finished, looking at her.

She took the painting from him and stored it against the wall, relieved that the tour was over. When the men headed to the living room for nightcaps she hurried in the other direction, taking the opportunity to clean the kitchen.

Rosemary was still working when Dylan appeared, a frown on his face. "Why didn't you leave this until later? Now Yasir has gone to bed and…"

She turned to face her husband, wiping her wet hands on her apron. "And what? I carried on a conversation at dinner, I showed him my work—what more do you want from me?"

"He was interested in pursuing the reincarnation theme again."

"Well, I wasn't. I don't want to revisit that topic at all, Dylan. Why did you bring this man down here?"

"Because he was interested in you and the outdoors. I told him I'd take him hunting."

"Interested in me—why?"

"I told him what happened between us."

"You mean your defection once you got over the residual trauma of war?"

"My defection, as you call it, was not that at all. I simply needed to go back to work in the real world. Men need that, or haven't you noticed? Yasir was interested in my time in prison camp and how I felt when I was released. He wanted to know how all those years apart affected us. He seemed genuinely interested."

"He seems rather shady to me. There's something too slick, too all-knowing about him. And as far as the past lives and the bardo…well…" She shook her head and turned back to the sink full of dishes.

Dylan picked up a towel and began to dry. "That was as much a surprise to me as it was to you. He's a complicated man with many sides to him."

"Muslim or Hindu?"

"I'm not sure. He's lived in various places during his life. Did you know he's in his late seventies? He carries a lot of weight in the Pakistani government."

"I would guess so if he's in charge of weaponry for their military. Will you take him back to Washington tomorrow morning?"

Dylan nodded, placing a dried plate in the cabinet. "Can Mary come over to fix breakfast?"

Rosemary scoffed. "I'm not going to call her for that! I am perfectly capable of cooking a decent breakfast."

"That's not the point."

"What is the point—having him think we live the good life out here? He already knows we don't share a bed. I'd rather he see us the way we really are. Are you afraid he won't buy from Raytheon because I don't have a cook?"

"He'll buy. He's already begun negotiations. I just wanted you to feel free—you know—to be able to sit around and talk instead of cooking and cleaning."

"Frankly I feel more comfortable in the kitchen, especially with all his talk about reincarnation."

"Millions of people believe in reincarnation. And I thought you did too. Why the change of heart?"

Rosemary shook her head. "I don't know. I'm just skeptical of him, that's all." She hung the dishtowel on the rack attached to the wall and took off her apron, hanging it over the back of a chair. "I'm heading to bed—I need to get some sleep tonight."

"Are you implying you didn't sleep last night? I have a remedy for that."

"No, Dylan." When she gave him a peck on the cheek he grabbed her arm. "I like what he said about us—that the past is bleeding through because we need to mend our relationship."

"That is not what he said. Good night." She headed away before he could respond, her measured footsteps taking her up the narrow stairwell to what had been their shared bedroom. Once inside the room she closed and locked her door.

She stared at herself in the mirror, not surprised to see a tired woman who seemed on the verge of tears. She pulled her hair back the way it had been in her self-portrait, tugging her sweater off her shoulders to expose them. If it wasn't for the wrinkles on her forehead, the confusion behind her eyes, she hadn't changed that much. But inside she did not feel at all the same.

That day in the Philippines when she'd decided to use herself as a model she'd been full of life, filled with joy at what she and Dylan had created between them. Dylan had come back while she in the middle of it, tubes of color spread across the porch next to her easel, a mirror propped up against the outside wall of the cottage so that she could see herself and the banana trees behind her. He stood next to her, watching it progress. He was the one who pulled her loose-fitting peasant blouse down to expose her shoulders. "Creamy white with a hint of rose and gold tones against the backdrop of lush green," he'd said, kissing the back of her neck. A few moments later she'd left her paints and followed him into the bedroom.

It was as though their marriage had begun once they moved far away from everything they knew. And when he returned a broken man, that love had very slowly been ignited again. They'd begun to build something here. And despite his protestations about it all being her idea, he had been fully present for all of it. Unfortunately the flames had not been able to withstand the physical distance created by his work in Washington. They'd flared for a while, but soon there was only ash. She took off her clothes and climbed not bed, closing her eyes against the past.

"I want to be with you forever," the voice said. Rosemary looked around for the source, noticing Dylan standing with another woman. His arm was around her shoulders, and when his eyes discovered Rosemary in the shadows, a wicked grin appeared on his face. It taunted her and she had to turn away. Why was he being so cruel? What had she done to deserve this betrayal? Instead of confronting him she moved further into the shadows, but when she looked back she was dismayed to see the two of them locked into an embrace, their lips clinging as they kissed.

Rosemary woke with a gasp, her heart pounding. This dream was just a dream, she told herself. It had come because of her suppressed feelings for her husband, desires that she had to keep to herself. Tears filled her eyes and she brushed them away. She had made her decision long ago, her life circumscribed and simple now. She had a hired man who helped her with the heavier chores. She was managing quite well.

But managing the farm was not the problem. She was still in love with Dylan and the very sight of him drove her nearly to distraction. Trying to keep this to herself required tremendous energy. If he found out it would only humiliate her further. His mistress wasn't a woman, it was his work and his social life in Washington. Nothing she could do or say would change that. He said he wanted to spend time with her, but she would always play second fiddle to the life he'd created for himself.

Breakfast went by in a whirl of conversation that Rosemary did not follow. She heard herself from afar answering questions, laughing at a joke, offering food, but her concentration was on distancing herself. Her dream about Dylan came back in lurid detail and she pushed it away. There was no use…no point…

Once breakfast was over she let out a sigh of relief. Soon she would be alone, able to let go of the strict control she'd placed on herself. But Yasir's parting words troubled her, repeating inside her mind.

"Something is calling to you, Rosemary, and you must give it your full attention if you wish to move on with your life."

By the time she'd formulated a question, Yasir and Dylan were already in the car. The tires crunched across the gravel as Dylan backed up and turned around. And a moment later they were heading up the driveway toward the main road. Did he mean the feelings for Dylan she kept hidden? What else could it be?

She went to the horse barn, trying to let go of her rising uneasiness. That man seemed to have some sort of hold over Dylan, and knew way too many details of their inner lives. When she opened the stall doors, the horses ran by her, bucking before settling down to graze on the thick grass. She watched them for a moment, letting the peace of the bucolic scene wash over her and soothe the mood that had come from the weekend.

Back in the house Rosemary pulled the sheets off the guest bed, removing the one towel Yasir had used and carrying them down to the washing machine. She loaded them in, added detergent, and turned it on before heading to the room reserved for family members where her husband slept now. She made up his bed and returned the wet towel to the bathroom, hanging it over the curtain rod.

Yasir said that she and Dylan needed to work out the past to find out where they'd gone wrong. But she knew where they'd gone wrong—it was the job with Raytheon that had done it, seducing Dylan as surely as if it had been another woman. There was no competing with that. She had a sudden wish to be free of it all. And the only way to do that was to get a divorce. Sleeping together every six months or so only made matters worse. Continuing with these interludes and knowing it would never change, was sheer torture.

She was preparing an afternoon snack and removing an open bottle of wine from the fridge when her phone rang. She hurried to pick it up.

"Mrs. Hughes?"

"This is she."

"Your husband has been in an accident, Mrs. Hughes. He's at Memorial hospital and asking for you."

"What kind of accident—is he all right? What happened?"

"I was only told to call you; I don't have details."

"Who is the doctor—where…"

"Please, Mrs. Hughes. It would be best if you came as soon as possible."

My gods! Was he about to die? Ten minutes later she was in her car speeding toward Washington with her heart in her throat.

On the frantic trip to the hospital, her mind careened into the past, scenes of their life together moving by like the reel of a movie. If he died there would be no more chance to change anything. He couldn't die—he simply couldn't.

She pressed her foot down harder, speeding up to get past several slow drivers. Dizziness sent her careening off the road for a second—she must have been holding her breath. She pulled back into traffic but something was happening to her—was she having a stroke?

"I refuse to go!"

"You will not refuse, Rebecca. You have been sick for a long time."

"You call grieving sick, Father? I lost my baby, and my husband is gone for good. I have seen him with another woman, an African woman, they have a child together now."

"Get into the carriage."

Rebecca pulled away, but the driver who was waiting to take her to her terrible destination was able to grab her.

"Thank you, Nathan," her father said, pushing her into the carriage. He got in behind her, staring at her with narrowed eyes. "I never thought we would come to such an impasse, daughter. Your vision of Edgar is an embarrassment. He died serving his country and you are painting him as a philanderer? You should be ashamed of yourself. What did he ever do to deserve such enmity? You have thwarted me at every step and made me ashamed to claim you as my child. You shall be hidden from sight until such time that you can promise to do better."

"If by, do better, you mean not have visions, I am afraid I cannot comply."

She felt the sting as he slapped her across the face. "You will not be insolent with me!"

Tears filled her eyes. "No one comes out of that place," she muttered, but her father either did not hear her, or chose not to reply.

Rosemary was suddenly aware of horns honking and people shouting. She was still behind the wheel of her car, but how she'd managed to keep driving was anyone's guess. At the moment the car straddled the yellow line at the edge, two wheels on the verge and two wheels on the roadway. She quickly pulled over and shut off the engine, catching her breath while angry drivers hurtled by. Her heart was beating wildly. She reached up to adjust her hat before realizing that she wore no hat. Looking into the rear view mirror revealed the pale oval of her face, gray-green eyes wide with disbelief and terror.

It took her fifteen minutes before she felt able to continue toward the hospital, the fear of Dylan's imminent death driving her on. The hell with Rebecca—her own life was falling apart. *Dylan,* she thought...*please be all right.* Tears squeezed out of her eyes, blinding her for a moment.

By the time she reached the hospital she was shaking with fear. She parked the car and ran inside.

"Just down the hall," the woman at the desk of the trauma unit told her. "He's just come back from surgery."

Surgery? Once she reached the room she stopped for a moment to take a deep breath. She had no idea what injuries he'd sustained, or even whether he would live or die. She pushed the door open into a darkened room, the beep of monitors frighteningly loud. Dylan lay with eyes closed, his face nearly the same color as the sheets. One leg was in a cast from ankle to hip and held suspended in the air, and his left arm was bandaged from wrist to shoulder. Purple bruising lay beneath his eyes and across his right cheek. She picked up his good hand in hers. "What happened to you?" she whispered, tears brimming.

She heard the whoosh of the door, turning to see a white-coated man arrive. "He's stable now," he said, checking Dylan's vitals. "It was nip and tuck there for a while."

"You operated on him?"

The man nodded. "I'm Doctor Adderly. You must be Rosemary."

She nodded, wiping at her eyes.

"He was calling for you when he came into emergency. It's why we were able to get in touch so quickly."

"What happened to him?"

"He walked in front of a car on Massachusetts Avenue. His leg is broken in two places, his arm is severely cut and bruised, but no broken bones there. He sustained some internal injuries that we were able to repair. He's a lucky man."

"Lucky? He doesn't look lucky to me."

"Lucky to be alive, Mrs. Hughes. If that car had been traveling a few miles faster your husband would be in the morgue instead of lying in this hospital bed."

Rosemary shivered, her arms going around her body. "Thank you for saving his life."

"I did everything I've been trained to do, but honestly I think it was you who kept this man alive. He kept mumbling about unfinished business, things he needed to tell you. He was incoherent most of the time, but he did manage to give us your name and number before he lost consciousness."

"What now? How long will he have to stay?"

"We'll want him to have physical therapy for a month or two after he gets the cast off, but in the meantime he can go home—as long as he has someone to care for him." The doctor picked up the chart hanging on the foot of the bed and checked something off. "He'll need to be with us for another few days, but after that you're welcome to come and get him."

Rosemary stared at him. "We…I mean I…we don't live together."

The doctor looked surprised. "You don't live together? By the way he was shouting you'd think you were his true north."

Rosemary smiled. "He tends to be overly romantic at times."

"If you can't take care of him he'll need a private nurse around the clock—at least until we can get that cast off his leg."

Rosemary gazed at the man in the bed. "I can take care of him until then."

The doctor smiled. "Good. One thing settled." He glanced at Dylan. "You may as well come back in the morning. He won't wake up anytime soon."

Instead of taking the doctor's advice, Rosemary went into the hall to place a call to Mary. "Can you watch things for the next few days? Dylan's in the hospital."

"Of course, Mrs. Hughes. Is Mr. Hughes all right?"

"He will be." After the call Rosemary settled on the chair next to the bed and closed her eyes.

The room was dark, the smell of disinfectant strong. Rebecca stood on tiptoe to see out of the window but it was too high for her. She'd been here a week already, a terrible week filled with the sound of screaming and crying, some of it hers.

"Come along now, dear. It is time for your treatments."

The nurse was built like a house, iron gray hair cut short around her square pasty white face. She grabbed Rebecca and dragged her from the room and down a long hallway into another part of the facility.

When she saw the chair again her heart rose into her throat and she thought she might faint from terror. "But I had one yesterday."

"You will have them daily if it helps you. Your father insisted on the latest techniques and encouraged us to use as many as we deemed beneficial. You will also be bled today to rid you of ill humors. You are lucky to be in this facility where you have access to such things. Many asylums use other more drastic means to bring their patients back to reality. Luckily we have the money to afford the newest machines."

Rebecca shuddered. What they had done to her was like going to hell and barely coming back. She had not been able to utter one word for hours after it was over, her hands still shaking from it.

But before she could argue further she was dragged to the chair, her arms and legs fastened to keep her still. Claustrophobia made her struggle but it was of no use. As the 'treatment' began, darkness came over her, and she fell into a place where nothing mattered.

Rosemary screamed, waking herself in the process. She was shaking all over.

"Rosie?"

She jumped up and hurried to the bed. "Dylan, my gods. You scared the life out of me."

"Is that why you were screaming?"

She shook her head, shuddering. "I had a terrible dream."

"One of *those* dreams?"

"Yes. But let's not talk of it. You look terrible."

Dylan's glazed eyes took in his casted leg. When he shifted he let out a moan of pain. "Good God. I feel like I was run over by a truck."

"You got hit by a car. Do you have any memory of it?"

Dylan's eyebrows pulled together in concentration. "Not really. The last thing I remember is walking home."

"You were crossing Massachusetts Avenue."

"Why would I do that? From what I recall I'd been down at the Cook n' Captain Bar and Grill. My apartment's on the same side of the road."

"Who were you with?"

"Only Yasir. He wanted to have a drink before he left for the airport."

"Was he with you on the sidewalk?"

Dylan looked perplexed. "Honestly, I don't remember."

Rosemary spent two nights at Dylan's apartment waiting for the hospital to release him into her care. Finally she drove back to the farm after they told her he would need to stay longer than they'd originally thought. It would be at least another week before his leg could come down from where it was suspended—there was just too much swelling.

Back in her bedroom at the farm her dreams took her into the past again, Rebecca's life taking on a macabre reality. It was becoming increasingly more difficult to deal with, the poor woman's body and mind weakened on a daily basis by the asylum's cruel methods.

The reasons for why this was happening confounded her, making her ask the same questions over and over. Was she supposed to fix the past or was the past merely trying to point out something that she couldn't seem to fathom? When she was there her own consciousness disappeared. She *was* Rebecca and felt every single horrible thing that Rebecca felt. And Rebecca was at the breaking point.

CHAPTER TWENTY-THREE

Virginia
August 1957

Rosemary had chosen the small sitting room off the kitchen to act as Dylan's bedroom, making up the couch with sheets and blankets to serve as his bed. The office and the fold-up cot would not do for his current needs.

This was her favorite room in the house, the low-ceilings and dark beams reminding her of eras long past--one of the reasons she'd purchased the 1700's farmhouse. A stone fireplace nestled against one wall and held logs for when the weather turned chilly. Dylan would have everything he needed, including a bathroom close by. He was walking on crutches now, his daily excursions around the house giving him something to do. The stack of books she'd left on the table next to the couch had helped at first, but he was becoming bored and out of sorts without his daily exercise and the usual work that occupied his active mind.

"Rosie?" His voice jarred her out of her thoughts; she wasn't used to having another person in the house.

She hurried from the kitchen, hoping he hadn't fallen. "What is it?"

He sat on the edge of the couch, his face drawn in pain. "I need to talk to you. We haven't had a chance yet, and..."

"Yes, Dylan. Too many things between us have been left unsaid."

His face relaxed and he leaned back against the cushions. "Can you spare me a few moments now? I know you have chores to do. Did you remember that today is our wedding anniversary?"

"I did remember that. I was thinking about that day when I was out doing chores and you were still snoring."

Dylan laughed. "You always were an early riser."

"Not like you who always wanted to spend your free mornings in bed."

"Only when I had the pleasure of your body next to mine."

Rosemary ignored the comment, pushing away the intimate image that rose up in her mind. "What would you like to talk about?"

"Mainly us, to be blunt. My accident has given me a lot of time to think." He readjusted his leg position, an expression of pain crossing his features. He breathed in and went on. "After the war we never discussed anything but what was happening at the time."

"As I recall we tried but you didn't wanted to talk about it. It was too fresh. I could tell from your moods how much emotional pain you were in. And we had a lot of other things going on at the time."

"Don't remind me. What I want to talk about is how we came to be in this predicament."

"By predicament, you mean our living situation?"

He nodded. "When I came back all I wanted was to be with you. And if memory serves, you felt the same—that is, after we worked through what happened in the interim. To me it was a chance to start over—and yet here we are."

"You took a job with Raytheon and forgot everything you wrote in your journals."

"That isn't fair. When the job came up we discussed it. You thought it would help my sense of failure, the insecurity brought about by the army. I never thought it would keep us from being together."

Rosemary sat next to him, adjusting the pillows behind his back. "I just didn't realize how Raytheon would consume you, Dylan. We had the farm then; you promised to help with the planting and the animals. You left me here to fend for myself. Those first few months without you were very hard on me. I had to make a decision to let go of what I'd envisioned—that was the start of my new life."

Dylan was silent, his gaze on the floor. "You told me that the beginning of your life was when we went to the Philippines."

Rosemary fiddled with the edge of the sheet. The bedding needed to be washed. "Instead of laying blame, why don't we move on to the present. What is it you're trying to say?"

"I want to share the rest of my life with you. I'm sick of living apart."

"Let's revisit this after you get well, all right? You aren't thinking straight right now."

When she moved to stand Dylan grabbed her hand. "I heard from Raytheon yesterday while you were out mucking stalls. I am no longer welcome there."

Rosemary stared at him. "They fired you? Why?"

"I lost them the contract with Yasir. And to add to that he left without settling his bill."

"It's very possible that Yasir tried to kill you. That man took off because he knew the police would arrest him if he didn't get out of the country."

"No one I've spoken with has mentioned that. You're the only one who thinks he's responsible."

"You told me he was with you. Even if you were drunk, I can't see you stepping in front of a car. Face facts, Dylan."

Dylan let out a heavy sigh. "Even if he did it, he's gone. My being reinstated at Raytheon because he tried to kill me is not going to happen."

"Ah. I see. The reason you want to resume living together is because you have no job."

"Godammit, Rosemary! Why can't you ever take me at face value? You must have a very poor opinion of me to think that."

"I know you, Dylan. This sudden change of heart does not make sense to me."

"It isn't sudden. I've been thinking about it for months now."

Rosemary stood. "I thought this conversation would have more substance. I need to write some letters."

"Rosemary, please! I'm at your mercy here."

"We've talked about all this ad nauseam. I'll be back to fix you lunch." She left the room before he could persuade her to stay. She had yet to admit how very frightened she'd been about his accident. She had not had the nerve to open herself up to him at all. Why was she keeping this distance between them? Had Yasir pushed her husband into traffic? And if so, why?

Instead of writing letters she hurried out the door into the misty rain. Admitting to herself that she enjoyed having Dylan around was one thing, but if she allowed him back into her life what was to keep him from hurting her again? She was not emotionally strong enough to go through the pain.

She thought again of his journals, how she'd cried nearly every day as she read them through. She'd been so sure of his love back then, his declarations of how he felt for her on nearly every page. And yet they had not discussed what he'd written, his need to be done with it keeping her questions at bay. Now it was too late to go over it all again. He was not the same man who'd written those words, nor was he the man she'd married. They hardly knew one another now, their lives having diverged into two very separate worlds.

Dylan watched his wife hurry from the room. As usual the proper words had eluded him. He had wanted to tell her about the dreams, *his* dreams. He'd only mentioned them briefly, letting her believe that her forays into the past were on her shoulders when in reality they shared them, and had done so for years. The day he found that locket something had shifted inside him, as though those two people were closer to him than his brothers or his parents. But he'd neglected to open up about that either, his casual comments belying how he really felt.

And here he was again, helpless to stop the thoughts and dreams that had returned full force. Why was it so hard for him to admit his vulnerability in the face of things that couldn't be explained? Something was not right and he was sure Yasir had known exactly what it was. Being Edgar had made him hate himself, the man's dealings with his wife and patronizing attitudes making him cringe once his consciousness returned to this reality. Damn Yasir and his mystical nonsense! Now it was too late to question him.

He was dozing when he felt the air shift around him, a tingle going through his body. A moment later he was floating, his mind letting go of the present as he drifted into a familiar world.

"Edgar, why did you keep this from me?"

Edgar watched her face turn into an angry mask. He longed to hold her but he knew how she would react if he tried. "I was afraid you wouldn't go through with the wedding if you knew."

Rebecca rose from the new velvet settee they'd purchased together just after their wedding a month before. "You might be correct in that assumption, but with the plans already in place I would not have wanted to disappoint anyone. We have barely established a routine or become used to sharing a bed. How am I to deal with you going off to war?"

He watched her pace, wishing he could make her be still. "We should have married earlier. I begged you not to let so much time elapse between my proposal and the ceremony. You could have had a baby by now if you had listened to me."

"A baby? I had hoped to wait a year or two before beginning a family, Edgar. How can you be so cavalier about this?"

"I have been called to do my duty. The conflicts with the Ashanti must be curtailed."

"But so far away in Africa! Why does it matter so much?"

"Because the British assumed control in 1821."

"And yet these wars are between tribal members, not us."

He shook his head in exasperation. "No, Becca. It is our duty to put these skirmishes down. I will be leaving early tomorrow to join my regiment."

"Dylan? Are you all right?"

Dylan came back with a gasp. "I was…I was in the past, Rosemary. I was the man—the man in your locket. I was about to go off to war in Africa."

Rosemary eyed him worriedly. "You were sitting here with your eyes wide open, and you did not look yourself. You scared me."

"The dreams have been coming more and more."

"That was no dream—you were gone." She sat down next to him. "I had something very similar happen to me on my way to the hospital right after your accident."

Dylan watched her eyes fill, the way she bent her head as though embarrassed to admit it. "Why didn't you say?"

"Why didn't *you* say, Dylan? Why do we always keep these things to ourselves? This is what stands between us, not some job or your need for excitement or my need for solitude. It is exactly what Yasir said."

Dylan took in a deep breath. "Yasir knows something that we don't. I wonder now if he's settling a score from long ago."

"What do you mean?"

"I think I knew him in that past life, and I think I know what I did to have him carry a grudge into another lifetime."

"Listen to yourself—any sane person who heard us right now would have us locked up in a loony bin."

Visions crowded Dylan's mind—places, people, *women*. At some point he'd been with Yasir's wife. He could see an African woman, knew intuitively who she was.

"I did something I feel ashamed of. And I've been hearing these words in my mind, but I'm not sure from where or who said them: *You bastard! You took my woman—she was meant to be with me!* And they're said with such force and anger." He turned his face away.

"How can you be ashamed of something that happened in another life?"

"He knew. It's why he made arrangements to come down here. He hoped to jog my past life memories by going over what I'd told him about you. It's why he may have pushed me in front of that car."

"But if you didn't remember what you did, why would he get any satisfaction out of killing you?"

Dylan shook his head, his hands going to his casted leg. "My leg itches intolerably. When can I get this damnable cast off?"

Rosemary didn't answer, her gaze in the middle distance. "I'm getting us some drinks and then we're going to go through this piece by piece."

"Happy anniversary," Dylan said bitterly, watching her leave the room. So much for champagne and laughter. He hoped they could hash this out and come to some resolution. But after the many failings between them he was certain she wouldn't ever trust him again. At this point he didn't even know if he trusted himself.

CHAPTER TWENTY-FOUR

Virginia
August, 1957

"Please, Rosemary. For once can we have a civil conversation without laying blame?"

"I hardly think talking about your affairs to be laying blame. I had one, you've had them—why is it such a big thing?"

He let out an exasperated sigh, trying to come up with the right words. Rosemary had an attitude about him that he'd fostered in order to assuage his battered ego. He'd let her believe in his happy-go-lucky attitude, his involvement with other women. She thought of him as a shallow womanizer, and instead of being honest about his feelings he'd let it continue. He had not been with another woman the entire time they'd lived apart. But if he admitted this, it was tantamount to admitting he was still hopelessly in love with her.

He looked up from where he lay on the couch, his leg propped on pillows. He took in a breath and let it out. "Because I haven't had any, that's why. You can choose not to believe me, but I have no reason to lie to you. I've let the falsehoods between us go on and on. They have to stop now. I am not who you think I am."

Rosemary's eyes narrowed. "You expect me to believe you haven't slept with other women? I see how they look at you, Dylan. And that sparkle in your eyes is a dead giveaway."

"Just because I like to look doesn't mean I partake. I take full responsibility for leading you on. It seemed easier than admitting my reluctance. But it's time to move past this."

Rosemary pulled the chair closer to the couch and took a sip of the drink she held, her gaze on him. "Now that you bring this up, I'm afraid I've been doing the same. You think I'm a snob, but in reality I'm ashamed of being wealthy. I've been sending money to charities for years as well as trying my best to do what I can for the less fortunate. I've felt guilty my entire life."

"So we've both put forward a false persona. You believe me now?"

"You look too serious not to be taken that way. Honestly, I don't think I've ever see this particular expression on your face."

"Lying here helpless while past life visions and scenes from prison camp march by has brought me full circle. You can't lie in a bed hour after hour without having regrets arise."

"Tell me about Yasir. You believe he shared a past life with us?"

"There was a man I remember from my time, Edgar's time, in the war—the Ashanti war that is. He was African, a member of one of the tribes on the side of the Brits. His wife took me in while he was still fighting. How I found my way to her, I don't really know. Something happened between us.

I'm sure that's the reason he came here, and it's why he pushed me into traffic. He's obsessed with her."

"An African woman who lived over a hundred years ago?"

"Yes, Rosemary—does that offend you?"

"Of course not! Do you think I'm racist on top of everything else? Rebecca had a vision of Edgar with an African woman—they had a baby together. Was this woman beautiful, exotic?"

Dylan grinned, watching her expression. "If I was with her I'm sure she was, considering my taste in women. But that was back in the eighteen hundreds. Maybe we should bring the discussion into the present."

"We can't talk about the present if we don't get to the bottom of why we keep visiting the past. Those lives are inextricably mixed up with ours, and I don't know why. And Yasir is a big part of it all."

"I'll tell you one reason why: I left Rebecca and went to war and never saw her again. Maybe this life we share is a way to undo some of the hurt I caused."

"Rebecca lost the baby and was put into an asylum."

Dylan whipped his head around to look at her, nearly knocking his drink off the table. "What? Who put her into an asylum?"

"Her father, a despicable man who couldn't stand the fact that she could see into the future."

Dylan had a hollow feeling in his belly, tears forming in his eyes. "I don't know why that affects me so much over a hundred years later, but it does."

"It affects you because those lives still haunt us."

He gazed at her. "And maybe because we never had a child."

"You didn't want a child."

He scoffed. "Another part of me I didn't reveal, Rosemary. I very much wanted a child, but after the war I was afraid my semen might not be up to snuff, and then life took over."

Rosemary leaned over to place her drink on the table. "As long as we're admitting secrets, I have one. I was pregnant when I left Manila. I had a miscarriage when I was five months along."

Dylan's mouth felt open in shock. "Jesus Christ, Rosie. Why didn't you tell me?"

"I couldn't reach you at the time and then once you got back I figured what was the point? Four years had gone by—you were in no shape to hear about it. I didn't want to add more pain."

Dylan grabbed her hand. "I'm so sorry I wasn't here to support you. That makes me terribly sad."

Rosemary's eyes filled with tears. "It does me too."

He pulled her close, avoiding his leg, which lay inert along the couch like a pallid monster. "I wish we could have a do-over. I had visions of a baby during those years, hoping when I got back we could start a family."

"Maybe if I'd told you sooner..."

"As you said, I could not have dealt with it. I was a mess, barely able to get through each day."

She pulled back, her eyes meeting his. "How do we cross these chasms between us, Dylan? There are so many lies and so much hurt."

"We start over—it's as simple as that."

"Start over--from when? From what we've revealed tonight the lies have been going on since day one. On our wedding day I thought I was marrying a charmer, a womanizer who had managed to sweep me off my feet. I wondered if I'd made the right choice. I was worried that we didn't have anything in common other than a physical attraction. Are you saying that even back then you didn't have eyes for other women?"

"I've always appreciated women, Rosie. But as far as eyes for others? No. I was devoted to you from day one. I do have to admit that I was seduced somewhat by your wealth and place in society. But after we got to know one another I got over that. I was a social climber back then, my fervent desire to rise above my humble beginnings. If you felt that way, why did you go through with the wedding?"

"I couldn't back out and let everyone down. We'd booked the National Cathedral, for God's sake." Her expression turned bitter. "You married me for my money."

"In the beginning your money was part of the attraction, yes. But the army brought me the prestige I needed, and I began to see things differently, especially after the long talks I had with your father. His take on life seeped into me and made me appreciate my own abilities. He believed in me." Dylan leaned back, his eyes closing. "I can't think anymore. Can we take this up tomorrow?"

When Rosemary leaned over to give him a quick kiss goodnight his arms came around her, his mouth pressing against hers. He was gratified when she didn't pull away.

Rosemary turned off the light, her thoughts on what she and Dylan had discussed. The kiss between them had not been chaste. Were they falling in love again? She was too old to be feeling tingly all over, her body on fire.

She fell asleep to wind whistling around the old windows, her dreams of Dylan taking her places she'd never been before. His arms were around her as she soared from this reality to some kind of ethereal palace of pleasure. When she woke in the morning she was almost embarrassed by what she remembered.

She knew it was the confessions that had opened up that place inside her, the shell cracking as they divulged their long held secrets. But in the light of a new day she wondered—did she have the strength to be vulnerable again—to trust that what he told her was true? If they came out of this still living apart there was no hope for them. That would signal it was time for a divorce. But something niggled inside—a tiny seedling had begun to sprout. She wanted to protect it, nourish it, and keep it growing. But Dylan would have to want the same thing for the plant to survive.

CHAPTER TWENTY-FIVE

Virginia
Late October 1957

While mucking out the stalls Rosemary thought about the first time she'd seen Dylan after his release from prison camp. He was emaciated, hollow cheeked, a haunted look in his eyes. She didn't know him. From what she'd read in his journals he'd barely survived. Now they were going over all these past times, emotions rising like bubbles in a champagne glass. Except this was no champagne. It was bitter and nasty, something she did not want to swallow. What she still didn't understand was how they'd reached this impasse. Yes, she understood the lies, the pretending they'd both engaged in over the ensuing years. But every couple had things between them, and mostly they managed to move forward without hashing out every tiny detail. But then again, most couples did not have prison camp between them, or a past life that loomed large.

Today was the day he was to have his cast removed. Finally. Would he decide to move back to his apartment? As usual they had not discussed it. So much for keeping the lines of communication open.

"Are you excited about getting the cast off?" she asked as she drove toward Washington and the hospital.

"Are you kidding? I can't wait! I want to take walks, swim, maybe ride that old nag, Ulysses."

"Really?"

"Yes, really." He smiled at her.

She turned back to the road as a squirrel darted across, making her swerve. "What are we doing, Dylan? I thought we were divorcing."

"Is that what you want?"

"I don't know. I haven't really thought about it."

"And yet you've had six weeks to think about it. Sounds like old habits die hard."

She chuckled. "I was just thinking the same thing, wondering if you wanted to stay here or move back to Washington."

"There's nothing for me in Washington without a job. But I do need to look into the Yasir issue."

"Yasir. I'd forgotten all about him. Who can you talk to—CIA, FBI?"

"I've got some connections with the CIA from my time in the service. Maybe I'll start there."

"And the apartment?"

"I'll keep it for now. Who knows, we may want to come in for a weekend from time to time."

So he didn't want a divorce. Did she want a divorce? When she thought about the house empty again it didn't sit well. She enjoyed having him around, even with the painful talks they'd been having. When she reached the hospital she parked and helped him get his crutches out of the back seat.

An attendant came to escort him back, leaving her in the waiting room. It was over an hour before she saw him again, his face drawn with pain as he limped toward her, a cane in his hand. "Leg's kind of weak."

"I would imagine it is," she said, taking hold of his arm. "Lunch at our favorite place?"

"You bet."

After they were seated at a table by the window he turned to her. "Just to keep things clear, the doctor wants me to come in once a week for physical therapy."

"Can't we do it on our own?"

"No, Rosemary. They have machines and things. I'll drive in and either spend the night or come home the same day."

Rosemary remembered the last time he'd said these words. His trips had gone from five days to seven in short order. At least this time he didn't have a job to disappear into. "How does it feel, your leg?"

"It feels out of shape. You won't want to see how shriveled it's become."

❦

"Where do you want to sleep tonight?" she asked once they got back to the farm.

"Where do you think?"

"Well, we haven't...I mean, we don't know..."

"You want me to stay downstairs?"

Rosemary felt a tingle that she couldn't ignore. "Is your leg strong enough to get up the stairs?"

"If it isn't, I'll crawl."

It was sometime later that she caught sight of his leg for the first time. It didn't look right, but her focus was on other things. They were about to sleep in the same bed, the look in his eyes alerting her to what he had in mind. This would be the first time since their drunken foray at his apartment, and the tension between them had been building. Before she could pull her nightgown on he grabbed it away and tossed it on the floor. And a moment later she forgot everything but the feel of him, his familiar spicy smell, and the gentle way he touched her.

They were still unclothed and leaning against pillows when Dylan reached for his cigarettes, lighting one. "Remember what you said when I began staying down in Washington?"

"Which time?"

"When I got the job with Raytheon."

"What was it?"

"You said you didn't want to lose me again. And yet you did."

"I hardly think that's my fault. It was you who decided to spend all your time in the city. I figured you weren't in love with me anymore and that I'd better get my head together. My expectations about our life here had been dashed. I was heartbroken."

Dylan blew out a plume of smoke. "I missed you so much, but I was damned if I was going to beg to see you. I thought at first you were punishing me, and then I decided you just weren't in love with me."

"Dylan, it was your decision, not mine."

"But as usual we never talked about it or tried to come to some compromise."

"I can't think how a compromise would have worked in that situation. We had a dream together, a life I hoped we shared, and then one day you were gone."

"You never understood my needs, Rosie. I felt like a failure. Even the army hammered that fact home. I needed the city, my friends, work that made me feel like I was worth something."

Rosemary gazed at him, suddenly understanding. "And all this time I thought your defection was about me, when really it was all about you."

"I never stopped loving you. I figured we'd work it out somehow, but as time went by we got further and further apart, and finally you seemed to hate me."

"I never hated you. I was disappointed, and I guess I took that disappointment out on you."

They stared at one another until he stubbed out his cigarette. He reached for her. "Come here."

CHAPTER TWENTY-SIX

Washington, D.C.
November 1957

Dylan paced his small apartment thinking about Rosemary. He'd come down to Washington only because she insisted. "You have to do what the doctors told you, Dylan. Your leg is not strong and never will be if you don't heed their advice."

During his leg's lengthy recovery they'd become close again. It felt good. But now he was in the thick of it, friend's calling and asking him to meet them in bars, and colleagues suggesting jobs he might be interested in. Every day found him at the clinic, doing the prescribed exercises, grimacing through the pain. He'd told her he wanted to move down to the farm, but there was a part of him that didn't want to stir up the old hurts. In order to truly have a relationship with Rosemary he had to confront his demons. She'd already mentioned his journals, insisting that they go through those pages and talk about what he'd written there. "We need to reconnect," she'd said. Apparently the one night of loving each other wasn't enough for her, despite how wonderful it had been.

She was right of course—Rosemary was seldom wrong. But how could he rehash that terrible time in his life? He'd tried once and broken apart. And now she expected him to lay himself bare for her. What would he get in return? She didn't have the same wounded soul and couldn't possibly understand what it meant to face that part of his life. And then he remembered her words, "Until you share those experiences, I will always feel shut out."

He let out a roar of frustration and knocked a glass ashtray across the room, watching it shatter against the wall. He let out a grunt of anger and went to pick up the pieces, his mind going to Yasir. He'd spoken to his contact in the CIA but so far he hadn't heard if they'd found him or not.

His phone rang, jarring him out of his musings. "I was just thinking about you," he said when he heard Rosemary's voice.

"When are you planning to come...dare I say...home?" Dylan chuckled. "A few more days yet. After this next round they want me to take a few days off. This regimen will go on for several more months I'm told."

"So no putting your apartment up for sale?"

"Not yet. We need to discuss that."

There was a long silence. "You're having second thoughts."

Dylan sighed. "Not second thoughts exactly, more trepidation about the hoops you want me to jump through."

"Talking about the past is jumping through hoops? From what you told me that night, you know the one, you wanted to spend the rest of your life lying next to my...and I quote... 'sublime body'."

Dylan let out a laugh despite himself. "Well, yes, I did say that, didn't I? I only hope you won't torture me to the point where I forget those prophetic words or what brought them to mind."

"Come home and we can talk about it face to face."

"I know what you're up to, Rosie. If we have another night like that one it will be curtains for me."

She laughed. "Are you so weak? I can give you some strengthening exercises—turning the earth in the vegetable garden, carrying bags of feed and loading the hay off the truck into the barn. Your leg will be stronger in no time."

"The strength I'm worried about is emotional, and you know it. As I remember, the physical therapy was at your insistence. Are you upset that now I'm here you have no control over me? These past months I've been completely at your mercy."

"Yes, well…"

"I'll let you know when I'm on my way."

Yes, he was that weak, he thought as he hung up the phone. He had to think things through carefully before he let it all happen again. Despite her light tone about the farm work, if he were unable to face the journals he was sure she'd decide to live without him—it was that important to her. He poured himself a whiskey and stared out the window at the overcast sky.

༄༅

Rosemary hung up the phone. The thick, legal sized, bound pages lay on the desk, several pieces of paper marking the spots she wanted to go over with Dylan. He'd sounded so remote on the phone. It was as though he'd left a part of his soul in that prison camp, hence his need to be with the men he'd shared it with. If he couldn't reclaim it he was like an empty ghost.

She didn't want to stop those friendships, far from it—she only wanted to have his attention on her more of the time. The question inside her rose again—what did she really want? But this time the answer came. She wanted something new, something deep and enduring, a relationship like the one his fantasies created during his years in prison camp. She wanted a trusting closeness in which they shared their innermost desires and fears. It didn't have to be sexual in nature, although that part was exceedingly pleasurable.

Working in the garden, planting and preparing the beds for winter set her mind at rest. She loved it here, loved kneeling in the dirt, her fingernails filled with it, streaks of mud across her cheeks. She pushed a wisp of hair back, running her hand across her forehead. Could Dylan give up the life down there in Washington as his diary had indicated? That was a long time ago, now. What had happened to that man, the one who was awed and reverent inside an antique church and declared his life devoted to her? These were the questions she wanted to ask him.

When she went into the house for lunch she heard the phone ringing. She hurried to answer, thinking it was Dylan telling her he was on his way, but instead it was her aunt Cecilia."

"My dear," Cecilia began in a somber tone, "I've unearthed some rather disturbing letters. When will you be down in Washington again?"

"I haven't any plans to come down. What letters?"

There was a pause before her aunt said, "They are between your father and mother. I had no idea..."

"No idea about what?"

"I hesitate to reveal it on the phone."

Rosemary tensed. "You can't stop now."

"Your mother was in a sanitarium for a while, Rosemary. Your father put her there because of her alcoholism."

Rosemary frowned. "What alcoholism? When was this? I don't remember her ever drinking."

"I knew she tippled a few once in a while, but I was not aware of what your father referred to as abuse. Apparently she had shock treatments. After reading through the letters I believe that what she endured there led to her suicide."

Rosemary couldn't speak for a moment. "Why didn't my father tell me about this?"

"I think he felt guilty. You probably have no recollection of this, but I remember how he was after her death. I worried about his health."

"Have you told Amanda?"

"Not yet. If you can get away I'd like to meet the two of you for lunch one day this week. These letters are important and you and Amanda should have the chance to read through them. Will you come down?"

"Of course I will. What day is good for you?"

"Give Amanda a call and set it up with her. My schedule is flexible."

"Is this what you were referring to on the day the estate was dispersed?"

"Yes. I had just discovered them. It's taken a while for me to get up the nerve to talk to you about them. I was so very disturbed myself. Your mother did not have to die, Rosemary." Cecelia began to cry.

"I'll get in touch with Amanda and call you back."

CHAPTER TWENTY-SEVEN

Washington, D.C.
November 1957

The day Rosemary drove to the teahouse to meet her sister and her aunt was nasty and cold, low clouds reminding her of a shroud. Dylan knew nothing about this unexpected trip. Until she'd read the letters and digested them herself she didn't want to talk about it.

Rosemary met Amanda at the teahouse entrance and stopped to give her a hug. Her sister was wearing a green wool coat that made her eyes sparkle. Apparently this new marriage was working out well. Rosemary had come to like number three, chalking her earlier misgivings up to fatigue and grief. The last few times she'd been in Washington she'd made a point to visit with them and found that he was a congenial man who loved her sister very much. And Amanda had changed because of him; she was a nicer person now. Rosemary no longer held it against them that they'd managed to snag the best pieces of furniture from the estate. They were not as well off as Rosemary and they had children to think about.

"Grant wanted to come along. He's so protective of me!" Amanda said as they entered the restaurant. "How did Dylan take it?"

"I haven't said anything yet. He's due to come home any day now, and I figured I'd wait until I know more."

"You two really do keep a lot of secrets, don't you?"

Rosemary stared at her sister. "I'd hardly call this a secret. I'll tell him as soon as I read through them myself."

Amanda shook her head. "You are so defensive. I told Grant because he's my confidant, my best friend. It made me feel better to know he's there for me."

Rosemary realized that Amanda was right. She was used to her solitary life now, and had forgotten how to do the one thing she expected of Dylan. Her aunt waved them over to a table.

Once they were settled and had ordered tea and sandwiches, her aunt opened her purse and pulled out two letters. "The first one is from your mother to your father," she said, handing it to Rosemary. "I'll let you read that one before I talk about the second."

Rosemary placed the letter on the table between herself and Amanda, their heads going together as they read Ilise's wavy handwriting.

Dearest: I have been too upset to write after I found out that it was you who had made the arrangement to leave me here for three months. Why, Boyd? Have I been such a burden on you that you felt it necessary to deliver me into the hands of doctors who could care less about me? At least at home I knew I had your love—here I am at their mercy. I am not blaming you for anything; I know that you are trying to do the best for me, and that you are as lonely as I am. Please come back when you said you would; time drags for me terribly, but if I can look forward to the time my sentence will end, it won't be as bad. But again I am confounded by what the purpose of it all is. My drinking was not such a great burden on you, was it? I don't think I behaved badly because of it. Maybe one or two times I may have stumbled in front of guests or spoken a bit too loudly. Shame is a hard thing to admit—so it comes out as belligerence when the doctors force me to open up.

I feel physically fine and see no reason why I can't face the world and not fall into the trap again. ...If I felt I was profiting from being here, I would stay! I hardly see the point in spending your hard-earned dollars to live in a room with three other women, be treated like a prisoner and humiliated at every turn. I am not prepared to spend that much time here when already the place and people are getting on my nerves. I feel that a long stay will make me bitter and frustrated.

Do you really think that delving into the past will help? And if so, shouldn't you be here to explain your role in all of this? After all, my drinking came from my grief and upset about your dalliance, as you well know. It is not fair for you to treat it as my problem alone when you have such a large part in its inception. You do remember that I also lost a baby—does that count for anything? I refuse to speak to these doctors about my pain. It is mine and mine alone.

I have put up with all of the indignation, the shoving around by young nurses, and the rules made for the mentally unbalanced with as much cheeriness as I could muster, and without complaint. ...I propose to leave here as soon as possible. I have no one to turn to except you and now it seems that you are on the side of the doctors. What of Rosemary and Amanda? Do they know what you have done with their mother? Do they know they might have had a baby sister or brother?

You do realize that this is a mental hospital and that if anyone gets wind of it, my time here will be a social blight you will never erase...as to the treatments I've had to endure, they are horrifying and leave me unable to speak for several hours. Do you wish to see me turned into a vegetable? Please at least have them stop the shock treatments.

The day I turn my back on these grim walls will be one of the great days of my life. If you make me stay here longer than the prescribed three months, I don't know what I shall do. These beastly doctors easily talked you into this and will probably try for longer. I will kill myself if you do not get me out of here soon.

Rosemary's hand went to the locket around her neck. This was so similar to Rebecca's life. The parallels were uncanny. She wiped her eyes with her napkin. "This is too horrible to contemplate. She lost a child. That poor woman. I'm so angry."

"He must have thought it was for the best," Amanda said softly, looking down. "I don't remember her drinking, but I do remember lots of times when she was 'indisposed'. I just figured she was sick, and Daddy never clarified. I had no idea she was pregnant, did you?"

Rosemary shook her head, looking at the letter resting on the table. The handwriting moved up and down across the page, as though their mother had been in distress at the time she put pen to paper. "Is there an answer from Father?"

Cecilia dug through her bag, producing an envelope. "Here it is."

Rosemary removed the folded piece of paper and held it between herself and Amanda.

My dearest, Ilise,

I am sorry for your unhappiness, but it is for your own good. You were fast becoming a danger to yourself and to your children. I grieve for you but I cannot let you out any sooner than what these doctors recommend. I understand that your unhappiness over my latest 'venture' has taken a toll, but my involvement with the woman you refer to as a dalliance was short-lived. It is all over and done with now. Why are you unable to let it go? As far as the baby, what happened was not caused by my affair. I was sorry for it, but your age and the fact that it was unplanned were never positive factors. The doctors do not hold me responsible for your actions, and nor should you.

I went to war for this country and came back a changed man. Our two girls have changed me in ways I would never have expected. It is time for you to join the real world, Ilise, and stop relying on your unhappiness to carry you through. You must learn to let go of what is over and done with. Just as my indiscretion, your drinking and the loss of the child will be topics that we will never mention again. These are unhappy secrets that we share between us. Let us do what the British do—keep a stiff upper lip and carry on. No one will ever know about any of it. Now please listen to the doctors and do as they tell you. They come highly recommended in this new field they call psychiatry. As to the shock treatments, I'm sure they are good for what ails you.

Your loving husband,

Boyd

"How could he do this to her? I wish I could remember more about that time in our lives. It seemed she was always off in her bedroom with the door closed. I don't remember her being gone for three months. Do you, Amanda?"

Amanda shook her head, attempting to stop the tears that spilled over. "I hate him now," she muttered. "He betrayed her."

"Maybe his affair is what caused her unhappiness in the first place."

"There is no point in hating him, girls. Boyd Hewitt is dead and buried. He made a very bad call when it came to your mother. She was a fragile soul—those shock treatments probably fried her brain. No wonder she did what she did."

"I don't remember her before or after," Amanda said, looking toward Rosemary. "When did this happen?"

"It was the summer you turned eleven and I turned thirteen," Rosemary supplied. "Father was never around, probably still involved with his affair."

"His letter said it was over," Amanda said.

"Ilise was terribly upset about that. I remember her saying that she could never trust him again," Cecilia said.

Rosemary picked up her tea cup and took a sip. It had turned cold. The plate of sandwiches sat untouched in the middle of the table. "I feel sick inside, as though everything I thought I knew about my father has been smashed into bits. He killed her as surely as if he'd stuck a knife in her heart."

Cecilia reached over and placed a hand on Rosemary's arm. "He was doing what he thought would help her, Rosemary. I do know how much your father loved her. And she loved him just as much. But I also remember the affair. It was devastating for her. As you know your mother was a recluse, a woman who didn't cope well with the outside world. Boyd confided in me that he liked that about her. He'd grown up with an overbearing mother and a henpecked father. He described your mother as a breath of fresh air. 'Our lives were simple because of it,' he said to me once." Cecilia stared into space. "I knew what was happening to her but there was nothing I could do. She simply walled herself off."

"What about the miscarriage? Did you know about that?" Amanda asked.

"She never mentioned the pregnancy. It must have been around the same time as the affair. I didn't see her much during that time."

"Secrets," Rosemary mumbled to herself.

"Secrets that ended up killing her," Amanda said, beginning to cry again. "I think this must be why I hate secrets so much. For once I'm married to a man who doesn't keep anything from me. He's like an open book."

Rosemary looked up from her careful perusal of the lace doily. "This is exactly what's between Dylan and me, and why we haven't made a decision about a divorce."

"A divorce? I thought you two were together again," Cecilia said.

"We've been trying, but this news makes me realize why it's so hard for us. He grew up in a family with secrets, and apparently, so did I. No wonder we've been struggling." When Rosemary closed her eyes for a moment she was taken into a scene with the locket people, as she now thought of them. She tried to stay in the present, using the room as an anchor, but the more she tried the stronger the past became...

"Please! I must see the sky again. I am so unhappy. And look at my hands— I can barely hold them still. Please contact my father and let me speak with him. He cannot mean to keep me here indefinitely."

"Your father is a regular visitor here. He may not come to see you but he does keep up on your progress. He has specifically insisted that we are to continue as we have been. He and your doctors are in agreement, Rebecca. You are improving as evidenced by your quieter demeanor. Do not work yourself up again or I will be forced to tell the matron. And you know what that will mean."

"More treatments?" she asked in a small voice.

The nurse smiled and left the room, locking the door from the outside. Rebecca stared at the white walls, the gray loose-fitting dress she wore. She sat heavily, her gaze going to the dingy, patched off-white blanket. There was not a bright color anywhere. If only she could be allowed to paint. But that had been denied as well. Why, she did not know. It was time to make a plan to end things.

Rosemary gasped, her hand going to the locket around her neck. The scene was so vivid, so real.

"What is it, Rosemary?" her aunt asked.

But she couldn't answer, her gaze going to the old mullioned windows fitted with wavy antique glass. This building was an old one, possibly built in the early eighteen hundreds. She breathed in and out, trying to let go of the images from the past. If something wasn't done soon Rebecca's life was over.

"Rosie?" Rosemary felt a hand on her arm.

"I'm sorry, Amanda. I had kind of a waking dream."

"I can certainly understand that reaction after what we just found out." She picked up her teacup and took a sip.

Rosemary pulled herself into the present. She was clearly going round the bend. She reached up to pull off her loathsome bonnet, instead encountering the chignon twisted hastily in the car. It had loosened, several strands of curly hair hanging around her face. She removed a few bobby pins and re-attached them.

It was becoming more difficult to separate past and present, as though she was in both of them at the same time. Maybe she needed shock therapy. That thought did nothing to cheer her up.

"If you have no further questions I must get on with my day," Cecilia said.

Rosemary picked up the two letters. "Are there more of these?"

"There may be, but I have to dig further into the box where I found them."

"I feel like we should do something, but I don't know what it would be. It's too late to save our mother." Amanda turned to Rosemary. "Do we need to perform some sort of ritual?"

"Like burning the letters? Or maybe we could hang up an effigy of Father and light it on fire."

Cecilia stared at her with wide eyes. "My goodness, Rosemary—your thoughts do turn to the macabre!"

Suddenly it seemed like a very good idea, as though the burning would assuage the past and the present at the same time. "I'm angry, and it seems a good way to release it, that's all. We haven't yet put the house on the market. Perhaps we need to do this out in the garden—what do you say, Amanda?"

Amanda grinned. "I think it's a wonderful idea. And Grant will be thrilled with the romantic aspect of it all."

"Romantic? I would hardly call it romantic. But it does have a certain poetic justice about it."

"You two girls will be the death of me! Are you planning a naked dance around this burning effigy? Will there be chanting and spells as well?"

When Rosemary and Amanda looked at each other, they both burst out laughing. "Can I borrow the letters so that Dylan can read them? I'm afraid if I pull my father down off the pedestal where Dylan has placed him, it could destroy his world. He will never believe it without reading it for himself."

"Is that all right with you, Amanda?" Cecilia asked.

"As long as we get them back. I plan to personally throw them into the fire."

Rosemary nodded. "What can we do for Ilise?"

"The best thing we can do for Mother is to burn Father—to punish him for what he did to her."

"I will not be coming to this witch's coven," Cecilia announced.

But Rosemary barely heard her as she planned the event in her mind. "We should probably try to have an auspicious number of attendees—six for the goddess."

"Six for the goddess—what does that mean?" Amanda asked.

Rosemary frowned, wondering where that thought had come from. "I don't really know. It just popped into my mind. I'll look it up at the library."

Amanda scoffed. "You are not yourself today, Rosemary. I guess I can chalk it up to the shock of the letters?"

"Possibly."

"I have a book at home about witches and spells. I'll find out for you."

Now it was Rosemary's turn to stare at her sister. "Why do you have a book like that?"

Amanda let out a sigh. "I became interested in the occult after Grant told me several strange stories about things that have happened to him over the years—unexplained things."

"I hate to interrupt this fascinating discussion, but I must be on my way," Cecilia said, standing. "You two girls figure things out and give me a call. I want to hear what you decide. In the meantime I'll search for more letters."

Once Cecilia was gone, Rosemary turned to her sister. "I should be going too."

"I'm looking forward to the burning; when do you think we should do it?"

"Soon, because the house needs to be sold. We'll both be getting a sizable endowment when it does."

Amanda looked surprised. "Really? I could use it right about now with Grant's kids about to go off to college."

Rosemary felt a pang. It would have been nice to have children, even if it meant coming up with cash for their educations. "According to the will it gets split between the two of us. I do feel bad planning this when our father was kind enough to will us this wonderful house." She rose and collected her purse. "As soon as I talk with Dylan and look at our schedule I'll call you."

"I don't feel bad at all. He hurt us by his behavior and was terrible to our mother. I hope we can do it soon," Amanda said, rising. She gave Rosemary a peck on the cheek. "I'll check in my book for details about the number six thing." She gave Rosemary an enigmatic smile.

Rosemary thought about her visions, wondering why she was reluctant to mention them to Amanda. With her sister's recent interest in the occult she might be intrigued. They walked out of the shop together and headed toward their separate cars.

Instead of driving straight home Rosemary decided to stop by Dylan's apartment. She didn't want to put off telling him about the letters. She patted her purse and turned the key in the ignition. Peering up at the sky she wondered if it might snow. Perhaps she should stay the night with Dylan and head home in the morning. She could use the comfort of his arms right about now. The thought of it made her smile.

CHAPTER TWENTY-EIGHT

Washington, D.C.
November 1957

Rosemary knocked, but when there was no answer she reached into her purse, retrieving her key to Dylan's apartment. She hadn't been wrong about the snow, it was already collecting on his stoop. The lock clicked and the door swung open, revealing a dark interior that smelled musty. "Dylan, are you here?" she called out. She switched on a couple of lamps and pulled off her coat, throwing it across a chair. The kitchen revealed a sink full of dirty dishes, and several empty cocktail glasses. She put her nose to one— bourbon.

While she was in the bathroom she heard the door open, the sound of voices, one of them female. She froze. A moment later she heard Dylan call out, "Rosemary? Are you here?"

She flushed the toilet, washed her hands and straightened her hair.

When she walked out of the bathroom her husband was waiting for her, a surprised expression on his face. "I didn't expect you."

"I didn't expect to be here. I came down to see Amanda and Cecilia and it got late—and the snow," she added, indicating the window in his bedroom. It was then that she noticed the rumpled sheets, and the smell of perfume. "I heard voices. What's going on?"

Dylan frowned. "I could ask you the same thing. Come meet my, um, friend, Lillian."

Rosemary followed him into the living room to where a statuesque blonde woman waited. She looked to be in her early twenties, her navy linen dress and hat to match obviously purchased from some of the very best stores. She removed a hatpin and placed the hat on the chair, her fingers moving through her waved shoulder length hair. Blue eyes peered at Rosemary curiously. Rosemary smoothed her sweater over her rumpled tweed skirt, feeling frumpy and old.

Lillian held out her hand. "I've heard so much about you," she said with a southern drawl.

Rosemary shook her hand, trying to make sense of things. Was Dylan now having an affair? It certainly seemed that way. "Maybe I should go," she said, turning to her husband. "I've obviously interrupted something."

Dylan and Lillian exchanged a look before Dylan said, "Lillian is…she's…she's my physical therapist. She's dressed up today because of a party she's attending later," he added quickly. "She only came by to go over the last exercises, since I won't be going to the clinic after today. I tried to call you. Where have you been?"

"As I said, I was meeting Aunt Cecilia and my sister. I had planned to let you know, but…"

"Sit down, Rosie. I'll make you a drink—you're as white as a sheet."

"I should be going," Lillian said, reaching for her coat. "I don't want to be late for…the party."

Dylan hurried to her side and helped her on with her designer lambs wool jacket, his fingers lightly brushing across her cheek. When he accompanied her to the front door Rosemary could hear them whispering, but couldn't make out the words.

"So, my sweet," Dylan said moments later, arriving with two glasses filled with amber liquid. He handed her one and sat down in the chair across from the couch. "Why are you in Washington?"

"Who is Lillian?"

"I told you—she's my…"

"I know that's not true. The way you two looked at each other, your caring manner, did not say working relationship. I smelled perfume in the bedroom. Are you having an affair?"

"After all we've been through? Have a little faith in me."

"How can I have faith when you show up with a beautiful young woman on your arm? I'm going home." Rosemary stood and grabbed her coat off the back of the chair. "She's a gorgeous woman, Dylan, there's the aroma of Chanel no. 5 in your bedroom, and your sheets are rumpled, the bed unmade. What else am I to think?"

Dylan was on his feet, a pained expression on his face. "If I tell you the truth will you stay?"

Rosemary paused. "I'll make that decision when I hear what it is."

"Lily's my daughter."

Rosemary stared at her husband. "What? Since when?"

Dylan laughed. "Since she was conceived? I was involved with a woman a few years before I met you. She had a baby."

Rosemary placed her coat carefully on the chair. "How long have you known about her?"

"I knew Bethany was pregnant when we broke up. She refused to have anything to do with me, said she didn't need my help."

Rosemary could not take in this news, her mind whirling. "I have to go." She grabbed her coat, slipping it on, and picked up her purse.

"Please, Rosemary. This happened a long time ago."

"And you neglected to mention that you had a child? Have you seen her over the years?"

"No. Beth got married and I never saw her again. I want to know why you instantly assumed I was having an affair. We just talked about this."

Rosemary met his angry gaze, the frustration clear in his eyes. "I just wasn't expecting you to arrive home with a beautiful woman."

"Without trust we can't move forward."

Exactly what Rosemary had been thinking. But how could she trust him when he held something this important back from her? She was on her way toward the door when Dylan grabbed her arm and spun her around.

"I find your lack of trust very unsettling, especially after everything we've been discussing."

Rosemary's tears were right on the surface and she did not want to break down in front of him. She pulled out his grasp and opened the door.

Dylan was right behind her. "It's snowing out there—this is no time for meaningless gestures."

She didn't look at him as she hurried down the steps, trying to keep from slipping. By the time she reached the car tears were on her cheeks. She wiped them away and turned the key in the ignition. As she drove away Dylan was still silhouetted in the doorway, his face a mask of bewilderment.

Dylan watched his wife pull out of her parking space, worried about her state of mind. It was snowing hard now, she was upset, and her car was not equipped with the proper tires. Her shock about Lillian was to be expected, but there was something more going on, something she'd come by to tell him—the reason she was in Washington.

He closed and locked the door, worried about his daughter. She was already shy about this new relationship with a father she never knew existed, and now he'd pulled her into his lies. And on top of all that he had to face Rosemary and explain to her why it had taken him over a month to mention Lillian's appearance in his life. He had planned to tell her once he moved back to Virginia, but his social life with comrades from the war, plus the physical therapy, had kept him in town. The way things were going it was a good thing he hadn't put this apartment on the market.

He picked up his glass and drained it. Damn it all to hell! Tomorrow he would have to call Lillian and try to explain his behavior, and then, if the snow stopped, drive down to Virginia and have it out with her. To what avail, he did not know. He loved her as much as he could love a woman, but he had other needs as well, needs she couldn't seem to understand. The men with whom he had shared those war-torn years were closer to him than anyone, including his wife.

The trip home seemed to take forever, what with the haze of tears that blinded her and the snow that had her sliding all over the road. It was dark when she reached the farm, glad she'd left the stall doors open for the horses. They had the choice of where they wanted to be. And thank goodness she'd left the chickens shut up in the chicken coop, safe from the snow and marauding foxes on the prowl.

She left the car out, too enervated to open the garage and pull it inside. When would they invent a device to open garage doors automatically? Maybe they already had, but if so she knew nothing about it. Perhaps she was secluding herself too much. Life was passing her by. That thought brought another bout of tears. She wasn't usually so emotional, and this sudden onslaught of utter despair frightened her. Why couldn't she get herself under control?

Inside the house she went straight to her bedroom and threw herself face down. None of this made any sense. How had Lillian suddenly come into his life? She couldn't believe a word he said; so much for working out their secrets. This might just be the end for them. More tears came and she finally gave up, allowing the grief and disappointment to flow over her. Images of Rebecca, lost in a gray world, collided with Edgar and Rebecca's early happiness, and her own with Dylan. Into this scene her mother appeared, her eyes filled with unshed tears, the silhouette of her father in the shadowy distance. "Go away!" she shouted.

CHAPTER TWENTY-NINE

Virginia
December 1957

Two weeks had gone by with no word from Dylan. Rosemary had spoken with Amanda, both of them deciding to put off the effigy burning until the weather improved.

Rosemary was having her first cup of coffee when the phone rang. She picked it up, hoping it was Dylan, but instead Amanda's voice, chirpy and happy, said, "I ran into Dylan yesterday. He seemed depressed. What's going on?"

Rosemary sucked in her breath and reached for a cigarette and then thought better of it. For some reason they turned her stomach these days. "He lied to me, Amanda. He has a grown daughter he never mentioned. Did he tell you about it?"

"He didn't say a word about that—he did ask me if I'd spoken with you."

"And you said?"

"I told him we talked often on the phone. He was in a hurry to go somewhere, so we didn't get very far. So tell me about this daughter—what's she like? Did you meet her?"

"She was at his apartment the day we had tea with Aunt Cecilia. She's blonde, beautiful, and apparently well off—she has a southern accent."

"You sound angry."

"I am angry. He has never once mentioned Lillian's mother, nor has he mentioned Lillian. We've been attempting to get beyond the secrets and he comes up with this?"

"Maybe he didn't know about her."

"He told me he knew, but he lost touch with the mother. Apparently she's married now."

"Did he provide for her?"

"No. He said the mother refused his help."

"What will you do?"

"I expect him to apologize. If he doesn't our marriage is over."

"Sounds as though you haven't heard all the details yet."

"He hasn't bothered to call me, if that's what you mean."

"What did he think of the letters—our plan?"

"I didn't get a chance to mention any of it."

Amanda scoffed. "So now you have secrets too. The two of you are bound and determined to make things as difficult as possible, aren't you? Why don't you just call him and invite him down? I know he loves you, Rosemary. Doesn't that count for anything?"

"If I can't trust him, his love means nothing."

"Call him. I have to ring off now, but as soon as the weather improves let's make a plan, okay?"

Dylan picked up the phone and put it down again. Several things were on his mind, not the least of which were the fucking recurring dreams he was having. Rosemary was the only person he could talk to about this, but Rosemary wasn't speaking to him. Last time he'd called she'd hung up the phone before he could say a word. He picked up the phone and dialed her number before he lost his nerve.

"Before you hang up on me, I need your help. I've been having those dreams about the past—and I don't like what they seem to be indicating. Can I come down and see you?"

There was a long silence before Rosemary's voice, sounding remote, answered. "I'm about to file for a divorce, so if you have any objections you'd best get down here and explain them."

"Jesus Christ, woman! What in hell is wrong with you? Is this because of Lily?"

"It's not Lillian, it's your lies. I seriously cannot handle them anymore."

"I'm leaving now. And please, do not shoot me before we have a chance to talk." Dylan hung up the phone, stopping himself from hurling the contraption across the room. What had gotten into Rosemary? This could not just be about the delay in telling her about Lillian.

He drove like a mad man, reaching the farm in record time. He left the car parked in the driveway and went around the house to the kitchen where he was sure Rosemary would be. Snow still covered the grass between the house and the vegetable garden, the fir trees they'd planted years before turning the scene into a winter wonderland. Christmas was coming. Where would he be for it?

He stopped to look around, his gaze going to the small pond covered in ice, the bare branches of the fruit trees. He missed this place, missed planning their next project. They'd done so much together, building a life that rooted them, connecting them to each other. He glanced into the fallow garden, missing the feel of dirt on his hands, the smells of damp earth, and Rosemary next to him, streaks of mud across her face. The smile she always had for him.

His time in prison camp had shown him the pleasures of growing food, raising the pigs and ducks the prisoners subsisted on. He'd been in charge of it all. But many of his projects had been claimed by the guards, the pigs and ducks taken to feed them. His mind recoiled as the memory of his hollow stomach returned. His hands went to his belly as he recalled his craving for fat. He let out a low moan, returning to the present. Would he ever be free of those years? And now this other life had overtaken him, the one in the distant past where two people seemed to be leading parallel lives. What in hell was happening?

The steps up had not been cleaned off, slush saturating his wingtips as he climbed to the kitchen door. He peered inside before letting himself in. Despite his warnings she never locked her doors. "Hello? Anyone here?"

Rosemary appeared in the doorway to the dining room, her eyes red-rimmed. "Take your shoes off, Dylan. You've made a muddy puddle on my clean kitchen floor."

He did as she asked, moving toward her in his stocking feet. "I think you've lost whatever shred of common sense you had," he muttered. "Shall we sit somewhere and hash this out, or would you rather just kill me and get it over with?"

"Your jokes are not funny. I've had a shock and you seem to think it means nothing. When exactly did you meet this long lost daughter of yours?"

He followed her into the dining room and sat across from her at the table. Papers were strewn everywhere, her account books and letters scattered. "What's all this?"

"I'm trying to organize things for when we get our divorce. I've had a heck of a time figuring out what price would be fair for a buy-out."

"Buy-out—you mean buying me out of my share of this place? What if I don't want to sell? What happened to making amends, starting fresh? Tell me what's really going on."

Rosemary pulled several pieces of paper together in a neat pile. "I have some news I haven't shared yet, about my father and mother." She pulled two letters from the pile and handed them across.

He began to read, his shock deepening the further he got. He finally looked up. "When did this happen, and why didn't you tell me about it?"

"I only found out the day I met Lillian. I was planning on telling you, but in light of everything that happened, it slipped my mind."

"Understandable," Dylan acknowledged, sitting back. "Were you born when this sanitarium business took place?"

"It was my thirteenth year. The same year she committed suicide."

Dylan reached for her hand but she pulled it back. "Rosemary, I want to know why you're treating me like a pariah. I only met Lillian a month ago. I was planning to tell you about it. I only lied that day because of the awkwardness of her being there when you found out. I didn't want either of you to feel uncomfortable."

"Can we concentrate on one thing at a time? What do you think about the letters?"

Dylan stared into the distance for a moment before turning back to her. "This news about your father and mother—well, it's surprising considering what I know of Boyd Hewitt. He hardly seemed the type to hurt her like that.

There has to be a reason for why he did this. Have you other letters?"

"I had a feeling you'd take his side."

"That's unfair. I knew him. He would never do something like this without being sure it was the right thing. Letters, Rosemary—are there others?"

"There may be. Cecilia hasn't said. She found these quite by accident, going through a box she got from the house."

Dylan sighed. "Back to Lillian—can you accept that I had a good reason for not blurting out the truth that day?"

"But why didn't you ever mention this woman, Beth? You knew she was carrying your child and you never looked back?"

"I told you already. She refused to let me in her life and then she disappeared. I did try to find her, but then I met you. After that I just decided to let it go."

❧

Rosemary felt herself softening toward her husband. He was obviously distraught about her talk of a divorce, and his explanations of why he'd lied that day made some sense. At least the desire to throttle him had passed. "How old were you when you were with Beth?"

"Barely twenty. She was eighteen."

"We didn't meet until you were twenty-five. What happened during those missing years?"

"I was with her for close to two years. The three years before I met you were taken up with West Point and my budding career." He paused and let out a sigh. "I feel blessed to have met my daughter. She's the one who sought me out. I couldn't wait to share her with you."

Rosemary smiled despite herself. "I'm glad to have met her. She seems very poised for one so young."

"She plans to go into politics, can you imagine that?"

Rosemary heard the proud note in his voice. "I'm sorry she isn't ours, Dylan."

He looked up at her. "I am too. Are you willing to include her in our family? That is, if we're staying together."

"Yes, if we decide to make a go of it. It isn't her fault that her father can be such an imbecile."

Dylan grinned, running fingers through his hair and making it stick up. "Now what's this about an effigy burning?"

"Amanda told you? She said she didn't mention it."

"Actually, after you left I called your aunt. She filled me in on some of it. That's why I had to get down here before you did something rash."

"You knew about the letters?"

"No. She told me you had some important news and that you were planning an effigy burning. When I asked her what she meant, she said for me to take it up with you. Apparently she is not in favor."

Rosemary rose from the table. "How about a glass of wine?"

Dylan looked at his watch. "It's barely noon."

"It's five o'clock somewhere, and I feel the need to calm my nerves." She headed to the kitchen, arriving back with two full glasses. "On the phone you said something about dreams." She took a gulp and looked over at him. "I've been having them too. Terrible things are happening in the past, things that parallel what happened to my mother. And not only that, but Edgar and Rebecca were so close and then…"

"And then Edgar went off to war, met another woman and had a child with her. I know all about it."

"But there's more, Dylan. My latest dreams feel like waking nightmares. Rebecca is in an asylum. I have a feeling she may die there."

Dylan stared out the window, where snow had begun to fall. "I think we're supposed to mend the past. But I have no idea how."

"That sounds rather fanciful. Are you saying we need to mend our relationship to mend theirs?"

"Maybe we need to do what they didn't. If we had a baby, or…"

"A baby? Are you out of your mind? I'm forty years old!"

"That isn't so old. My grandmother had babies up until she turned forty-six."

"How many children did she have?"

"Seven all together, although two died within their first year."

"I don't think us having a baby will help Edgar and Rebecca. He left her for another woman, and she lost his baby. We can't change that."

"Then why are they plaguing my dreams? I get the distinct feeling they want something."

Rosemary thought of her recent nights spent worrying about Rebecca's fate. "I've felt that way too. I'm sure Rebecca is about to kill herself. But it's already happened. Whatever we do won't make any difference."

The phone rang and Rosemary got up to answer it.

"I looked up the number six," Amanda said. "It refers to the triple goddess, and Aphrodite, the goddess of love. Oh and Venus—well, I guess Venus is the same as Aphrodite. Six represents harmony. It's very auspicious, Rosemary. I think you're right about needing that number of witnesses for our burning. But how? Even if you have Dylan along and I have Grant, Aunt Cecilia only makes five."

"I have another person who might like to come," Rosemary told her sister.

"Who was that?" Dylan asked when Rosemary returned to the dining room.

"My sister—she wanted to tell me about the number six."

"The number six is considered lucky in Asian cultures. And remember, my birthday is on the sixth of August. It's a balanced number—harmonious."

Rosemary stared at her husband. "You know more than I do. Do you think Lillian would like to attend our ritual effigy burning? With you and me, Grant and Amanda, Aunt Cecilia and Lillian, we would be six."

Now it was Dylan's turn to stare. "You're serious about this. What do you hope to accomplish?"

"I hope to burn away all my anger."

"Anger with me as well?"

Rosemary cocked her head to one side. "I hadn't thought of that, but yes. The burning could release all sorts of pent-up emotions."

"I'm in."

CHAPTER THIRTY

Virginia
December 1957

Dylan spent the night in the room reserved for him, leaving his wife to her musings. He wanted very much to go to her, but he knew it was too soon. She was still mulling over the revelations about his daughter. He wasn't even sure whether she'd given up her intentions to file for divorce. She could certainly be a hot head when the mood took her.

"Dylan?"

He turned to see her backlit in the doorway, a sheer nightgown wafting about her legs. He sat up. "What's wrong?"

She moved into the room and sat down on the edge of the cot. "I've been thinking. Maybe we should invite Lillian down here before we have the burning. It would be nice to get to know her a bit before she sees us dancing naked around a burning effigy."

"Dancing naked—are you serious?"

Rosemary chuckled. "Just a metaphor for behaving like heathens."

Dylan let out a low laugh. "You had me excited there for a minute. Yes, I think inviting her here is a good idea. I'll run it by her when I go back tomorrow."

"Do you have to leave so soon?"

Dylan gazed at her in disbelief. "This morning you were talking divorce and now you don't want me to leave?"

"I'm all mixed up. One minute I see us together, and in the next…" She let out a long sigh. "Between that and the visions I don't know what's going on with me."

"I do. You love me and you know I love you. We've complicated things, made them insurmountable, when all that counts is loving one another."

"I wonder if it's Edgar and Rebecca who are doing this. The dreams have ramped up—I don't want to feel my death when she kills herself."

Dylan had a sharp pang in his chest. "The mere idea of that is overwhelming."

"We have so much—your daughter, this place, our past together. You managed to live through three and a half years of pure hell. We're so lucky."

Dylan reached for her, pulling her close. He slid the silky straps of her nightgown off her shoulders and kissed her collarbone before finding her mouth.

It was sometime later that they began to talk, Dylan's arm wrapped loosely around her shoulders where she lay against him. The cot was overturned, blankets scattered. They leaned against a wall, pillows behind them. "After all our talk about being together I've realized that being with the men from prison camp is too important to let slide. I hesitated to tell you this for fear you wouldn't understand. I know it takes me away from you, from us, but I need to see them, to talk about what went on. The more I talk the further it seems to recede. Does that make sense?"

"Not really, but I can accept what you're saying. We were planning to revisit those journals. I have several passages marked I would like to talk to you about."

Dylan groaned. "When do you want to do that? It seems we've gone over everything too many times already."

"Too many times? We've barely discussed what went on over there. I have questions."

"Why, Rosemary? Why do you want me to revisit that time? It doesn't do either of us any good, only makes me feel the horror all over again. You've read them, you know all about it. You just referred to it as pure hell."

Rosemary hesitated, her arms wrapping around her middle. "But that's what you do with the men, isn't it? Why can't you share it with me? You said there were marks you made on pages, ways to remember things you didn't write in the journals. What's happened with that?"

"I changed my mind. Talking to the men, my comrades in arms, works it out for me. Talking to you about it would not be the same. You could never understand. If you don't let it go there's no future for us."

Rosemary rose to her knees to turn on the lamp, staring at him. "You would have something this small keep us apart?"

His eyebrows pulled together. "What you term as small was so horrible that I couldn't even write about some of it. I thought maybe with time I could revisit those incidents, but I don't want to anymore. It's finished. Try to imagine the horror of starving, seeing your friends die and having to dig graves and bury them. Every day was a living hell that I couldn't get away from—flies, mosquitoes, the stench of human feces every time I turned around. Benjos overflowed and we were the ones who had to clean it up. Friends coming down with illnesses, sickness spreading across the camp so fast I was sure I would contract one and die. Hunger. You wouldn't believe how it feels to be truly hungry, day after day. Why would you want to put me through that again?"

Rosemary turned away, her eyes filling with tears. "I'm sorry, Dylan. I didn't understand."

He grabbed her arm, making her look up. "Do you understand now?"

Tears tracked down her cheeks. "Yes. I'll leave it alone—I promise."

He let her go and fell back against the pillow. "If we get back together, I would like to go down to Washington periodically. Maybe every two weeks or so, for a few days. You can come with me if you like, get Mary to take care of things here. We could take in a show or visit a museum, go shopping."

Rosemary wiped her eyes, trying to smile. "And at night you'll meet with your buddies, stay out late and come back stinking drunk?"

He chuckled. "Something like that."

"I could handle that, as long as you sleep on the couch." Her eyes filled again. "We've wasted a lot of time over silly stuff. As far as secrets go, there have to be some between us. Men and women are too different not to have them."

"One last puzzle to solve," Dylan said, his eyes meeting hers. "Yasir. He left me in the road for dead and now there's no trace of him. My CIA contact has had no leads. And even if he's found there's no way to prove anything."

"What do you suggest?"

"I think I have a way to find him. Maybe if we talk and I explain…"

"Dylan, he could kill you! The man is obviously demented!"

"He was drunk that night. He went off his rocker for a moment. I know him pretty well and I doubt he would try it again."

"How will you find him?"

"I'd rather not say for fear of you trying to talk me out of it."

"Dylan!"

"Didn't you just say we had to have some secrets?"

Dylan was off early the next morning, citing talking to Lillian as his reason. "If she agrees I'll bring her down this weekend. Once there's a forecast for clear weather give your aunt a call and set things up for the burning."

CHAPTER THIRTY-ONE

Virginia
January 1958

"Aren't you over that flu yet?" Amanda sounded irritated, their recent plans stymied because of Rosemary's ongoing illness.

"I can't believe it's lasting this long. I feel great one minute and in the next I'm running for the toilet."

"You missed a good party over Christmas at Aunt Cecilia's house. Dylan came and I got to meet Lillian. She's lovely, such a sweetheart." There was a pause in which it sounded like Amanda inhaled, but as far as Rosemary knew, her sister didn't smoke. A moment later she continued. "Do you realize how long you've been ill? We've come up with two dates now for our ritual, and you've been sick for both of them. You need to see a doctor, Rosemary."

Rosemary pictured her husband making the rounds with Lillian. The weekend they'd planned for him to bring Lillian down to the farm had never materialized. Lily was a busy girl, involved with her studies and clerking for a congressman. And when they came up with another available time, Rosemary had already contracted the flu. Her stomach gave a heave. "Have to go," she managed to say before hanging up the phone. She ran for the bathroom, throwing up everything she'd had for breakfast. She lay on the cool linoleum, exhausted, trying not to see Dylan happy with his daughter on his arm.

Dylan had called several times over the past month, but once she'd contracted the flu she told him not to come down. "I don't want to give it to you or to Lillian." She was suddenly crying, weak with self-pity. She'd not only missed Christmas, but the New Year as well. Her body felt like it didn't belong to her anymore.

It was later that day, after she'd managed to get some tea and toast into her stomach, that the phone rang.

"How are you feeling, my sweet?"

"Not good."

"Have you been to the doctor? I think it's time to see what's going on. Flu does not last this long."

"Are you saying I have some dire disease?"

Dylan chuckled. "I doubt that you're even sick, Rosie. When I mentioned your symptoms to Lily she suggested something that I hadn't thought of. Could you be pregnant?"

Rosemary felt a little twinge in her stomach. She placed a hand there to keep the nausea at bay, at least until she got off the phone. "I can't imagine how."

"Well, you see it goes like this—the man and the woman take off their clothes, and then…"

"Stop it, Dylan. We've hardly…"

"Oh really? If I remember correctly there have been several times that could account for this. Remember the 'sublime body' incident? That was back in November, as I recall, and now is about the right time for the morning sickness to kick in. Were you using birth control?"

"Well, no. But I'm too old. My periods have been irregular. I thought I was going into menopause."

"Get yourself to a doctor and find out, okay? I would certainly like to know if I'm going to be a father."

❦

He'd been thinking about Rosemary, wondering if she had news when Dylan heard a knock on the door. He opened it, surprised to find himself face to face with the man who tried to kill him.

"Before you slam the door in my face, I came to apologize and try to make it up to you."

"Apologizing for trying to kill a man is hardly worthy of the effort."

"Please, Dylan. I was wrong to take it out on you. You were not responsible for what happened to my former wife."

"You mean the African woman who died over a hundred years ago?"

Yasir stared into the distance. "That woman was my one true love, the one I'm destined to find in every lifetime, but in this one she's been sadly absent."

"And you blamed me. What happened to change your mind?"

Yasir crossed his arms, looking around at the swirling snow. "Can I come inside?"

Dylan stepped aside to let you older man walk past. He wasn't at all sure this was a good idea. "You didn't answer my question."

"I was drunk that night. I was not thinking straight."

"And yet you nearly killed me over something I didn't even remember."

"You did remember it—we talked about it that very night. You told me all about your dreams of an African woman who you fell in love with. You were blubbering about Rebecca, your wife who you left behind. You felt guilty about it."

Dylan frowned. "I have no memory of that."

Yasir laughed. "After that many drinks I'm not surprised."

"Where have you been? The CIA couldn't even find you."

Yasir gazed around the small living room before settling into an armchair. "I am very good at disappearing, my friend. I have a proposition for you to make up for what I did. I want to go through with my order, finish the transaction before you leave Raytheon for good. That way it will be you who gets the commission on the sale."

"You do know they fired me. "

"I'll go in with you. With me along they won't be able to deny a sale this big. If they don't I'll threaten to withdraw my offer. Monday?"

Dylan nodded hesitantly. "I was planning to go by anyway to clear out my desk and collect my last check. After that I'm heading down to Virginia."

"You will join your wife and the baby she carries."

Dylan scowled. "How do you know about that?"

"I told you I'm psychic, didn't I?"

"But she hasn't even confirmed it with a doctor."

"The flu that won't go away?" Yasir chuckled. "Your daughter, Lillian, is quite astute. There is no doubt."

Dylan wanted to put his hands around Yasir's neck and squeeze the life out of him.

"I've been tracking your activities ever since I went underground. Did you misunderstand what I said about the bardo? We travel in groups, my friend, and I'm afraid you're stuck with me for many lifetimes to come."

"Oh great. Just what I needed to hear."

"Oh, come, come. I'm not so bad, am I? I'm here now and saying I am most sorry for my actions. Congratulations, by the way."

Dylan didn't react to this statement, anger right at the surface.

Yasir rose. "I suppose I must be going. I will meet you on Monday to cement our deal. Please alert anyone you've told that I did not push you into traffic. I would hate to be hauled away to jail when I was about to give you your independence. Your wife will no longer have the upper hand in matters of finance." He moved toward the door, only stopping to turn back. "And by the way, the six includes Edgar and Rebecca. Tell your wife."

After Yasir left, Dylan poured himself a stiff drink and lit a cigarette, sitting on the couch to think. Yasir's timing was uncanny. Dylan had been churning over his inability to provide for his wife, the possibility of a child complicating matters even further. With his firing he had no income, and having her control the purse strings made him feel powerless. Yasir had arrived just when he was feeling his most insecure and seriously wondering if his ego could tolerate retirement. And what about his comment about the six? Was he spying on every part of their lives?

He picked up the phone and called Rosemary. "Did you go to the doctor?"

"Yes, I went to the doctor," she said in an irritated tone.

"And?"

"I'm pregnant, Dylan. I'm at my wits end about it. I haven't decided yet what to do."

"What choice do you have?"

There was a long sigh. "I could have an abortion."

"Rosemary, if you have an abortion after all this, I will find a way to make your life a living hell."

"A baby will make it a living hell, Dylan. What in the world am I going to do with an infant?"

Dylan let out an exasperated sound. "You'll be a mother to him or her. You have the money to hire help. How bad can it be? Women have been doing this for eons."

"You're not the one who has to get fat and then go through the birth, not to mention dirty diapers and all the rest of it."

"Like breast-feeding?"

"Who said I would breast feed? But yes, that too."

Dylan let out a roar of laughter. "I'll be down there in two hours and we can discuss this properly."

❦

True to his word Dylan let himself into the house at six p.m. "Rosemary?" He found her on her knees in front of the toilet, her face white and sweaty. He grabbed a towel and dabbed at her brow before helping her to her feet. "I can understand your reluctance after going through this for a month, but the morning sickness will pass."

"Since when are you such an expert? And this isn't morning sickness, it's all day sickness."

"The doc didn't give you anything for it?" he asked, supporting her to the living room.

"Crackers—saltines. But I don't have any."

"Stay here," Dylan said, helping her onto the couch. "I'll be back in a jiffy."

Dylan found himself humming all the way to the store.

When he got back Rosemary was on the couch with her eyes closed. "I'm due in July."

Dylan smiled, handing over the box of saltines. "We want this baby, Rosie. It's a symbol."

She scoffed, popping a saltine into her mouth. "A symbol of what? Idiocy? I'm too old for this, and so are you."

"You're barely forty. I'm forty-five. We're in the prime of life. You need to get out more."

"Get out more? How is that going to happen? Once I'm saddled with this," she gestured expansively toward her stomach, "I'm stuck here."

Dylan sat down next to her. "You don't have to be stuck anywhere. People with children actually take them along on their trips into town. There's equipment now, prams, to wheel them about. Why do you have this old lady attitude?"

Rosemary stared into the distance, crunching on another cracker. "I don't know. I was just thinking about the garage door. Are there ways to open garages with an electric device?"

Dylan laughed. "Yes, Rosemary. We can have one installed. I'm thinking that perhaps we should spend more time in Washington. It wouldn't hurt you to go to a nightclub or see a show. I have a television now, did I tell you?"

"A television? I decided they weren't worth the money. What in the world do you watch?"

"News, Perry Mason, Dragnet." Dylan pulled her close. "I'm so happy. I don't think I've ever felt like this."

"Don't get your hopes up. I had a miscarriage the last time."

"Yasir says it's a done deal."

"Yasir? When did you see him?"

"He came by to apologize. The man knows everything about us, including the number six and the burning."

"The number six—how...?"

"Your guess is as good as mine. He wanted me to tell you that Edgar and Rebecca could be included to make it six."

"What? How does he know that? Is he a ghost from the past?"

"I don't think so. He says he's part of our bardo. To tell you the truth it was hard for me not to throttle the shit out of him."

"Understandable considering he tried to kill you."

"He's meeting me on Monday at the office to go through with our deal—says he wants me to get the commission—his way of apologizing."

"Will you reapply for your job?"

Dylan noticed the wistful expression in her tired eyes. "No, Rosie. I want to be with you through every minute of this. As soon as the deal with Yasir is completed I'm out of there."

CHAPTER THIRTY-TWO

Washington, D.C.
February, 1958

Rosemary rolled over in bed, her arm reaching for Dylan. She opened her eyes. "Dylan?"

"I'm getting us coffee," he called back.

Rosemary stretched, her mind going to the night before. Dylan had taken his daughter and Rosemary to a club in Georgetown where they saw a man named Elvis Presley who played the guitar and sang. He had a backup piano player and a base guitarist. Dylan had told her that Elvis was in the army, stationed in Germany, but had to come back to the U.S. for a few days to deal with family matters. "This concert was serendipity," he'd told her. "We are extremely lucky to see him at all, and especially in such small venue. He's a major celebrity."

Rosemary smiled, thinking about the antics of the singer and the wildness of his music. Dylan had forced her to dance, showing off his new moves while Lily watched them. That is until the single men in the club noticed Dylan's gorgeous daughter; from then on she never left the dance floor.

Dylan appeared in the doorway. "How are you feeling? We had a rather late night."

"Made later by you," she murmured, thinking about what they'd engaged in before they went to sleep.

He handed her the coffee cup. "I didn't hear any complaints."

Rosemary smiled, taking her first sip of coffee. "I liked the music after I got used to it. It isn't my usual style, but..."

"You never listen to music—how could you have a style?"

Rosemary reached for the saltines next to bed, crunching on one. Her morning sickness had all but vanished, but she was not about to give up on the crackers just yet. "My inner self has a style--the part of me that has traveled through many lifetimes? The bardo me."

Dylan laughed. "You like to make fun, but I have to say I believe the man. He followed through on his promise. I can now take care of you in the style to which you're accustomed."

Rosemary stared at her husband. "You were upset about not being the provider?"

"Yes, Rosemary, I was. But now it's a non-issue. The money is invested, and barring any major downturns, will provide a steady income for years to come."

She sipped her coffee, surprised by his confession. She had no idea the depth of his insecurities. He'd never taken her money or allowed her to pay for things, with the exception of this farm and the two horses that now languished in the barn. And that was only because he was too psychically weakened at the time to argue. Yasir had arrived at the perfect moment.

She sighed, leaning back against the pillows, her arm brushing Dylan's. Even with all their late night talks, the secrets shared, she felt like they didn't know each other very well. There had been years of living apart, years in which they'd changed.

She put her coffee cup down on the nightstand. "Dylan, tell me your thoughts now that you've been through war and prison camp. Do you still believe in honor and duty to country, that right will prevail? Do you still think God is behind who wins or loses because he knows who's in the right?"

Dylan swiveled toward her, his eyes wide. "Where did that come from?"

"I was thinking about war, past and present. Despite Rebecca trying to stop him, Edgar went off with stars in his eyes. Why do we keep having wars?"

"We do it because we have to. If we didn't, evil would prevail."

"So you do believe in good and evil."

"Some things are evil, yes. There are atrocities that we can't condone, like gassing millions of Jews."

"But why do we have to glorify war? Isn't it enough to go because we want to stop evil?"

"We glorify it to keep ourselves from thinking about the reality of it. I, for one, will probably never get past the terrible images that appear in my mind. If we didn't build it up we would go mad…and no one would enlist or be willing to fight."

"If you were asked to serve again, would you go?"

"With you pregnant? Hell no."

"So for you having a baby is more important than duty and honor and serving one's country."

251

"Now it is. Back then, when I was young and foolish, I didn't understand what it meant."

"Do you agree that the glorification is not a good thing?"

Dylan frowned, his eyebrows knitting together. "I think men should understand what they're getting into, if that's what you mean. It's not pretty, it's not glamorous, and the chance of getting maimed or killed is very high. But someone has to do it. Both sides in every war believe they are doing the right thing and that God is on their side. "

"What if there were no more wars?"

"Wars are inevitable, Rosie. I can't imagine a time when they won't exist. Human nature, such as it is, brings them on. There will always be a cause, a reason to keep fueling the war machine. It's what my business is all about."

"Raytheon is no longer your business, is it?"

"Slip of the tongue. I'm finished with Raytheon and devoted to you and that one." He placed his hand on the bulge of her lower belly. His eyebrows rose. "You'll need maternity clothes soon."

She slapped his hand away.

Dylan laughed and rose from next to her. "Lily will be here in an hour. I'm going to start breakfast."

"I'll get dressed then. I thought, perhaps…"

Dylan grinned, gazing down on her. "It did cross my mind, but it's a bit late now. I wouldn't have time to do it justice."

Rosemary reached for her robe.

Lily had already left for an appointment when the phone

rang. Rosemary looked around for Dylan but he was in the bathroom. She lifted the receiver from its cradle. "Hello?"

"Is that Rosemary?" a male voice asked.

"Yes, who's this?"

"I know you are still angry with me, but this is Yasir. Is your husband available?"

"He is not, but I'll tell him you called."

"Who are you talking to?" Dylan asked, coming up behind her. She handed the phone over and rolled her eyes.

"Yes?"

Rosemary walked into the other room, but she couldn't help eavesdropping. Her husband sounded business-like and serious, his mumbled responses making her wonder what Yasir was saying. "It won't work," Dylan said, followed by, "That's impossible!" followed by a pause and then, "Tell her yourself!" He banged the phone down.

"What was that about?" she asked, joining him.

"Yasir wants you to contact Rebecca and try and talk with her. He thinks he can change what happened in the past by interfering now."

"What? For one thing these dislocations happen on their own. I can't control when I go. And I'm not me when I go there...I see the world from her perspective. What does he want?"

"He wants Rebecca to keep Edgar from entering the war so that he'll never meet Yasir's wife. He thinks we can meddle with time, Rosemary. The man is off his rocker." He ran agitated fingers through his hair. "And he's on his way over."

"Rebecca tried to keep Edgar out of it. There's no way now—they've moved beyond all that. I told you, she's in an asylum."

Forty-five minutes later Yasir was standing in their living room, his avid gaze focused on Rosemary. "I know you can do this, Rosemary. All I have to do is hypnotize you."

"And then what? I don't have any influence over her."

"You will if you go back as yourself. She knows you now. You can talk to her, get her to stop Edgar from going to war."

"And how exactly will you be able to place me there at the correct time? Did you know her father had her put away?"

"I did know that. As far as the timing, I know the date."

Rosemary glanced at her husband who watched the two of them with a frown. "What do you think, Dylan?"

"I think Yasir is crazy. You can't go back in time and change things. It doesn't work."

"And how would you know?" Yasir yelled angrily. "Have you been in touch with all your lives, seen yourself in every timeline as I have?"

Dylan threw up his hands. "If Rosemary is willing to try, it's all right with me. As long as this isn't dangerous."

"Could I get stuck back there, Yasir?" Rosemary asked.

He smiled and shook his head. "You will be under my control at all times. All I want you to do is talk to her, convince her to keep her husband from going to war. If it means lying, and saying she's pregnant, then so be it."

"You want me to ask Rebecca to lie?"

Yasir let out an exasperated sigh. "She knows he won't come back. I doubt there will be much convincing about it. She didn't know she was pregnant when he left. Now she'll know."

"If I tell her."

"That is correct." Yasir moved toward the couch, gesturing for her to lie down. "Shall we get started?"

Rosemary glanced at her husband.

"If you're willing to do this, then go ahead," he said, looking skeptical.

Once she was stretched out on the couch Yasir lit a candle and turned off the lights, moving next to her. His dark eyes looked like two ebony stones as he stared into hers. "I want you to watch this necklace," he said, beginning to swing her locket.

Her hand went to her bare neck. When had he removed it? "How did you do that?"

"Watch the locket, Rosemary," he said in a sing-song voice. "Keep watching the locket."

Rosemary began to feel drowsy, his voice droning on and on. She heard him say, "Tell Rebecca she's pregnant—Edgar cannot leave her alone. He will die and never see his child."

Rosemary began to visualize Rebecca and the small stone house with the thatch, the yard where chickens pecked in the grass. She was so tired, too tired to even pick up her hand.

"That's right, Rosemary. You are there now. You see Rebecca coming out of the house. She sees you. You know one anther and she pauses to listen to what you have to say. Say it, Rosemary. Tell her what will happen if Edgar leaves. She is pregnant—tell her."

Rosemary saw Rebecca through a smoky haze. She tried to move past the fog, but she was trapped on the other side of a veil. Rebecca stopped on her way across the yard, her eyes going wild when she saw Rosemary. She opened her mouth and said something but Rosemary couldn't hear it.

"Rebecca," Rosemary said, her voice echoing inside her head. "You are with child. You must keep Edgar at home with you. He will die and never see his child if he goes to war."

Rebecca watched her, but Rosemary knew the woman couldn't hear her and had no idea what she was saying. She tried to mime it, using her hand to indicate her belly growing big, but Rebecca shook her head, her eyes filling with tears. Rosemary gasped as the realization hit her. Rebecca knew. She was fully aware of what would happen to Edgar, but she also knew she could not stop him. It had been Yasir who had waited in the shadows the day of Edgar's appointment with the printers, Yasir who pushed Edgar in front of the carriage, trying to kill him before he left for war. Falling in love with another woman was Edgar's life, his destiny. Rosemary lurched into the present with a gasp.

Dylan was beside her, his hand on her cheek. "You're crying. Are you all right?"

"She knows. She knew all along." She glared at Yasir. "And you did the same thing to Edgar that you tried with my husband."

"What are you saying?"

Rosemary met his gaze. "You tried to kill him before he met your wife, but it didn't work. It's his destiny, Yasir. There's nothing to be done."

"That can't be true—Jaleh is my destiny—she's mine!"

Dylan helped Rosemary up. "Let her rest for a minute, Yasir."

But he ranted on, his face turning red. "Did you impress upon her how important this is for her and her child? She will have to raise the child on her own!"

Rosemary met his gaze. "She understands everything. She's known all along. She will lose the baby. You cannot change the past."

Yasir put his hands over his face, sobbing. "My beautiful Jaleh. I need you."

Dylan took hold of his arm. "Enough, Yasir. It's time for you to go."

Without speaking Yasir handed the locket to Rosemary and headed toward the door. A moment later the door clicked closed behind him.

"Are you really all right? I almost stopped him. You seemed so far away, as though…"

"As though I was more than a hundred years in the past? I went there, I saw Rebecca. It was as though I had a bubble around me, a membrane that separated us."

Dylan pulled her into his arms. "That bastard. Why did I let him go ahead with this insane idea?"

"I'm fine, Dylan. He didn't hurt me."

"But he could have. That man would do anything to connect with his former wife."

CHAPTER THIRTY-THREE

Washington D.C.
March 1958

Rosemary, Dylan, Grant and Amanda huddled in the front hall of Boyd Hewitt's house. The heat had been turned off for some time and the place was frigid. A layer of dust covered everything, including the black and white marble tiled floor, a musty smell from closed windows wafting around them. "Where's the effigy?" Amanda asked.

"I set it up in the garden," Dylan told her. "It's quite the work of art."

Amanda looked from Dylan to her sister. "Did you make it?"

"I did," Rosemary answered, smiling.

"You look amazing," Amanda said suddenly. "Your skin glows."

When Rosemary glanced at Dylan he smiled. "That's what the hormones do."

Amanda laughed. "Oh yes, I'd forgotten about that aspect of pregnancy—the only nice thing that can be said about it. Just wait until the birth. I definitely don't envy you."

"Thanks for that, Amanda. I needed to have your doom and gloom today."

Amanda smirked. "Just take the drugs—you'll do fine." She glanced toward the door. "Where are the other two to make us six?"

"Cecilia didn't have any interest in what we're doing and Lillian is at work."

Amanda looked taken aback. "But...that was an important aspect of all this."

Rosemary smiled, glad she'd finally shared her experiences of a past life with her sister. "We're hoping two others will join us."

Amanda frowned, turning to Grant. "I hope this doesn't mean what I think it does."

"You're right on target, Amanda," Dylan said, grinning.

"Oh good God."

"Put on coats, hats and gloves, it's cold out there," Rosemary reminded them, heading toward the French doors. She opened one and waited for them to come through, before pulling it shut behind her. It was late afternoon, the sky a flat gray. The temperature was dipping by the minute—a freeze was predicted. At least there was no wind. But as soon as that thought went through her mind the breeze came up, blowing her wool scarf off her neck. She grabbed it off the path and wound it tightly, tucking the ends into her coat.

When she came to the fountain she could smell the boxwoods, their distinctive aroma invoking memories of her childhood. She'd played here with Amanda, their hide and seek games taking them under these bushes. They were now chest high and lush after the wet winter. She ran her fingers over their small leaves, images of herself as a little girl appearing in her mind.

After the line of boxwoods the path turned right, leading down three wooden steps into the lower garden. The fruit trees were bare, the lawn dried out from the cold winter. The planting beds were filled with dead weeds. She had a momentary dread at the sight of it all, wondering if what they were about to do was something the goddess might not approve of. She sent a mental prayer to Venus/Aphrodite. "It's all about love, isn't it?" she whispered.

"What did you say?" Amanda caught up with her and grabbed her arm.

"I just sent a message to the goddess, the one who will preside over our burning."

Amanda made a derisive sound in the back of her throat. "You and your hocus-pocus. Since when did you become so irrational?"

"Traveling into the past might have had something to do with it."

Amanda scoffed. "I halfway don't believe you. It could have been some mental state brought on by stress. Our mother was obviously prone to those—maybe you inherited it."

Rosemary stopped to face her sister. "How can you say that after everything I've shared?"

Amanda looked abashed. "I guess I'm just nervous. I've never done anything like this." Grant came up behind her and put his big hands on her shoulders. "You were the one interested in researching the number six, and you seemed to believe me when I told you about some of my experiences. Why the sudden doubt?"

Amanda shrugged and smiled up at her husband. "You're right. I've been excited about this for months."

As Rosemary turned away Dylan grabbed hold of her hand. "Come this way everyone," he said, heading toward the back garden.

The 'effigy' was tacked to a large board. Around the base, kindling and logs had been stacked just as it might be in a fireplace. "What's this?" Amanda asked, staring at the canvas covered in images.

Rosemary moved to her creation, pointing out the antique clock face with roman numerals at the right edge of the canvas, the hands of which were both at the number twelve. "This represents the past and the future," she said. "The future is yet to be seen, here," she pointed to the space to the right, outside the painting. "The past is everything to the left of the clock." Behind the clock and covering the rest of the canvas were hazy figures of people, houses, and cars. The colors ranged from bright orange to dark charcoal, with many shades in between, every bit of white covered in color. Seen from afar it looked like a flowerbed, everything connected and blending into the interlocking composition. The clock was the only part of the painting that stood out, distinct and real, the thick black roman numerals catching the eye.

"Is that a wedding?" Amanda asked, pointing to a woman dressed in white, the man in black. They stood close together, the woman's hair pale blonde, the man's the color of coal.

"Yes, that represents Father and Mother. They are also depicted down here." She pointed to an indistinct embracing couple done in purples and orange.

"And the two little girls over there are us?"

Rosemary nodded. "There are other figures scattered about—family members, friends, and the cars I recall from when we were young."

Amanda clapped her hands. "I remember this one—the Desoto!" She pointed. "But I thought we would burn Father, punish him for what he did."

"When I began the painting, so did I. But then I realized that we really know nothing about why he did what he did. And I believe he loved our mother very much. He made a mistake just as we all do. And I'm sure he paid for it for the rest of his life. Do you remember how hollow-eyed and depressed he was? It took him years to get over her death. I am certain he blamed himself. So why should we blame him too? No. This is for us, to let go of our past, to embrace what is to come." Rosemary looked around for Dylan, reaching for his hand "Do you want to do the honors?"

Amanda touched her fingers lightly to the surface. "That's wet oil paint, Rosemary."

"It's still slightly tacky, but I'm sure it will burn." She moved out of the way so that Dylan could light the paper and kindling beneath, and then they all stepped back.

The fire was crackling, flames lifting into the sky when Rosemary noticed Rebecca and Edgar. She grabbed Dylan's sleeve and pointed to where they hovered, as indistinct as two wispy ghosts. But they were there, witnesses to the burning away of what was no longer needed. Rosemary was sure that Rebecca smiled at her just before she turned to Edgar, placing her small hand in his larger one. A moment later they were gone.

Rosemary produced the two letters from her pocket and handed them to Amanda who threw them into the flames. "Goodbye," Amanda whispered, watching them curl and blacken, turning into ash. Her face was wet with tears. Grant stood next to her, a bear of a man, his arm around her shoulders.

The fire was still going, although not as strongly, when two uniformed policeman arrived. "We got a call that a fire had started back here. We came to investigate."

"We decided to have a bonfire," Dylan said. "It's full moon, isn't it?"

One of the men laughed. "If you could see it. Since I recognize you lot, we'll leave you to it. Seems as though you have things under control. Make sure you douse those coals before you leave."

It was another half hour before the fire burned down sufficiently to leave on its own. Dylan did the honors, using a stick to disperse the coals and covering them all with fresh dirt. "Shall we go and have a drink to celebrate?" he asked brightly.

Rosemary glanced at her sister, who still looked done in by emotions. "Amanda?"

"Yes," Grant answered for both of them. "I could use a drink, if not to celebrate, at least to warm up."

The small group wiped their feet carefully before entering the house. Rosemary locked the French doors and headed across the marble tiles. "I really wish we didn't need to sell this place," Amanda said wistfully.

"We could keep it, but for what? It's too big and none of us want to live here. It would require a staff of thousands just to keep it clean."

"I suppose you're right," she said, looking around, "but so many memories here."

"Yes. And that's exactly why we need to sell. Remember what we just did out in the garden?"

Dylan drove them to their old haunt, the hotel restaurant bar they all knew. Once settled around the table with various drinks in their hands, Rosemary picked up her glass. "I propose a toast to the future."

Dylan smiled widely. "I'm on board with that." He lifted his glass.

Amanda and Grant lifted theirs as well, all of them taking a sip. A moment of silence followed. Finally Rosemary broke through the reverie. "Did anyone else notice our friends from the past?"

Amanda frowned and shook her head. "All I saw were the flames and your beautiful painting turning into a horrible mess."

Grant shook his head, looking confused.

"I saw them," Dylan said. "They came to say goodbye."

Rosemary glanced at her husband. "I don't understand how they could be together."

Dylan shrugged. "Neither do I. What I do know is that we will never see them again."

Rosemary scoffed. "You're sure of that, are you?"

But Dylan's expression remained serious. "I'm very sure of it."

"What are you talking about?" Grant asked.

Amanda turned to her husband. "The people from the past, Grant. Remember, I told you about them?"

"Ah, yes. I had a similar experience back when I was in my twenties. It felt like I was living two lives for a week or so."

"You too?" Rosemary stared at him.

"I told you about him, Rosemary. He's the one who convinced me you weren't making this entire thing up."

"So glad I have your trust."

"Okay, girls—no bickering tonight," Dylan said. "Tonight is for looking forward. In five months we'll have a baby. We're in process of deciding our living arrangements." He turned to Rosemary. "I'm keeping the apartment for when we want to be in Washington, and that includes the month before your due date until you're strong enough to travel back to Virginia."

Rosemary blanched. "I can't think that far ahead, Dylan. I'm too superstitious after what happened the last time."

"Yasir said that we *will* have a baby. And he knows."

Rosemary shivered and put her attention on her wine glass. The memory of her miscarriage moved through her mind. She wouldn't feel safe until she was holding the baby in her arms.

CHAPTER THIRTY-FOUR

Virginia
May 1958

Rosemary shifted on the couch, her hand going to her belly where a kick had brought her out of her dozing state. These signs of an active baby were coming more frequently now. A moment later the dream fragments returned. She was holding a baby in her arms, a boy child who looked like Dylan. She smiled despite her trepidation about what was to come.

"Hello, my sweet," Dylan said, arriving from the kitchen with a plate of crackers and cheese. "Did you get a short rest?"

Rosemary sat up and reached for the plate, placing it on the coffee table. "I seem to fall asleep at a moment's notice now."

Dylan sat next to her, his hand going to her protruding stomach. "It won't be long."

"Only two more harrowing months," Rosemary replied, putting her hand on his. "He's been kicking a lot."

"So it's a boy?"

Rosemary shrugged, picking up a cracker. "I don't know, but I've dreamed about a boy a couple of times."

Dylan leaned back on the couch. "What of the other dreams? Have you had any more?"

"Not since the burning ceremony. How about you?"

"Nothing. We did what Yasir wanted—healed the past."

"I don't know what we did, but I'm glad it's over. Rebecca's terrible unhappiness was seeping into me. I'm sure she killed herself, Dylan. She had it all planned out."

"What was she planning?"

"She was going to hang herself."

"Maybe we righted things before that happened."

"I don't know how past lives work, but I hope you're right."

Dylan stood and grabbed her hand, pulling her up. "Okay, lazy bones. We have to go and pen the chickens and take care of the beasties. You've done nothing all day."

"You expect me to waddle out to the barn and work?"

Dylan laughed. "Yes, indeed I do. Women all over the world work until the day they deliver. You're still months away."

He tugged her toward the door.

༄

It was nine in the evening when the phone rang, startling them from where they sat together reading. "I'll get it," Dylan said, jumping up.

Rosemary wondered who was calling, but the phone was in the kitchen and she was too relaxed to bother heaving herself up to eavesdrop. Calls this late were rare. She put her mind back on the Daphne Du Maurier novel she was reading, but a few minutes later when Dylan came into the room looking like he'd seen a ghost, she placed the book aside. "What is it?"

Dylan shook his head, running fingers through his already mussed hair. "Yasir is dead. He committed suicide."

Rosemary sat up straight, adrenaline coursing through her body. "How? When? Who was that on the phone?"

"It was my CIA contact, Rand. They've been keeping an eye on Yasir, but when he stopped coming and going from his apartment they decided to investigate. They found him hanging from the ceiling fan." Dylan sat next to Rosemary, his head in his hands. "He left a note for me."

"What did it say?"

"I don't know. It's in a sealed envelope with my name on it."

"He was so depressed that last time we saw him—I'm actually not that surprised."

Dylan nodded, staring off into space. "I've got to go down to Washington tomorrow." He turned. "Will you be all right on your own?"

"Why wouldn't I be? And contrary to popular belief I am entirely capable of taking care of the garden, the chickens and the horses."

Dylan smiled. "I don't want you straining yourself."

She scoffed. "You've grown very protective."

He frowned. "I worry, that's all. You're close to the birth date."

"And too old for this?" she added.

"I never said that, nor do I think it. The doctor isn't worried, why should we be?"

Rosemary sighed. "At least I've held on to him for seven months."

"Don't do that, Rosemary. This baby will be fine and so will you."

Dylan fell asleep quickly while Rosemary stared at the ceiling, trying to make out the wooden beams. It was the dark of the moon and being so far away from a town made the darkness even denser. She thought about Yasir, wondering why he'd decided to take his life. Wouldn't suicide disrupt the bardo? She glanced at her husband sleeping on his side. So far this new life seemed to suit him, but then again they'd gone through this before. Would the addition of a baby keep him from getting bored? She'd already agreed to head down to Washington a month before her birth date, and also promised to make it a regular part of their lives. As much as she loved her solitude, she knew he was right. And besides, how much solitude would she have once the baby was born? She let out a laugh.

"What is it?" Dylan mumbled, turning.

"Nothing. Go back to sleep."

In all truth what they'd managed so far had pleased her greatly. Despite her growing girth they'd remained intimate, Dylan oddly entranced by the changes in her body. As far as day-to-day activities, he'd taken to gardening with his former gusto, laying out rows with the precision of an army general marshaling his troops. He helped her with the cooking, finding recipes in old dusty cookbooks she'd forgotten about. He seemed very happy. But her pessimistic nature worried. Would this honeymoon period last?

By the time Rosemary woke in the morning Dylan was long gone, a note on the kitchen table. *"I'll be back tonight.*

Don't hesitate to call the doctor if something untoward happens. Take care, my love."

So he was worried too. She poured coffee and made a piece of toast before heading outside to begin her morning chores.

It was mid-morning when she felt the first twinge. Must have been something she ate or didn't eat, she thought, continuing to muck out the stall she was working on. By noon the twinges had turned into intermittent pain. She tried to remember what the doctor had told her. Was this normal or not? It was too early for the birth. Her back ached from working.

By five she was huddled on the couch sweating. The pains were happening at regular intervals now. And when they came it was all she could do not to scream.

It was seven when she heard the door open, the sound of Dylan's voice. "Rosie? Where are you?"

He arrived in the dark room, taking in the scene. He switched on a lamp, peering into her face. "Jesus Christ! Are you in labor?"

"I don't know," she managed, grimacing when another pain rolled through her.

"We're heading to town."

"Washington? It's too late for that."

"What do you suggest?"

Rosemary couldn't speak for a minute or two. "Berry Hill has a hospital."

Dylan picked her up and carried her to the car. "Why didn't you call the doctor?" he asked, placing her inside.

"I thought it would pass. It's too early."

"Clearly it is not too early, Rosie."

270

"But what if it is?" She stared at him, tears moving down her cheeks.

"The doctors got the date wrong," was all he would say as he sped through the night.

Her water broke in the car, scaring her even further. "I hope you know how to deliver a baby," she muttered. A moment later she let out a scream that echoed into the darkness.

"Hold on, Rosie, we're almost there."

But Rosemary barely heard him, her body telling her to do things that she couldn't ignore. By the time they reached the small hospital she was crouched on the seat, her face sweaty and red.

Dylan took one look at her, jumped out of the car and shouted for help.

CHAPTER THIRTY-FIVE

Berry Hill Hospital
May 21, 1958

Dylan paced and smoked outside the waiting room. He kept seeing his wife, her face contorted in pain, as they carted her off on the gurney. The baby had been on the way, he was sure of it. If they hadn't reached the hospital when they did she would have given birth in the goddamned car! He kicked himself for leaving her, for going into Washington and staying so long. If something happened to her...*don't go down that road*, he told himself. He sucked in smoke and expelled it, stubbing the cigarette out under his heel. He stared toward the cars moving past on the road, but he didn't see them, his mind back in the car with Rosie. She'd already begun to push, her animal-like grunts driving his foot down hard on the gas pedal. He must have been going close to ninety by the time they reached the emergency entrance.

Jesus, please! He wasn't religious but found himself praying to some unknown force that he hoped would help. He thought of the church he'd bunked in during the war, the serenity he'd felt there. He tried to recapture that memory, but it was a no go. This woman was everything to him. "If it's a choice let the baby go," he heard himself say. Luckily he was the only one in the room. Why wasn't the doctor coming out to let him know what was happening? He'd been out here for what felt like days, but when he looked at his watch it had only been two and a half hours—but still. Someone should have…at that moment the doctor arrived through the swinging doors, his expression serious. Oh God.

"You have a baby boy," he said.

"And my wife—is she…?"

"She's exhausted and she lost a lot of blood, but she'll be fine."

Dylan nearly collapsed. "Thank God. Can I see her?"

The doctor smiled for the first time. "Follow me."

Dylan entered an antiseptic room, his gaze going to the still figure in the bed. He hurried over. "Rosie?"

She opened her eyes and smiled. "We have him. He's all right. I did it, Dylan. He's all right."

"And you're all right, my sweet. Thank everything holy." He bent over her and kissed her forehead. "I was so worried."

"Sir?" Dylan turned to see the night nurse. "Perhaps you should let her rest. I can show you your baby if you like."

Dylan looked down on his wife again, taking in the paleness of her skin, the dark circles under her eyes. He picked up her hand.

"Go and see him, Dylan. They told me I can't have him until I've rested for a little while." Her eyes drifted closed.

Dylan followed the nurse down the corridor to a room that held an incubator. The baby inside was tiny and red, sleeping. "Is he all right?"

"He's a preemie, but strong for being so early. Doctor Edwards wants to monitor them both for a few days. What is his name?"

He pulled his gaze from his infant son, suddenly bewildered. "I don't know."

Dylan dozed in the chair in the waiting room. His wife was asleep, his son as well. The doctor had told him to go home and come back late the next morning. "We need to run some tests on your son and on your wife. After ten would be best."

Finally he headed out to the car and stretched out on the back seat.

❧❧❧

Dylan woke with a start—he'd been dreaming, but about what he couldn't remember. Were Edgar and Rebecca still hovering about? And what of Yasir's suicide? Had that affected them? And then he remembered his tiny new baby and his wife. My gods! He was up and out of the car in a flash, running for the hospital.

"What did you do, Dylan—sleep in your clothes?"

He laughed. "Afraid so. I spent the night in the car." It was early still, not even seven a.m., but he'd managed to wheedle his way into his wife's room. The nurse had taken pity on him with his mussed up hair, wrinkled clothes and unshaven face. "Where is our baby?"

"They told me they'd bring him in early this morning. I'm sure he needs to eat. And from how I feel, I need to feed him."

Dylan grinned. "Doing it the natural way?"

"I hope so. I've heard there can be trouble, especially with a premature baby."

Dylan sat on the bed next to her. "You look so much better this morning. I was really worried about you."

"The birth was harrowing. I was afraid I wouldn't make it through."

"Looked to me like you were well into it when they wheeled you away."

"I was, but there were some complications. He wasn't quite in the right position. They had to maneuver him."

Dylan grabbed her hand. "Jesus, Rosie. I had no idea."

"It's all over now. And he's fine."

"Speaking of the baby, what will we name him?"

They stared at one another. "I can't believe we never talked about this!"

"We both thought you had two more months to go."

The door whooshed open and the nurse arrived, carrying a tiny bundle. "He needs you," she said, smiling. She placed the baby in Rosemary's waiting arms. "You may need some help," she said hesitantly, glancing at Dylan.

"Yes, I might. But don't worry about my husband. He can stay for it."

"If you say so."

The next few minutes were taken up with getting the baby into the right position and teaching Rosemary how to deal with it all. Once the baby was latched on the nurse left the room.

"Oh my goodness," Rosemary said, looking over at Dylan. "I'm already exhausted."

"But he looks fine," he answered, standing to look down on the baby at her breast. "What a beautiful picture this would be. Camera's in the car."

ROSEMARY FOR REMEMBRANCE

"Don't you dare!"

CHAPTER THIRTY-SIX

Virginia
May 1958

It was a full week before they released Rosemary and the new baby, who was still un-named.

"Baby no-name?" Dylan joked as he helped her into the car.

"Anonymous," she quipped.

Back at the farmhouse Dylan settled his wife into bed, and brought up the bassinet, placing it next to her. "Good thing we had the good sense to buy this early," he said, taking the sleeping baby from her. He placed him down and covered him with the soft wool blanket.

"I can't just lie here, Dylan. I have things to do."

"You can and you will, Rosie. The doctor told me that you need to rest. When he agreed to release you he made me promise to keep you in bed for at least two more days."

"So you're going to cook?"

"I am. Do you doubt I can?"

She scoffed. "Maybe."

❦

When Dylan brought up lunch Rosie was standing next to the dormer window staring out. She turned when she heard him. "You never told me what happened with Yasir."

Dylan put the tray down. "I nearly forgot about it with all the excitement."

"What did the note say?"

Dylan reached into his pocket and pulled out a folded piece of paper. "You can read it for yourself."

"You've been carrying it around with you?"

"I put it in these pants so that I could share it earlier, but then it never came up."

"How many days have you worn those trousers?" she asked, looking him over critically.

He smirked. "A few more than I intended." He ran a hand over his unshaven cheeks. "I've neglected quite a few things this past week."

Rosemary took the piece of paper and unfolded it, heading back to sit on the bed to read.

Dylan,

I must apologize for my actions. As you know I have been obsessed with my dear sweet Jaleh. As far as Edgar and Rebecca, I think perhaps your ceremony has managed to heal things for them. I sincerely hope so, since that would mean that Jaleh is now there for me.

My death means nothing so please do not mourn me. I will be back in the bardo where I will reconnect with my one true love. Know that I never wished to do harm. Circumstances only got the best of me. Remember me to your wife, and take good care of little Vihaan. I will see you in another lifetime.

Most sincerely,
Your friend always, Yasir

Rosemary looked up, meeting Dylan's gaze. "Vihaan? What does that mean?"

"I have no idea."

When the baby made a mewling sound she picked him up, settling on the bed to feed him. "I like the sound of the word."

"I do too. If it's a name it's very different. I'd expected to name him after my father or yours, but for some reason Boyd doesn't seem to fit and neither does Samuel." His eyes met hers.

"Can you find out the meaning? Yasir must have mentioned it for some reason."

༄༄

After a day long visit to Washington, Dylan arrived home carrying a heavy leather tome and several pamphlets. "How did your day go?" he asked, coming into the kitchen where Rosemary was cooking. "Where's the baby?"

"Day went fine. Baby's in there." She pointed toward the dining room. "I was afraid I'd wake him banging pans."

Dylan hurried through the swinging door between kitchen and dining room, arriving back a minute or two later. "Did he grow today or is it my imagination?"

Rosemary laughed. "He's been eating like a pig, so maybe."

Dylan came up behind her and wrapped his arms around her waist. "I missed you two."

She wriggled away. "Honestly, Dylan, you have become the most sentimental man I've ever known. How long before you decide to get another job and leave us to fend for ourselves?"

He twirled her around to face him, placing a kiss on her mouth. "Never. This is my life now, I swear it. Now, about Vihaan…"

"Oh. What did you find out?"

"It's Sanskrit, possibly the oldest language on earth. It was written purely for religious and philosophical purposes. It's a language of the divine."

"Hindu?"

"It's the classical language of Hinduism, mostly spoken by the priests. Vihaan means dawn, or first ray of light, or possibly awakening. It also translates to the beginning of a new age."

"I like that."

"So do I. Do you want to have him baptized? The reason I ask is because I ran into your sister today. She's rather annoyed that she hasn't heard from us since the day I called to let her know about the baby."

"I would rather have a naming ceremony, Dylan. Since I haven't yet managed to put Father's house on the market we could have the party in the garden. It's a perfect time of year. I want everyone to be there to meet him and we can do our own sort of baptism."

"You mean like everyone kissing him or something along those lines?"

Rosemary smiled, her eyes lighting up as she visualized the party. "Everyone could bring one small gift for him which we will keep until he's old enough to appreciate whatever it is. We can hire a band and the champagne will flow."

"I like how you think, Mrs. Hughes. Shall I take charge of the music?"

"Yes. And please ask Lily to bring any friends she'd like. Does she have a beau?"

"She might, although I have yet to meet him."

Rosemary turned back to the stove, stirring the curry she'd prepared. But before she could finish cooking the baby woke and gave a high-pitched cry. "Time to feed him. Again," she added, smirking. "He takes after his father. Can you please stir?" She handed him the wooden spoon and hurried into the other room.

EPILOGUE

Late July 1958

The entire family, including children of current marriages and children of previous marriages, plus grown children who had recently appeared in their lives, all gathered in the garden for the naming ceremony. Amanda and Grant and Aunt Cecilia had hired a catering service for the food, and a bartender for the drinks. Dresses were light and gauzy, with conversation to match, and most of the women did not wear shoes.

"What a perfect baby," Lillian gushed, reaching for Vihaan. "My brother!" she added in a surprised tone, glancing at Rosemary. Beside her a handsome blonde man crowded close, as though afraid she might disappear.

Rosemary gazed around at the crowd of people, surprised by how large the family had grown. Cecilia's loud voice boomed, waxing eloquent about the gardens and the house for those who were not familiar with the property. "But soon it will be gone," Rosemary heard her say, "Sold to the highest bidder."

Rosemary had a moment of misgiving until she realized the folly of the wayward thought. Yes, she loved the house, yes, it held many wonderful memories, but it was utterly impractical and way too big for her family. Her family. What an odd concept that was. It was then that she had the distinct impression that there was more to this gathering that met the eye. She had the sense of other entities, long gone, floating around her—her mother, her father, possibly even Edgar and Rebecca. She smiled and acknowledged them.

She watched Dylan take Vihaan out of his daughter's arms and move toward her.

"Would you like a glass of champagne?" he asked.

Rosemary nodded, thinking how very handsome he was. A wave of love surged through her when she glanced at their baby who already resembled Dylan, with his dark hair and secret smile. He handed him over and went off to the bar.

The jazz band began to play Rhapsody in Blue, the notes rising up like bubbles and sliding down the scale, only to lift again. The music curled through her, the languid tones so different from other music she'd heard. This she liked.

It had grown dark and fireflies moved through the fruit trees, vying with the fairy lights strung through their branches. The velvet sky echoed the earth bound scene, billions of bright pinpricks blinking on and off. By the time Dylan arrived with the champagne Rosemary had placed the sleeping baby in his bassinet.

"Are you crying?" he asked, crouching next to her.

She wiped her eyes. "Only from happiness."

AUTHOR'S NOTE

In case you did not read the foreword, I just want to reiterate that the journal entries kept by Dylan during the war and prison camp are my father's. Most are verbatim with slight alterations due to the story I created around them. I hope this story does his journals justice.

To find out more about John Ramsey Pugh and his part in the conflict and subsequent surrender in the Philippines, here is a link:
www.3ad.org/members_pages/newsletter_archives/2006_ne wsletters/Volume_06_Issue_1.pdf

To contact Nikki please visit www.nikkibroadwell.com/

Or visit her author page here: www.amazon.com/Nikki-Broadwell/e/B007EE1LN0

Please visit my website and claim your free book for joining my newsletter list here: nikkibroadwell.com/contact.html
And please, if you enjoyed this book, leave me a review on Amazon! They make all the difference!
Thank you for reading!